Totally Bound Publishing books by Zoe Normandie

Unbreakable Heroes
Under Control

Unbreakable Heroes

UNDER CONTROL

ZOE NORMANDIE

Under Control
ISBN # 978-1-83943-726-7
©Copyright Zoe Normandie 2021
Cover Art by Erin Dameron-Hill ©Copyright August 2021
Interior text design by Claire Siemaszkiewicz
Totally Bound Publishing

UNDER CONTROL

Dedication

For J.,
Thank you for sharing
your story with me.
And thank you for serving our country
with bravery and perseverance.

Chapter One

Carrick

"Moose, hold up. I haven't cleared the area," Delta called out to the man jumping out of the passenger side of the armored black SUV.

Former Navy SEAL and decorated war hero Carrick Byrne tilted his head back, giving Delta the usual 'don't even start' expression.

"Relax, big rig. This is just a little 'find and retrieve' contract," Carrick said in a skeptical voice tinted with the slightest Irish accent as he leaned back into the idling SUV. "I don't think we need to worry about one little girl."

Delta narrowed his brown eyes, and a lock of his slicked-back dark-blond fell onto his unimpressed face. "She's been on the run for years. Don't underestimate her."

Carrick looked around with obvious sarcasm at the fact that they were literally about to walk through a park on their way to finish the job. Glancing back,

Carrick raised his eyebrow to his friend, recognizing the face of someone who wanted to punch him.

"Come on. How much trouble could one chick cause?"

"Your client seems to think she can cause a lot of trouble," Delta reminded him. "And our intelligence suggests the same. She's slippery, Carrick—and I don't think your client is very forgiving."

"Don't overdramatize this," Carrick warned. "This is a nothing contract."

The two strong, opinionated men exchanged looks before Delta backed off, seemingly knowing that at the end of the day, Carrick was the CEO of Sea-to-Sky Security.

"Have it your way," Delta said, leaning back. "You're the boss."

Moving away from the SUV, Carrick slung his old black hockey skates over his shoulder, heading toward the rink. He flipped up the collar of his black work coat, even further concealing his identity. He had a target to follow. Years of urban reconnaissance and black ops had given him more than enough tactical training to handle the job.

Popping a black baseball hat on and smoothing back his black hair that was peppered with gray, the dark Irish-American moved stealthily.

Delta took off behind him with gusto, but Carrick didn't care. He just needed to get the job done and over with, then move on to the next one. It should be in and out—quick and easy. Those were the types of cases Carrick needed to build his client base and his reputation as the premiere private security firm in LA.

And, damn it, he was going to do the best job he could—because after losing everything that mattered to him, this new business venture was all he had left.

Carrick focused on the scene before him. The crowd had thinned. It was growing quiet. As he came up to the skating rink, a young couple passed him on the other side of the pathway leading out of the park. They seemed happy — in love. His only instinct was to scowl, and he pulled down the brim of his hat farther as he stooped to put on his skates.

The target was on the ice. It was time to get *closer*. *Then retrieve.*

Out on the rink, it was nearing closing time, and everyone was clearing out. He was the only one heading in. *Good.* He needed the space. It was much easier to keep eyes on the target.

At least, that was what he told himself. He wouldn't admit it, but at that moment — Valentine's Day night — he wanted nothing else than to have a reason to be alone — alone and away from everything to do with his life, away from the memories. *Is this my second Valentine's Day alone?* He shuddered, pushing the thought aside. That wasn't something he was prepared to feel.

He didn't have to. The girl was in sight.

Hockey skates on, Carrick moved hard down the bumpy outdoor ice — as hard as the restrictive leather strap of his shoulder holster would allow. Wearing a pistol was like wearing boxers. He did it every day, no matter what. It had come to feel like a second skin.

Keeping his eyes on the ice, not on her, his blood pumped to his engorged muscles and a sated grin crossed his lips. There were very few things in life that served to alleviate his stress — hockey being one. The other was a similar cardio-exhausting exercise that elevated his endorphins, pumped his blood and left him satisfied and spent.

Pushing forward, he observed her — the lone woman skating in the opposite direction, once again nearing his position. Her long brown hair had escaped her pink toque, and her warm breath visibly illustrated her panting chest, even from afar. Carrick had to admit that her form was more than pleasing to look at. Athletic and swift — he didn't doubt she could give him a run for his money in a race, but he kept his gaze down. He made sure to give her enough space so that he wouldn't scare her away.

Danica Petrova.

As she was skating past him, he stole one glance of her face, locking eyes. He *had* to see her face in person. All he'd seen was a picture.

He wasn't disappointed.

Her red cheeks flashed at him and her eyes sparkled. *So youthful and full of life.* What he'd seen in a blink of an eye held the promise of an eternity of pleasure as he took in her beautiful face.

But then, in an instant, just as her body floated by him, her skate hit a groove in the ice, an unmistakable sound — and common. Turning immediately, he thrust forward and reached out, catching the young woman as she fell. He quickly heaved her back onto her skates, rescuing her from a hard fall. As he held her, she fluttered her dark lashes at him, enchanting and stunning him.

"You okay?" he asked, looking her over, hoping she hadn't been hurt.

"I'm okay." A sweet, feminine voice escaped her full lips.

Holding her close, he realized that her eyes hadn't been sparkling. They were wet.

Has she been crying?

"I just caught an edge," she explained, like she'd been caught doing something wrong. "Thank you."

As she made to push away from his arms, he realized that he had been still holding her all this time. *I never let her go.*

She frowned as she probably realized the same thing. He released his grip on her thick sweater, letting her float back a foot into her own space. Silence filled the rink. Their gazes did not break, and she continued to blink at him, likely assessing him, given the look in her eyes.

There was something distrustful about the way she was evaluating him. Her body language screamed that she was scared and threatened that she was about to run. Before thinking, he threw out his hand, just knowing she was just about to pop smoke and disappear—and knowing he couldn't allow that. His client had warned him that she was a runner—and that she could slip out of any situation.

His client had also warned him of the importance of not letting her go.

"Carrick," he introduced himself, keeping her there.

She took his hand, though hers remained limp, and she retracted it right way. Clearly, she didn't know what to make of him—but her manners shone through.

"Dani."

Cute. She seemed very sweet, and not at all like the client had described. That was the first thing that brought on his suspicion that something might be wrong and not as he'd been led to believe.

"Nice to meet you," he replied with a little more meaning than he'd expected.

She responded slow and shy, her voice cracking, "I really do appreciate you saving me from the fall."

"Forget it." He shrugged as instinct urged him to back off a little.

But the caveman inside him couldn't take his eyes off her. Lithe and pert, she almost glowed under the soft lights. There was something different about this target. She continued averting her gaze, looking down at the hard ice and shaking her pretty heart-shaped face.

Something was brewing in his mind that he was unwilling to accept, and his strategy shifted. This was not how he'd planned the operation to go, but he had to adjust on the fly—right?

Carrick checked his watch and turned in the direction she was going. "Heading this way? Last five minutes."

He motioned, nearly regretting it as he did. Really, he knew better. They didn't have time for leisurely skating.

"I was." Her words poured out nervously, responding to his invitation. "But..."

"You aren't anymore?"

"I mean, I am." She toyed with her gray sweater buttons as she looked away, seemingly just as conflicted as him. She was a smart little coyote, and he wondered if she was ready to bolt.

She is definitely *ready to bolt.*

"Well, let's go then." He took the lead, pushing off the ice and gliding away from her.

If there was one thing Carrick was good at, it was controlling a situation. After a pause, there was the distinct sound of skates on the ice behind him, and she caught up to glide alongside him. He'd been sure she would follow—had just known it.

A sense of intrigue tugged at his senses as a cold burst of wind blew her long brunette locks across her shoulder.

So he decided to lay it on thick.

"Looks like you've got tough luck tonight," he said.

"It certainly wouldn't have been the worst thing to happen to me on Valentine's Day." The rebellious words seemed to slip from her mouth, and she glanced up with an embarrassed expression.

"That sounds like a good story," he replied.

Her wide gaze betrayed discomfort. The effect? He was able to observe her eye color more closely. They were a lighter brown, but mixed. *With green? Like camouflage.* He'd never seen a color like that before.

He continued looking around. "We must be two sad cases — out here alone on Valentine's night."

She brought her gloved hands together, rubbing them and offering him a shy smile. "*Or*, we must both just love skating."

He couldn't help but smirk, his chest flexing, "Guilty. I'm a hockey guy."

What the hell am I doing? He wiped the smile off his face, feeling like an idiot. However, it seemed her guard was lowering — and in return her shy tiny smile grew a bit.

"I can't believe you…*caught* me."

"Come on. I couldn't let you take a nosedive." He shrugged, pumping harder down the ice.

She kept up, showcasing just how good she was on blades.

She cocked her head and offered the slightest grin, tepid and testing. "You have quick reflexes."

He shrugged again. "Yeah, when I need to."

Built from years of Special Forces tactical training.

13

She shook her head again in apparent disbelief, then looked away. It was almost like she didn't believe someone *would* save her.

The bumpy ice on the rink was overdue for maintenance, which tended to be the case at the end of the skating day. There weren't many rinks in California — and fewer outdoor ones. Her skate caught an edge again, which she was too distracted to see. As she yelped and almost fell, he lunged instinctively, grabbing her against his body one more time.

"Christ." He exhaled.

Holding her in his arms again, he gazed down on her young, golden face. She bit her lip as she glanced up at him. He was aware of his great height and wide frame, which could be intimidating for some, especially when he was on skates.

"Want to keep going?" he asked, offering his arm. "Or should we head off?"

Danica grinned up to him, making him wait far too long before she answered, her glittery, innocent gaze flickering left and right. Never before had he wanted someone to take his arm so badly. As much as he hated to admit it, he had her exactly where he wanted her. He was forcing her to make a choice. It was going to play into the job nicely.

"One more round." She grinned her little smile, but her cooperation was tentative at best.

She slipped her hand in the crook of his elbow, only to then avert her gaze from his. The flush in her cheeks grew, and he guessed it was more than just the cool night wind coming in off the Pacific Ocean.

Comfortable silence found them briefly as they pushed along the ice side by side. She never let go of his arm, and for the first time, it felt like they were skating *together*. Something stirred inside him that hadn't been there before.

"How long have you been skating?" he asked, propelling the conversation forward.

"Oh, for as long as I can remember," Danica began, revealing more and more. "I grew up on skates and dreamed of becoming a figure skater."

Again, the admission was followed by caution that flashed across her eyes. She didn't want to share much, but she *was*. She recoiled slightly, as if realizing her mistake, and tried to create space between them until he decided he wouldn't let her. He didn't want her to withdraw.

Changing the tempo, he pushed her out a little from him, allowing her hand to slide down his forearm and slip to his just as he twirled her around on the ice. It was so smooth, so natural—like they'd been skating together for years. He didn't miss the wide smile that crossed her lips.

"It never hurts to dream," Carrick said as he pulled her back into him, running his gaze over her form for the hundredth time, his curiosity at maximum.

What does Danica want? What does she do? Questions sprang to the front of his mind. *Why did my client lie to me?*

"I have no shortage of dreams." Her sweet smile betrayed a longing, and it was clear she noticed the way he was looking at her.

"What do you do for work?" He pressed on as he ushered them farther down the ice.

"I'm a nurse."

"At the hospital?" His gaze caught the city worker beginning the process of closing the rink.

"No, at a family clinic," she replied.

"What else?" he probed. "Tell me more."

She let out a low laugh, as if in disbelief he would even say that. "I think it's time to go."

Then she let her hand slip out of his arm, gliding one perfect white skate in front of the other on her way to leave the rink. As he followed, he couldn't keep his eyes off her, watching her closely as she moved. It was like he'd never met a woman before, never seen one. If he were a wiser man, he'd notice that his chest didn't feel as tight as usual for the first time in too long.

If he were a wiser man, he'd notice that he'd grown very distracted.

"What about you?" She cut into his thoughts as she held on to the wall of the rink, stepping one foot through the gate. "Are you...?"

If it weren't for the sound of a man shouting as he sprinted toward them, Carrick would have caught what she said after that. The shouting was unmistakable, and for a second he felt like he could kill Delta for the interruption.

Danica snapped her eyes open like a doe caught in the headlights, clearly frightened by the six-foot-five man running up to the gate. Delta grabbed onto the side of the rink with his meaty SEAL-build as he spoke to Carrick in low tones.

"Moose, there's a situation. We have to go."

Chapter Two

Carrick

"Oh God." Danica sounded liked she'd been gutted.

Carrick saw the fear in her eyes and instinctively pulled her into his body, shielding her, as he trained his eyes from left to right. The rink was closing, and the park had emptied.

"Your four o'clock." Delta's voice was urgent. "Stay low."

As much as Carrick knew Delta had a tendency to overreact, he didn't like the look of the idling car behind him to the right and the shadowy figure who had just gotten out. They were being watched.

Shit, he thought, *I let myself get distracted.*

"What's going on?" Danica whispered in deep concern, looking all around. She recoiled, moving away from him. "Who *are* you?"

"Come with me," Carrick responded, his tone now cold and professional.

As she parted her lips, obviously searching for words, he held her hand in the crook of his elbow so she wouldn't run away. Handling her was growing too natural for him.

"Let's get out of here," Delta said, pushing back from the rink and into the shadows. "Follow me."

As Carrick moved them both off the rink, he once again glanced at the far edge of the park where a dark car was idling. He clutched Danica tighter and felt her nervous panting.

"I have to go..." Danica cried out, looking around for her escape. "I can't be here anymore."

"No," Carrick ordered her, and she sank back into him obediently. Her eyes betrayed the terror she must be feeling.

That was exactly what he was afraid was going to happen. The back of his mind revolted and scolded him ferociously for being a fucking cavalier idiot. It wouldn't have happened if he'd have stayed on plan, but he'd deviated from it and put them in danger.

"I'm here to help you, not hurt you," he informed as he helped her out of the skating rink and onto the rubber boards padding the ground.

As her lips trembled, she was seemingly out of words as he held her close. She was obviously very afraid. He just didn't know how much of it was directed at him.

Suddenly, something in his mind pivoted and all he saw was a girl in trouble.

"*Danica*," he urged, only to find her holding her breath. "Shit."

What type of contract did I take?

Carrick quickly shrugged off his black utility jacket and draped it over the shoulders of a reluctant Danica, and he put the hood up to conceal her identity.

He looked back into her eyes and squeezed her tightly to him. "Do you trust me?"

Her mouth dropped open and she shrugged in clear disbelief. She didn't say yes.

But she didn't say no.

As he kept her pressed against him, the moment felt like an eternity, and Carrick memorized every soft curve on her face. With that, he made a promise to protect her then turned his head to focus on the task at hand. Determined, he hoisted Danica up and carried her in his arms as he began a dash up the grassy mound of the park, not far behind Delta.

Even with his skates on, cutting into the soft ground underneath them to propel their way up the hill, his thighs, thickly muscled from years of hockey, easily handled her added weight. He'd been used to hard drills with skates on in hockey, along with harder drills in the SEALs. It was nothing to run with her in his arms—skates or not.

"Delta, where's the goddamn car?" Carrick barked irritably as they crested the top.

"Over there…waiting." Delta motioned and made a break for it as Carrick nodded.

Delta was used to how controlling Carrick could be.

Even in mid-sprint up a grassy hill with hockey skates on, Carrick's mind was grinding and calculating. All that SEAL training had taught him how to reassess on the fly. There was something really irking him. In no way was her reaction normal. It had been way over the top for a runaway girl. And in all their interactions, she'd seemed to be a sweet, put-together young woman. That was when Carrick knew beyond a shadow of a doubt that there was a lot more to the client's motives than what he'd been told.

Danica dug her fingers into his shoulders, clinging for dear life as she bounced up and down in his arms.

"Where are you taking me?" Danica sputtered.

"I'm protecting you," he growled, recognizing that it was growing more personal.

"From who, exactly?"

That's an excellent question.

At the top of the grassy hill in the park, Carrick steadied in the soft ground beneath him with Danica still in his arms. There was the black armored luxury SUV sitting at the top of the hill, just another couple of leaps across the concrete sidewalk. Carrick quickly lunged forward, whipping open the back door with one arm and hurling Danica onto the truck's back seat bench with the other. Delta was already stationed up front as their driver. It wasn't exactly how they'd planned the operation to go, but there they were.

"Moose, glad to see you could make it," Delta sniped with sarcasm. "Ready to blow this Popsicle stand?"

"Let's get the fuck out of here." Carrick pushed Danica across the bench, planting himself firmly beside her.

He began loosening the top buttons on his black long-sleeve shirt, because he was melting. The truck was roasting hot in the interior — or maybe it just felt that way after his blood had gotten pumping as they made their run for it. It wasn't just the level of effort to move two human bodies up a grassy hill on skates, but it was the anger that was bleeding across his eyes. He didn't like being deceived, being fooled with, which was becoming increasingly more obvious.

As the truck pulled away, the idling black car across the park moved as well, and Carrick had no doubt he would be seeing it again in short order. *Whoever those assholes are, they are in for a fucking treat.* Carrick narrowed his eyes, wondering who would willingly go up against a former SEAL, who was fresh out, and another SEAL, still enlisted. Battle rhythm coursed through Carrick's veins, and he could taste blood in the water. As he closely followed the movements of the car leaving the edge of the park, he just hoped and prayed they'd give him a fucking reason. He'd been pent up without release for too long, and giving these jokers some payback would be very satisfying.

"Where to, boss?" Delta asked as he pulled the truck out of the parkway, turning from downtown.

"Shake our tail first." Carrick pulled off his black baseball hat and smoothed his hair back again. "Then back to the roost."

Carrick gave a curt nod and Delta flipped open the keypad in the center console. There, he'd added features to the armored truck. Of course, when Carrick had opened the business the previous year, he had been aware that he had to equip the company truck to get the job done. Delta knew exactly what to do. He hit a green button that lifted a pane of tinted glass, sealing Carrick in the back seat with Danica. The glass was bulletproof, dark and meant to stymie surveillance and protect VIPs.

As the glass closed them in, Danica leaned back, her eyes wide, clutching her chest and taking labored breaths.

"What is happening?" she pleaded softly. "Please, tell me what's going on, Carrick."

"I'm taking you home," he responded matter-of-factly.

Carrick realized his tone wasn't reassuring, but somewhere along the line, he had been forced to switch back to being the cold professional. He couldn't let her in. He couldn't risk any more distractions — and she'd become the biggest one of all. That, he hadn't expected.

Her eyes were still wild with fright and sweat was beading on her forehead. Her cheeks had grown pale, and she looked faint. Clearly, that wasn't from running uphill on skates, since he'd carried her. He'd seen enough in battle to know when a rookie was in shock. Instinctively, as he'd been trained, he undid her seatbelt. Then he helped her from his hooded jacket and unbuttoned her thick gray sweater to help her breathe. As he got closer to her, drinking in her scent, her girlish vulnerability jumped out at him, threatening to once again pull him out of his military mindset. He gritted his teeth, continuing on. Pulling her sweater down her shoulders, he revealed her collarbone then her chest, letting her clutch the fabric of the loosened sweater across her lower arms and stomach. He didn't miss how her perfect plump breasts rose and fell with her inhalations, which caused his mouth to water.

Damn, he mumbled to himself, pushing the sight out of his mind.

"Carrick…" she pleaded again, and he knew exactly what she needed.

He just wasn't in a place to give it to her.

Focusing, he remained deep in battle mode and bent forward to take off her skates.

As he indelicately yanked her socked foot out of the hard skate, it occurred to him that maybe she wasn't just scared of the shadowy threat, but maybe she was also scared that she'd been kidnapped. *Maybe she thinks I'm the bad guy?* Taking a second to work through the problem, he moved to kick off his skates as well, then pulled on the well-worn black casual shoes he kept in the back.

"I think we were being watched, but *everything* is going to be fine," he grunted at her.

The last words were both true and false. It had been wrong for him to guarantee her safety. He wanted her to be all right, but he didn't know for sure that she would be.

"We'll take you home." He sat back up, studying her.

"No," she wheezed, the dazed look in her face worsening. "Please, just let me go. Let me out."

She's going to fucking pass out.

Carrick instantly reached over and took the thick sweater from her, tossing it across the back seat. He leaned in to triage her but found another problem — the tank-top-clad form that had been hiding under the bulk of her sweater.

Her very *attractive* form.

He was always a man who knew quality when he saw it.

"I can't let you go... like this." He trained his gaze up and down, unable to rip it away.

With every breath, her delicious cleavage seemed to pour out of her top, taunting him. Her long, thin torso was complimented by slender hips that looked fit and athletic. He clenched his jaw, feeling a deep, unwelcome urge. The carnal part of his brain wondered how wet she was. That same hot feeling crawled up the skin of his neck, flushing it with heat, permeating his throat. God was unhappy with him again and testing his resolve.

She's a goddamn rocket.

He found her gaze again — those unique eyes, heavily lashed and spellbinding. As if realizing her effect on him, Danica slumped backward, fear intensifying on her face. She was at his complete mercy.

Her nerves were causing her to fidget in anxiety and anticipation as he grew closer, as though she was questioning what he was going to do to her. For a second, he didn't know either.

The hunger in him rose. Pure desire.

It has been too long.

As Delta sped down the parkway, taking random turns to clear their tail, Carrick found that he had stopped thinking about the threat and had grown focused solely on the shape of her lips and how much of her thigh was pressed against his.

"Are you all right?" he asked in a low voice, while he lifted a rebellious hand to her cheek, just to feel it.

What the hell am I doing?

"No," she whispered back, her eyes growing tearful, "I'm *not* okay."

"I'm not going to hurt you."

"I don't know that." She blinked out a few small tears, but she held back, shutting her lips.

It was almost Carrick's undoing when he allowed himself to look down at those trembling full lips. It was almost what made him finally let go.

In that moment, he needed to wake up. The heat she made him feel was intoxicating. His discipline had faltered.

Before he could do anything else, he reached over her shoulder, grabbed her seatbelt and drew it across her body, fastening it again safely. The click of the safety belt punctuated the end of the heated moment, and Carrick recoiled to a stoic, confident position. The stability and strength that were in his DNA flushed back to the front of his body, like a shield, and he realized that he needed to protect her from more than just one thing that night.

Chapter Three

Danica

Sucking back the desire to sob, Danica took in a brave, deep breath as the black SUV barreled down the road. She tightened her fingers over the seatbelt that was across her chest and frantically searched back and forth, trying to process, to plan out her escape route. It wasn't a time to cry. It was a time to figure things out. She'd been free for far too long to lose it all now.

Who the hell is this guy? What the hell am I doing in his truck?

There was something so in control, so persuasive, about him. It shocked her how she hadn't just said no. That wasn't like her.

Her anxiety spiraling out of control, Danica tightened her lips as the SUV turned onto a downtown thoroughfare that was decorated for Valentine's Night. She observed carefree couples lining the sidewalks to make their way to their destinations. Meanwhile, she was imprisoned in the back seat of a truck, isolated. *This guy... I don't know the first thing about him.* But Danica felt an undeniable intensity coming off the mass of tall, strong muscle sitting beside her.

It was shaping up to be the worst Valentine's Day she'd ever had. She'd managed to lose her boot bag in the shuffle somewhere outside the rink. Now, in the back seat, in socks, she eyed the door for an escape. Could she subtly reach down, grab her skates and bolt? She bit her lip, wishing she had the guts.

Her frame stiff, she covertly glanced to the right, where Carrick sat beside her. As he studied their surroundings out of the window, she observed his powerful structure...presence. He slowly took in air, his mind clearly in deep focus. His masculine scent filled her nose. It was rich and warm and full of something she didn't understand. One thing was very different about them. He was collected, dominating.

Meanwhile, she was frozen in place, *shrinking*.

She surveyed the profile of his face. That long, patrician nose was perfectly situated in the middle of a face peppered with a dark five o'clock shadow. He had dark hair frosted with gray at the temples. Wise-looking yet virile, his face was framed by a powerful jaw. The lines at the corner of his eyes spoke of experience, something she wanted to know more about.

The more she knew, the more advantages she would have.

She always tried to feel what was inside people — what made them tick. Her instinct told her that Carrick was a born guardian, strong and stoic. Yet, something indicated that there was a shadow lurking inside him, an element that she couldn't quite put words to, something unusual.

A shadow flashed across his face as he turned back to her — assessing her from the passing streetlights in the poorly lit back seat. His dark eyes promised curiosity and depth. Calculation. Control.

"Who — who are you, really?" she asked, nearly tripping over the words.

"I'm Carrick. I told you that."

A steel vault — just perfect, she thought as she chewed her lip.

"And who's he?" Danica continued on slowly, motioning to the front. "Is he your driver? Bodyguard?"

Carrick smirked like she'd made a joke and shrugged her off. His lack of answers was telling and bothered her intensely. It was like he was talking down to her — as though she were a child. She should have guessed he would be that way, and the same wave of frosty wind chill splashed over her, just as if she were being dunked in icy-cold water.

A little voice in the back of her head reminded her not to let him make her feel small, but she still shrank involuntarily under his sight, feeling less and less like a someone — less and less like the two of them were on the same side.

As he watched her, the memory of his warm, weathered hand on her cheek flashed across her mind, sending her torment into overdrive. That intimacy was something she was even less prepared for. All the memories of the night came crashing down — how he'd saved her from the fall, how he'd spun her on the ice, how he'd made her wonder if he was really going to help her. And the way he looked at her… She'd allowed herself to believe that it was real.

It was never real.

Realizing her grave error, Danica shrank back from Carrick's cold gaze. She had no doubt that this was who he truly was. She'd made a fool of herself believing otherwise. She should have run when she'd had the chance.

She found the door handle of the SUV as they came to a stop at a red light. Her mind raced as she tried to silently talk herself into doing what she had to do. She had to bolt, to get away. There were trees right beside where they were. She could jump into them and run. She knew the parks better than anyone. She could find a way to escape.

But she wavered, blinking rapidly to hide unwanted tears.

As the tires slowly rolled to a stop, Carrick flexed his shoulders, and he let out a deep breath as he surveyed the area, shaking his head slightly. He didn't look impressed. In fact, he looked concerned. Then he was reaching back into his waistband as he craned his neck to look around.

It seemed he had good instincts. The same dark car that had watched her at the skating rink skidded to a halt in front of the truck, blocking them at the vacant traffic light.

"God!" She flinched, terror driving her to the breaking point.

Carrick reached across her lap and put his hand over her in what seemed like a natural movement of defense. With his wide body, he shielded her from threat. As he pulled a pistol out of his pants, their driver revved the truck's engine, sending a clear threat to the dark sedan blocking them.

"Get us the fuck out of here!" Carrick roared.

Danica could see through the tinted glass that the driver up front had his pistol in hand as well. Without pause, he hit the gas, screeching the tires. In immediate response, the dark sedan blocking them whirled out of the way, preventing a collision.

Her heart thumped rapidly, threatening to break through her chest. She refused to let those tears fall from her eyes, pursing her lips and tightening her body to encourage some semblance of self-control.

As silence engulfed the back seat, the SUV drove several miles down the road, darting in and out of side streets. Exhaling low, Carrick finally put his pistol back into his waistband, continuing to study everything surrounding the truck. And for a man who felt as cold as mercury, she sensed an anger within him. A fire. *A hunger.*

Danica looked at Carrick again, assessing his behavior, his intentions. *Actions speak louder than words.* Carrick had instinctively protected her—ferociously and without question. He'd thrown his body in the way.

"Carrick... what do you want from me?" Danica finally breathed out, realizing there was a lot more to his story.

"What do you want me to say, Dani?" Something flashed in his eyes, warning her. "I think you already know what's going on here."

Carrick's stare bored into her, seeming to observe her unease. She knew she really had to collect herself.

His voice grew low and daring, pushing her. "Is there going to be a problem?"

She heard his question as—are *you* going to be a problem?

She instinctively drew back. "*No.*"

That seemed to be exactly what he'd wanted to hear. A tension rose in her throat at the sight of him leaning toward her, challenging her. She raised her hands to cross across her chest, as if holding herself together.

He observed this, amused. "You don't have to protect yourself from me."

The entire world grew silent. She realized how close his body was to hers, how close his face was. He licked his full bottom lip, his gaze assessing her mouth.

I need to run.

She was frozen under his stare, her mind spinning. He was pure masculinity, and the very pheromones that poured off him sent warning alarms up and down her body. He was the most dangerous man she'd ever met, but not for the reasons she'd once thought.

Run.

As if he could hear her inner thoughts, an emotionless smirk ran up one side of his rugged mouth, framing straight white teeth. He had the mouth of a man determined to take what he wanted. And that was when she knew without a doubt that he *wanted* her. She wondered if he was going to kiss her.

Please, let me go.

Before either of them could lean together, the tinted glass rolled down in between the front and back seats. The driver leaned back to talk to Carrick.

"I think we shook them," he stated firmly, and Carrick nodded back.

Carrick turned to her, commanding. "It's time to shut this party down. Time to get you home."

"You can let me out here," she suggested, not wanting any more of his VIP service or to expose herself any further.

"No," Carrick responded, dismissing her immediately.

"You don't have to do this," Danica replied quickly. "I'm not far from home."

He cocked his head sardonically. "Are you crazy? Aside from the fact you have no shoes, I couldn't allow you to walk home *alone* now without knowing who the hell is behind this. I don't care how close by you live."

As the SUV turned off the parkway into her neighborhood, she realized they probably already knew where she lived. None of this had been a coincidence. Danica closed her eyes briefly, feeling the rumblings of the engine as the SUV wound its way around her block. *What the hell am I supposed to do?*

One thing was for sure. Danica had run out of options—and she only had herself to blame. The only choice she had then was to wait until her feet hit the pavement again, find a moment alone and run—run like her life depended on it and start over again somewhere else.

"Okay, take me home." She turned her chin to him. "You already know where I live, don't you?"

He flickered his eyes at her, his discontent palpable.

After a moment of thought, he finally let out, "Look... There's something I need to tell you."

Chapter Four

Danica

Danica shifted in the back seat under Carrick's gaze as the truck rolled down her street.

"What do you need to tell me?" she whispered, knowing that time was running out.

He reached up, rubbing his chin, definitely deep in thought. She noticed how he looked out of the window, his eyes locking on to her three-story historic brownstone down the street.

Nodding at the house coming closer into view, he replied, "Let's talk in there."

It was a beautiful million-dollar home among a stretch of them in the urban neighborhood. However, what wasn't immediately obvious was the fact that the home was divided into several separate rental apartments and none were all that luxurious inside. The rent was astronomical, and the finishes were dated, but the setup capitalized on young professionals who were trying to find their way in the world.

Danica and her roommate Addie were young women who couldn't afford to buy houses and cars, so they'd opted to live urban, close to transit. A nature lover, Danica didn't mind being without a vehicle and spent much of her time walking. There were worst places to be forced into that situation than San Francisco. There was something that had always been so appealing about being on her own two feet, grounded and steady. She felt the earth below her, making her feel safe, as though in an instant she could escape to wherever she needed to go.

And not having a driver's license kept her safely off the grid.

The armored SUV rolled quietly to a stop on the side of the street, about five houses down from her apartment. The driver turned off the engine and lights, staying still while watching the dark, silent neighborhood. Wasting no time, Carrick held on to Danica's hand and slid her across the leather SUV back seat behind him. The way he moved her body was unapologetic and determined — and again, she let him.

She followed him like she'd never followed anyone before, secretly enjoying how he reached across her body to grab her discarded thick gray sweater, throwing it over his shoulder.

Once he had slid them out of the back seat, Carrick reached down and picked her up in his strong arms — without asking. He acted like her socked feet were never going to touch the ground on his watch. Like a guardian, he looked around, holding her tight against his hard chest, carrying her like a princess. Danica gasped, realizing that the man really did what he wanted, and now he was doing something he really didn't have to do.

"You don't..." she sputtered as Carrick carried her down the sidewalk.

"Yes, I do," he said, tightening his grip.

As she let herself relax into his arms, a screaming voice at the back of Danica's head reminded her to ignore how good it felt. She needed to reject her desire to curl up and sink into the protection he was offering.

There is always a catch.

Finally, Carrick stopped in front of her apartment, seeming to take a second to assess the brownstone before them. Once he was seemingly satisfied, he grunted, "Got your keys?"

He waltzed them up the five-step porch staircase while she fumbled for her keys in her pocket. As soon as she had them out, he took them, as natural as could be. With one arm, he unlocked the exterior door like he'd lived there for years, moving them into the small foyer that had three more doors for different apartments.

"Now, let's talk," he said, putting her down, briefly gazing up at the large painting hanging in the foyer.

She found the dated, packed carpet underneath her, grounding her back in the reality of her life. She backed up, trying to understand him.

"You said you are here to help me. What does that mean?" she asked, knowing it was now or never.

"Well, Dani, I was asked to come find you," he explained, his eyes locked on her every move, sending chills up her spine, "and I have."

"And?" She crossed her arms, sinking back, determined to stay strong. "Who asked you to do this?"

"Your father."

Danica's mouth dropped open.

"Have you told him where I am?" She couldn't hold back the tone of desperation and fear in her voice.

The pure terror.

"Yes."

Winded, she took a step back, falling into anything that could help her find stability. She searched the man before her, trying to figure out what the hell his game was.

"Are you scared of him?" Carrick asked, watching her as she stepped farther away from him. "Will he hurt you?"

She bit her lip, unable to resist doing so. That was not something she was prepared to admit to. Her heart sank with the reality she faced and the need to uproot herself yet again. She dropped her gaze and shook her head. How many new identities would she have to fake before she could finally just get away?

"Talk to me," Carrick commanded. There was nothing soft in his voice.

But Danica didn't want to tell him anything.

"Are you going to leave me?" She regretted the words as she said them, and immediately felt the pain of being exposed.

"Only if you are safe," he assured, but then demanded more from her. "You need to tell me — Are you scared of *him*?"

Danica pressed her eyes shut momentarily. She couldn't tell him all of it. Never, not once, had she told anyone the truth about what that man had done to her, so she bit her tongue, holding her silence.

"I can't take action if I don't have answers." He pushed on, giving her the chance to speak. "All you have to do is *tell* me what's really going on."

Danica opened her eyes and shook her head as she counted the threads on the carpet beneath her socked feet. She was too ashamed to look up and face Carrick.

Changing the tone, he shifted his weight and leaned against the wall with her. As she looked through the top of her lashes, she realized he was focused on the painting behind her in the foyer, observing and considering. She turned toward the complex piece of artwork with its bright, vivid colors that loosely depicted a perfect female form wrapped in bright green vines.

"That's stunning."

"Thanks." Danica looked back up into Carrick's stormy eyes and tried to breathe.

He raised an eyebrow. He was clearly intrigued. "You painted that?"

"Yes," she replied softly, shier than ever. "The foyer needed some life."

"You're talented...very talented." Carrick nodded approvingly, looking back and forth between the nude female form and Danica.

A hot flush hit her cheeks, and it wasn't just from coming into a warm building from the cold night.

"She looks imprisoned by those vines. Is that the case?" His gaze shot to her more intensely.

He was analyzing her, looking for the deeper meaning. And he was right, so she nodded. As he cocked his head, further studying what she'd painted, Danica couldn't help but explain.

"The natural world plays a big part in my life."

"There's much more to you than meets the eye, isn't there?" he asked quietly, in a low, smooth voice. "I like that."

She shivered as his words spilled over her. He saw her. He was seeing her. The look in his eye continued to reveal a curious man, interested in learning all her secrets. And she so wanted to confide in him — the first person who had ever made her feel like that in a long, long time.

Looking at one of the doors to the rental units in the hall, right behind where she stood, he continued, "And you live with someone?"

"Yes, my friend." Her gaze flitted to her locked apartment door, which opened to a staircase leading up to her flat. She could never let him in. Never.

Even so, words continued to pour out against her will. "She's out for the night. It's... Valentine's Day, after all."

She clamped down on her tongue after she'd said it, regretting whatever it suggested. She was being an idiot. What would he think? She needed to stop...

"And what about you?" He leaned back, continuing to assess. The deep baritone of his questions — his apparent need to understand — planted something inside her that felt like a hot coil. "No boyfriend?"

"Are you really asking me that?"

He smirked, leaning a little closer. "Maybe."

"I don't date," she squeaked out, embarrassed at the truth. She looked down at her shoeless feet, frumpy and unpolished.

"You don't...date?" He laughed genuinely, natural and smooth. He had a rich, warm, hearty laugh, as he continued his questioning. "You mean to tell me that *you* don't date?"

The concept apparently seemed unbelievable to him, and he appeared highly amused.

She stood still, frozen.

"You must be delusional," Carrick concluded, shaking his head. "Or deeply religious — or both."

She crossed her arms tightly, trying to steady herself.

"Look... I think we should talk about what you are planning on doing now that you've found me. That's what matters here — not whether or not I'm dating."

He drew his teeth across his lip, something dangerous twinkling in his eye, as he looked her up and down slowly for the hundredth time. He reached out his thick hand and tilted her chin up toward him. He was still close to her and she was aware of his warm breath and his heat. Against her better judgment, she let her eyes connect with his and sink into his intensity. And she obediently tilted her chin up to match his great height.

"You undersell yourself."

"You don't know anything about me," she said to reject his words — reject everything that threatened her narrative.

"I know what I see."

What does he see? She parted her lips as she fell further into his darkly lashed, deep blue gemstone eyes. *Sapphires in a storm.*

He ran his hand up her throat, gripping her jaw and angling it, seemingly to get a better look at her. She obeyed as he moved her, revealing how much she was growing to love when he touched her like that. The intensity in his gaze was startling. It was clear he wanted to know her secrets.

"You have to trust me," he ordered, focusing intently on her. "You have to tell me what's really going on."

She tried to shake out of his spell, stiffening her spine. "I can't."

Her words left a faint echo in the foyer.

"Then there's nothing I can do." He pulled back and let his hand drop from her face.

He gave her a second to change her mind, but she couldn't. None of his rapport-building had made a difference. She wasn't going to tell him what he wanted to hear—because she just couldn't.

Carrick let out a seemingly frustrated breath and turned back to the door. Everything in Danica's heart ached as he moved to leave. *It shouldn't be like this.* With a quick nod goodbye, he disappeared out of the door, leaving her behind.

Alone.

Crushed, she leaned against the foyer wall then fell to the floor in her socked feet. For a minute or two, she just closed her eyes and rubbed her hands over her face. Finally, she decided to get up and make a move.

Then everything fell apart.

The front door whipped open, but instead of hearing the welcome voice of Carrick once again, an unwelcome, familiar paternal voice echoed through the foyer, filling her with unparalleled fear.

"*Dansa,*" an aging man wheezed as he walked in. "I have been looking for you for too long. You will not disobey me again."

Chapter Five

Carrick

Madder than an angry dog, Carrick leaned on the armored SUV with his elbow on Delta's driver-side window. He maintained a strong silence while watching events unfold before his and his partner's eyes — events he'd never planned to see.

About five houses down, a couple of stubby bouncer-type guys with dark suits stood at the sidewalk leading up to Danica's apartment. They'd locked it down because Carrick's client was inside — talking to his daughter.

It didn't feel right. Nothing about it felt right. It took everything in Carrick's power not to force his way back into that situation.

"I didn't take this 'search and rescue' contract thinking it would end up in 'hostage rescue'." Carrick finally broke the silence in a low, critical tone.

Delta nodded, sitting in the driver's seat beside Carrick, gripping the wheel of the SUV tightly. The engine was off, but both men were flexed and ready to make a move if they had to. Carrick's feet, firmly planted on the cold concrete of the road below, felt the rumbling of distant traffic in the urban residential community.

"Yeah—I'm not going to lie to you, Moose. This guy has been playing silly buggers with you," Delta grunted, looking around.

"For once, you might actually be right." Carrick shot his friend a sardonic look. "This isn't what I signed up for."

"How did this guy find you?"

"Said it was a recommendation from a *happy* customer, but he wouldn't say who," Carrick replied slowly, shaking his head in self-loathing. "Yup, Petrov cooked up some big fucking story, all right. His poor, estranged daughter is vulnerable and in danger. He can't find her to warn her. Then he went on and on about this fucking shadowy evil that's out to get her."

"You bought it."

"That's right. I fucking bought it all."

The two men grunted together, seething that some Russian asshole had gotten the better of them.

"That dark car chasing us from the rink was a goddamn ploy," Delta said, flipping his cell phone rhythmically in his hand, "trying to turn up the tempo."

Carrick sucked his teeth, seething in anger. "Fucking right. I think it's damn clear that no one is after Danica—no one, except for *him*."

The worst part spiraled in Carrick's mind, something he was unwilling to admit.

She's scared of Petrov and I left her alone with him.

Guilt crashed over him and he knew that was the final straw. It was time to make a move. He pushed off the SUV, Delta instantly calling after him in the background.

"Don't be a hero," were the last words he heard from his old crewmate.

That wasn't what Carrick was planning on doing, but he couldn't help but reach around to the rear waistband of his pants and grab the cold steel of his pistol's grip. Wrapping his hands around it, he concealed it underneath his thick, black sweater, watching the two bouncers as he approached. Like a jaguar stalking his prey, his senses heightened, and every move they made echoed through his mind. He could take them both in the fucking blink of an eye. That wasn't what he was worried about.

One of the bouncers turned to him and held up his hand.

"Hey, watch it, buddy."

"I'm not your fucking buddy," Carrick growled, moving forward without a pause.

He found his way to their position and was ready to push past them to get to the girl. He wasn't going to waste another second without answers.

But it didn't come to that.

Kosta Petrov, an American-Russian businessman, pushed open the front door to Danica's apartment and came walking out, clutching a cane to help him walk. Tall, round and snarling, he stopped when he saw Carrick steps away from him. Petrov's gaze floated from man to man, and it was clear he knew what was happening—for the most part.

"What the hell are you doing?" he wheezed at Carrick, a lock of his gray hair falling out of place onto his forehead.

Carrick narrowed his eyes but played it cool. "We need to talk."

Petrov grunted, smoothing his hair back, then continued moving forward down the sidewalk, nodding to the bouncers to bring around the car. That left Carrick alone with him. It was a good thing Carrick was taller—by a few inches at least. And for maybe the first time in the businessman's life, Petrov was looking up at someone.

Carrick held back, though—trained to be slick and smooth. He knew how to make things happen, how to talk to people. And chest-pointing or dick-measuring wasn't going to help.

"Your payment." Petrov nodded at the car that was pulling up. "In cash."

"I said check or wire transfer," Carrick replied, emotionless, matching the confidence and intensity of the drilling mogul. "We do things by the book."

"Is my money not good enough for you?" Petrov demanded, his dark eyes framed by gray eyebrows, which were narrowing as he challenged Carrick.

"I don't take cash," Carrick insisted, fully understanding what Petrov was after.

Petrov made no noise or any movement.

"You did a good job," Petrov finally spoke, cutting the silence. "And your observations?"

"She's being watched. You got that for sure," Carrick lied, choosing his words carefully. "I don't know by who, but I know they aren't amateurs. Do you have any enemies?"

Petrov shot a yellowing smile, like he knew something Carrick didn't and was pleased about it. It was poisonous, and Carrick knew what a slippery snake looked like. He was clearly not willing to provide any information.

"And who's going to keep her safe now?" Carrick followed up, probing.

"*You* will protect Dansa." The Russian accent came through harder when the businessman spoke his daughter's name.

There it was. Petrov wanted him to become the girl's bodyguard — or prison guard. Carrick's stare never left the man's face, confirming to Carrick that there were layers and layers of secrets to the story. There was something going on — something serious.

"Protect her?" Carrick demanded.

"I need someone to make sure she stays safe," Petrov smirked and took out a check, signing it. "Write your price on here and cash it tomorrow."

Carrick flexed his muscles and stretched, not answering immediately to give the conversation some air. He didn't like this. The undertone was clear. It wasn't about keeping her safe. It was about keeping her under control.

Before Carrick could respond, Petrov broke out into a coughing fit, unable to catch his breath. He reached into the pocket of his jacket and pulled out an inhaler, taking a deep breath from the mouthpiece. It was then that Carrick came to fully appreciate that the man was obviously not in good health.

"What do you want me to do with her?" Carrick asked.

"Let's start with you escorting her to LA tomorrow." Petrov continued wheezing. "Her cousin is getting married, and she needs to be there."

"Then what?" Carrick pressed.

Petrov continued, smirking. "I'll give you further instructions after the wedding."

Petrov reached out his shaking hand, the check between his fingers, holding it out to Carrick. He squinted through the shadowy night while Carrick let the cold night's air fill his lungs, unmoving. Petrov shifted in surprise at his lack of response, almost drawing back. Carrick shot his hand out to accept the check, relaxing the arm gripping the pistol in his sweater.

Seemingly relieved, Petrov nodded with a tone of finality and staggered away toward the idling black luxury car sitting on the road.

Carrick watched the car pull away, and he settled into deep focus.

Now I am in charge.

He looked back up at the brownstone apartment building. In the window on the second floor, he saw Dani's familiar face peeking through the curtain, but she quickly shut it upon realizing she'd been seen.

Delta sauntered toward him from the direction of the SUV. He took a position near Carrick, and they scanned the neighborhood — watching for anything and everything. The night was young, and something told Carrick it wasn't over yet.

"What the fuck was that all about?" Delta asked, keeping his voice down so that no one else could hear.

"Petrov extended my contract," Carrick replied though a clenched jaw. "Punishment for a job well done."

Delta snorted, "No—just fucking no. What does he want now?"

Carrick replied cautiously, knowing it wasn't going to land well. "He wants me to be her prison guard. He wants me to drag her by the hair to LA for a fucking wedding tomorrow."

"That's bullshit," Delta spat, calling a spade a spade. "I don't like this guy. Wash your hands of this."

Carrick let out a pinched breath. "Believe me, I fucking know. But what the hell am I supposed to do?"

"Drop it. It's not your problem," Delta pushed.

And that is the truth.

"I can't," Carrick replied, knowing his own limitations. "You've still got the SEALs, but this is all I've got now."

Delta took a step forward then turned to stare his friend down with visible seriousness. It was clear that Delta saw through Carrick's implication and recognized how unfounded it was, because Delta had been there every step of the last two years—every time Carrick had hit the bottom of another bottle, every time Carrick had whipped something breakable against the wall, every time Carrick had become swamped with feelings and had started missing her.

"Look... I know this is a difficult day for you," Delta levelled with him.

"No," Carrick grunted, warning his crewmate to stop. "That has nothing to do with it."

"Man, you can't spend your whole life trying to save every girl," Delta said, concern in his voice. "It wasn't your fault what happened with Lauren. There was nothing you could have done."

Her name hit Carrick like a bag of fucking bricks, and he immediately felt winded...absolutely. He didn't spend a lot of time thinking about Lauren anymore, about what had happened—and how his life had taken a nosedive after she was gone.

His throat became tight, and something started hurting in his head.

"Look... Let's just fucking get the girl to LA and be done with it," Carrick commanded, and Delta relented.

It was a promise Carrick wouldn't keep—and Delta likely knew it.

Chapter Six

Carrick

Carrick reclined the seat slightly in his rented pickup truck as he kept his eye on the street down the hill. In the distance, he could see Danica's apartment — dark and quiet — as it should be, considering it was the middle of the night. She was supposed to be sleeping.

As for him, it was going to be a long night — keeping his eyes locked on her place, making sure no one went in or came out. He still hadn't figured out how he was going to play it.

Hours ago, he'd ordered Delta to grab him a rental and take the armored SUV back to LA. Carrick hadn't expected to be working Danica's contract for an extended period of time, and he needed Delta to manage the office until he could get back. Thank God Delta was in between rotations and had a little time on his hands before his next deployment. Carrick didn't want to take any chances leaving the office cold.

It had turned out that weekends were even busier in the private security industry than weekdays—especially so in greater LA. If Carrick had been looking for a normal pace of life after retiring from the SEALs, he hadn't yet achieved it. Maybe he'd just lied to himself when he'd said he wanted to get his life together—when he'd woken up in a pool of booze and blood, unsure where he'd been or what he'd done. Those had been dark, dark days—and he still kept the memory of them close to his chest as a reminder.

A painful reminder of what had happened when he'd let himself love someone.

Suddenly, Carrick noticed movement. It wasn't at the front door of her apartment. It was a shadow cast on the brick wall on the side of her building. He sprang forward in the seat, knowing he had to make a move. Pistol safely stowed in his pants, hand on the truck's door, he was ready to stalk. But he didn't have to. A familiar, lithe figure with a hood up crouched in the bushes at the front of the house.

He knew it was her. He just knew.

He had to give it to her. No one would have seen her—no one, of course, except for a former SEAL who was trained in urban warfare and black ops, a warrior with precise eyes, naturally adept at night vision, someone who knew what he was looking for.

Slouching down farther into the seat of the dark, parked truck, he watched her slink through the front lawns, keeping herself hidden behind fences and shrubs. Eventually, she made her way to the end of the street, toward the main drag running through the neighborhood. Up ahead, he heard the distinct sounds of a big bus approaching and saw her move to the stop. She was catching a ride.

It was clear that she was making a break for it. With a heavy black bag on her back, she looked like she'd packed for more than just a night away.

After the bus stopped and took off again, he turned on the engine of the rental truck and followed. She would have no idea he was driving it, but he'd keep his distance anyway. Whatever she was doing only served to confirm what he'd thought. She was afraid. She was afraid of her father – and she had good enough reason to fucking split.

Grinding his teeth together, he drove behind the San Francisco city bus, keeping his distance. The roadways weren't packed, but they weren't dead either – just busy enough to cover him. Quickly, he found that the bus was taking them toward the edge of the city, toward the long-haul coach depot.

"She's getting out of Dodge," he grumbled to himself, slowing his speed.

He caught a red light but was able to watch her offload from the bus parked in the distance. She went into the coach bus depot, which obviously was open at all hours. Maybe she really was a wayward runaway.

"Shit," he grunted, as the light took too long.

A minute or two went by, and he realized that if he didn't move fast, he was going to lose her. When the light went green, he hit the gas and found his way toward the depot, but he didn't have time to turn into the drive. A charter bus exited the rear parking lot, and an LED display above the front window indicated that it was heading toward Fresno, California.

Is she on that bus?

Carrick slowed his speed yet again, allowing a car that was faster to merge in front of him as he tried to make a decision – turn into the depot or follow that bus? One choice was right, and the other was wrong. He had no idea which was which, but he had a fucking guess.

Call it instinct.

He hit the gas again, moving the heavy pickup truck into a faster lane, and found a safe distance behind the charter bus that was heading to Fresno.

"Committed now," Carrick said, flipping on the tunes in the truck, settling in for a long drive. Fresno was hours away.

As he followed, his mind spun with questions about whether or not he'd made the right choice, but the way he saw it, he only had one chance. If he'd gone into the depot and she wasn't there, he'd have missed her. The reality was that those charter buses had many, many stops on the way to their final destination, and he needed to keep his eye on it to make sure she didn't bail early.

Something in his gut told him he'd made the right choice, and he wasn't usually wrong.

As hours passed while he trailed the bus, thoughts of Petrov, the contract and the weird fucking situation danced around in his brain. What the fuck was it all about? And what the fuck was he going to do about it?

I have to protect her.

The coach eventually slowed down in an isolated town, partway to Fresno, in the interior of Northern California. They were far, far away from the city stretches of San Fran or LA. In fact, if he threw the sunroof back, he knew he'd see the stars on the clear night. This was his type of place.

Up ahead, the bus pulled over and let out a few people. Carrick slowed his truck and lowered the brim of his baseball hat as he drove by the travelers, milling about on the side of the road. As the bus took off again, he noticed a familiar girlish form with her hood up, wearing a heavy black bag.

He hadn't been wrong.

She was on the bus.

He immediately pulled the truck onto the side of the road—a small patch of concrete lit up by a single streetlight in the one-shop town. The other travelers dispersed quickly, heading wherever they needed or wanted to go.

Carrick jumped out of the truck, breathing in the cold air of the dry night. As soon as he let the driver's door shut, Danica whipped her head around, flashing her eyes at him. She realized who it was and she gasped. With what he assumed was instinct birthed by a habit, she bolted.

Running as fast as she could—far, far away from him.

"Well, this is fucking going well," he cracked, and instantly sprinted after her.

He easily closed the distance between them.

"Dani!" he bellowed. "Fucking slow down."

Finally close enough, he lunged and grabbed her arm, pulling her into him. She fought back, slapping and punching at his chest. She was damn strong— much stronger than she appeared. He quickly released her when he heard her breathing sharpen and her sobs start. It was easy to understand that was she desperate as hell.

She was terrified.

"Hey, it's okay," he assured her, making a mental note to give her real fighting lessons someday. "I'm not going to hurt you."

Danica cried out harder, tears streaming down her cheeks. "That's what he always said. That's always what he wanted me to hear."

Carrick sucked back whatever lump was in his throat, his eyes widening.

"Dani, talk to me." He took a stronger tone, feeling every muscle flex protectively as he yanked her into him. "Who said that? Your father?"

"He's not my father!" she pushed Carrick hard against his chest, her voice cracking in pain. She was beginning to hyperventilate, and he saw anger and deep hurt.

Suddenly, something Carrick had felt deep inside started making sense.

Kosta Petrov isn't her father?

She winced and twisted as she sputtered out tears, struggling to breathe. He felt that pain. Someone had really done a number on her. As she pushed harder and harder against his chest, shrieking as she cried, Carrick did the only thing he knew.

He wrapped his big, muscled arms around her small frame and hugged her tight against him. It was a bear hug she'd never be able to get out of. He sucked in air slowly and rhythmically, making sure to release his hot breath onto her soft hair as he gently smoothed the stray locks. He wasn't sure if it was going to work at first, but in a minute, her crying abated and she buried her face into his chest, breathing with him.

Finally, he pulled her back slightly so that he could see her face.

"Hey." He exhaled down on her, assessing where she was at. "Everything's going to be okay."

Under that one streetlight, he could see red eyes and a redder nose. Her heart-shaped face, dusted with a golden tan, was wet from tears and wincing in pain.

"Why are you doing this?" she challenged him, her eyes batting out tears. "Just leave me alone."

He let out another strong lungful, keeping her with him. "Well, congrats. I'm your bodyguard now."

She shot him a confused look and her mouth dropped. "What? Why? Is he paying you?"

He brought her back into his chest, holding her head against him again. The answer was obvious. He clenched his jaw, hating it all the same. That wasn't why he was there – but he obviously could never say that.

"Look… Let's just get you somewhere safe, somewhere to sleep. It's the middle of the night," he said, "and we can take it from there."

Her muscles flexed and she was trying to push away, but this time he let her go.

"No," she snorted, "I'm not going with you. You are not my bodyguard. I don't know why you chose to follow me, but I'll tell you this for free. I want nothing to do with you. Leave me alone!"

She turned on her heels and started marching away from him at a fast clip. Of course, Carrick couldn't let her get away again. He didn't want to kidnap her, but he didn't want to watch her go – not deep into the desert mountains in the middle of the night. She was obviously a girl in trouble – more trouble than he'd first expected.

In the darkness, his mind started flashing memories across his consciousness. At first, he was reminded of an operation he'd run with the SEALs in sub-Saharan Africa, then he remembered something much, much worse. A pang of fear shot through him, a fear he'd never admit or breathe out loud. He had to own the memories from his past, whether he liked them or not.

For a few moments, Carrick stalked behind her, taking in their surroundings and watching her. Danica hunched over, clutching the bag tighter to her back, and panting steadily, between the uphill hiking and stress. He had to admire her resolve. One thing had become damn clear. She was willful, strong and determined to survive. Carrick grew more and more drawn to her with the realization that she was much, much greater than what she appeared.

She's spirited as fuck.

As they moved farther away from the streetlight, they found themselves in deeper darkness, on the side of a deserted road in the middle of the night. Unfortunately for her, night raids were his bread and butter. He wasn't in danger of losing her.

"Go away!" she yelled back at him, as if her snarling voice could deter him.

Frowning and dogged, Carrick trailed her without pause, as though he were hunting challenging prey. The more she told him to leave, the more he wanted to stay.

It wasn't but a little farther down the road before Carrick heard a sound he knew well — one he'd never forget. Very much like a person whistling or a bird chirping, a strange sound emanated from the bushes on the edge of the road where a thick brush of trees sat, leading up the mountainside. Alarms rang in his mind — emergency. He immediately lunged toward Danica, reaching back into his waistband to grab his pistol.

Probably startled by his sudden movement, Danica whipped around to find him in the darkness. The unmistakable sound of a mountain lion charging out of the bushes echoed through Carrick's ears, and acting on pure instinct, he took a shot, pushing Danica down to protect her under his body.

Goddamn, he would fucking save her if it was the last thing he did.

The bullet tore through flesh, resulting in a yelp from the mountain lion and a hot mess of blood down Carrick's arm. Yet Carrick felt the unmistakable pain in his arm from teeth sinking in, resulting in a deep, angry groan from his own throat. The mountain lion fell backward, growling low and raspy. Carrick moved Danica farther back behind him, guarding her, and all grew still on the roadside. Slowly, the mountain lion slunk backward, the shuffling of paws and a low whine the only audible sounds. It was too dark to assess the wildcat, but Carrick guessed the animal wouldn't survive.

A damn shame.

After a moment, with enough space between them and the predator, Carrick turned slightly, putting his pistol back in his waistband, tactical and precise, then dropped to pick up Danica. He kicked up dust in the sandy dirt of the roadside as he marched back toward the truck, holding a trembling, terrified woman to his chest.

Carrick couldn't believe how the night was unfolding. Yet he had to admit that it still wasn't the worst Valentine's Day he'd ever had.

Without a word or asking permission to touch her, he heaved Danica into the passenger side of the truck, only to find that his arm was covered in blood — but he realized it wasn't the mountain lion's blood. Wrapping the wound in his sweater, unable to feel the pain, he made his way to the driver's side.

Starting the engine, he cocked his head to her. "Are we doing this?"

Danica nodded quickly as she looked up and over to him. "Where to?"

Carrick searched her beautiful face. Her innocent gaze was pleading and frightened, but then the air shifted, and for some reason, he no longer was looking into Danica's eyes but saw crisp blue eyes surrounded by brown lashes — blue eyes that weren't there. What he was looking at wasn't real, but he couldn't stop the vision. His entire body stiffened in the driver's seat as all he could see was Lauren's face — with her head on the hospital pillow. She was scared. She was helpless. She was dying.

And there is nothing I can do to save her.

Chapter Seven

Danica

Danica anxiously ran her finger up and down the scratchy bedsheet on the motel's lumpy mattress, trying hard to quell the rollercoaster of emotions she was experiencing. Even though it was dark inside the room, she still avoided the corner where Carrick was sitting, because she knew he was watching her. She was still damn mad that he'd forced his presence on her, but she'd grown equally glad that he'd shown up.

And it was exactly that juxtaposition that irritated her. She just didn't know how to react. *How am I supposed to feel?* While her mind spiraled, she could hear him stirring and crossing his arms in the corner of the dark motel room. Was he going to spend the rest of the night in that chair? Just looking at her?

"How am I supposed to fall asleep," she finally asked, narrowing her eyes on his darkened frame, "with you *watching* me like this?"

"Just close your eyes," he ordered her, cold and emotionless. "We've got just about six hours until check out."

"Then what?"

But he didn't reply.

Trying to get comfortable curled up under the starchy white duvet of the room, she flitted her eyes back to the red numbers on the digital clock — *four o' clock in the morning*. Her eyes felt weighted and her skin cold. She was exhausted, physically and mentally. Nothing seemed easy. Nothing.

"I'm not going to run," she lied.

"Good."

She exhaled, wishing she hadn't said anything at all and that the words would stop coming out of her mouth. But, in her heart, she knew there was something else she had to say. She had to stay true to herself — and true to the natural world around her.

"Thank you," she mumbled, needing to express her gratitude.

"What was that?" he asked, much louder than she'd spoken.

Frustrated, she cleared her throat. Was he testing her?

"I said — *thank you*." The words came out a little heavier than she'd expected, and a thickness filled the air. "For saving me, again."

"I heard you the first time," he replied, the sound of amusement in his voice. "I just needed a sanity check."

She squeezed the blanket harder and made a mental note never to open up to him again, since all he wanted to do was throw it in her face.

"Let this be a lesson," Carrick went on in a lecturing tone. "Listen to me the first time *and* trust me."

"No," she said sharply, making herself clear. She rolled onto her other side, away from him.

The least she could do was not look at him or what she could see of his tall, dark, muscular form. She pressed her eyes closed, willing it to all go away and the panic inside her chest to cease. *What am I going to do now?*

Quickly, sleep found her. Or to be more accurate, a state of unconsciousness took her under.

* * * *

Danica flickered her eyes open slowly what must have been hours and hours later, only to see soft beams of morning sunlight breaking through the aged curtains in the motel room. She kept the white blanket close to her chest, protecting herself out of sheer reflex. Hearing rumblings off to the side of the room, she turned her head.

A familiar tall man made solely out of sculpted hard muscle in a gray fitted long-sleeved T-shirt and fitted black jeans was bent over a black duffel bag on the floor by the front door. Still dopey from a rough night, she watched him for a second or two as he reached up and smoothed back his hair. Her waking mind just drank him in, too groggy to feel. The golden tan on the back of his neck spoke of life experience and plenty of time outside. At least, she thought, there was something they'd have in common.

He leaned back and looked over his shoulder at her. She sucked in breath as a ray of morning sun caught his face, illuminating his eyes. She'd thought they were dark brownish—but they were actually a dark bluish-green and they shocked and startled her. She sucked in her breath, feeling goosebumps crawl up her thighs. There was something so intense about the way he looked at her.

"Morning," he greeted her in his low, cool voice, looking her up and down as she sat up in bed.

Rubbing her hands over her cool, naked arms, she suddenly felt very exposed in just a gray tank top and a pair of purple bikini-cut underwear. Grabbing something from the black bag on the ground, he then moved to grab a chair and pulled it up to the bedside table, just feet from her. His scent filled her nose, and she couldn't help but flutter her lashes as she inhaled. He was so damn masculine, so resolute—and that was enough to give her pause.

"Breakfast," Carrick said, putting a napkin down on the bedside table and placing what appeared to be some sort of sandwich on it.

"What is this?" Danica's voice cracked as she reached over to inspect it while he unscrewed the top of a bottle of water for her.

"It's a breakfast sandwich." He raised his eyebrow, searching her. "Look... It's not much, but I only packed essentials for this...job."

The word hung briefly between them as she flitted her gaze up to his. It was clear that he felt deep discomfort at the current arrangement, which suited her well, since she didn't like it either. He was being paid to be there. He didn't want to be.

She reached out and picked at the sandwich—bread, cheese, a sausage patty and a tomato. Another chill ran up her spine as she looked up and saw his forehead furrowed as he watched her.

"Um..." she began, clearing her throat.

"Yes?" his tone turned to a growl.

She shifted on the edge of the bed and let out a breath. "I'm vegan."

"What the fuck does that mean?"

"I don't eat meat." Her voice grew small.

Groaning, he reached over and pulled out the sausage patty from the sandwich, reaffixing it back together as bread, cheese and a tomato.

She let out another breath, closing her eyes in regret. She was not a difficult person. She was *not*.

"Vegans don't eat dairy either," she specified.

He narrowed his eyes farther, and his jaw flexed. Without saying anything, he pulled out the piece of cheese and patted the sandwich back together as bread and a tomato.

"And bread usually has egg products in it...so," she began, but she couldn't continue as he let out a low growl and grabbed the tomato out, flinging it on the napkin alone.

"I'll find you a fucking apple," he grunted at her, pushing himself off the bed. "You need to eat. We've got things to do."

"We've?" she replied slowly. "Things to do?"

Carrick stood over her, looking down. Danica recalled the reality she was in. Nothing was going according to her plan. Now Carrick, on the other hand? He clearly had a plan and expected her to be the passenger along for the ride.

"What did Petrov say to you after I left?" he asked.

Her gaze fell, counting the threads on the carpet again. She was sure Carrick already knew, so what was the point in trying to hide it?

"He wants me in LA for my cousin's wedding this afternoon," she replied, finally, in a shaky tone. "Is that why he hired you?"

Carrick paused, rubbing his scruffy chin.

"I don't know Petrov's intentions. I only know what he told me," he explained, his body stiffening.

Danica couldn't help but tilt her head, trying to understand what he was saying.

Carrick continued, "Why don't *you* tell me what's going on here? Who the fuck is Petrov to you if he's not your father?"

Letting out some air, Danica searched for the most minimal amount of information she could cough up to placate Carrick. She needed him on her side.

"Petrov has tried to position himself as a father figure to me," she told him slowly, checking her tone, trying so hard to hold the deep, burning hatred out of it. "My parents died five years ago."

"How did your parents die?" he asked.

"Car accident," she replied, and opened her mouth to say more — but she stopped herself.

Carrick just watched, waiting for her to continue.

She confessed, "I ran as soon as I could. I ran away from his circle of influence, from his agenda."

"Let me guess. He never treated you like a real daughter?"

The question nearly made her laugh because of how truly disgusting the answer was. Not only had he not treated her like a daughter, but in that short time after her parents had died, he'd treated her like another member of his enterprise — to be controlled and punished accordingly. But she bit her tongue. Those were not stories for this man.

"This wedding —" Carrick started.

Danica anxiously cut him off. "Are you going to force me to go?"

"Hell no," Carrick scoffed. "Not a chance. Not without knowing what the fuck is going on here."

Her whole body froze, trying to let his words sink in.

"Tell me, Danica." He lowered his head, growling. "Is Petrov trying to hurt you? What do I need to know?"

"He's controlling, abusive." She formed words, curling her lips in anger as hatred rose from her core. "The man is a monster. You have no idea what he's done."

"Then tell me."

"I can't." She dropped her gaze as a choking feeling rose in her throat. The pain of her past shot through her nervous system.

She shook her head slightly. *Confide in him? Absolutely not.* Her trust didn't extend that far, and it *never* would. She knew she couldn't buckle — especially under the intensity of someone like Carrick.

He's just as dangerous.

"I'm going to take a shower," she announced, desperate to get away.

She popped off the bed, keeping her gaze away from his, and moved toward the bathroom with purpose. As distance grew between her and his looming form, Danica felt increasingly alone — and not in the way she usually wanted to be. It was a strange, strange feeling.

Shutting the bathroom door behind her, an emptiness grew like a hard lump in her chest, and even the beauty of the early morning sun beaming through the window couldn't refill her. Shaking her head, she wondered what had gotten into her.

Taking a long, deep breath in the bathroom, she looked around. She realized Carrick had left things out for her—toothbrush, toothpaste, shampoo and soap. And it wasn't the shitty motel stuff. He'd actually thoughtfully laid out necessities. As she whipped on the hottest water and stepped into the tub, she acknowledged that this was a man who was genuinely working to take care of her.

Trying to keep me safe.

The feeling was strange, and it was the only thing that had stopped her from making an effort to squeeze out of the bathroom window and bolt.

As she washed herself, she had a random thought that caused her to raise an eyebrow. *Maybe I'm looking at this situation all wrong*, she thought, as she rinsed her body in the hot water. Carrick clearly had excellent tactical, outdoorsman and survival skills—things she needed if she ever wanted her big plan to work. Danica flipped off the water, and grabbed a crisp white towel from the rack.

I could ask him to teach me?

Danica nodded to herself, realizing what a genius idea she'd just had. Once she'd learned enough from him, she could finally leave—reclaiming her life on her own, once and for all. That was something she'd wanted for a long, long time. She'd known friends who had reclaimed their lives by turning camping into a lifestyle, and she was just as happy to get lost in the Northern California forests—spending winters in a cabin in the woods while she climbed mountains and summers in a tent on the beach while she surfed the cool, salty water of the coast. Her deep connection to the natural world would heal her and put her broken spirit back together.

A smile crept over her lips—a wild, crazy kind of smile. Maybe the anxiety had finally spiraled to a point of insanity and she had grown just desperate enough. Whatever it was, Carrick was starting to look like an opportunity, not a curse.

As she got out of the shower, she could barely see because of the steam in the bathroom, and there was no working fan. She moved to open the small motel window there, but the damn thing was firmly shut. While she was heaving on it, pushing it hard, she slipped on the wet tile and lost her grip. It didn't help that little sleep and low blood sugar had clouded her mind and weakened her.

As her feet slipped out from underneath her, she yelped, and the bathroom door whipped open. Carrick lunged forward, grabbing her arms as she almost cracked her head on the wall. Lifting her to her feet, he smoothed his hands over and over her face, running his gaze up and down, likely to check that she was okay.

"You said you weren't going to run." He spoke in a low, warning tone, continuing to hold her face in his hands.

"I was just trying to open the window for air," she explained, but she didn't step back from his grasp.

As he held her jaw, he stared into her eyes. The towel had fallen off her body, and even through the steam, she had no doubt that he could see her naked form if he looked, but his gaze didn't drift down.

"You slipped because you are faint."

She said nothing, just blinked back up at him. Something in his eyes changed in that instant — and there was a flash of emotion. It was the opposite of what she'd seen of him before — collected, emotionless, cool. Something wild and passionate had flashed across his face as he'd looked at her.

"You aren't taking care of yourself."

"*Yes*, I am." Her words came out more defensive than she'd intended.

"I can't sit back and let all this bullshit happen." He let out, his head dropping lower to hers. "You *have* to talk to me. Give me something to go on."

Danica felt a heat rising in her chest, a deep stirring of emotion. She tilted her mouth up to his, drinking him in. He was very, very close and wasn't moving back. He ran his thick, coarse hand down her back, sending goosebumps up her spine as she arched toward him. Her lips parted, which he clearly noticed.

"Carrick, we can't," she whispered.

He only frowned in response and tightened his grip on her. It seemed as though his big hands took up half of her back.

"Goddamn it, just fucking talk to me," he gnashed through a flexed jaw. "I can't fucking protect you if I don't know what the hell is going on here."

Danica's mouth dropped open. Why hadn't she seen it before? Never before had a man fought so diligently to *hear* her, and it threw her off completely, clawing at the defenses she had worked so, so hard on.

Cautiously, she ran her hand up his arm, feeling the definition of his muscles. When she drew her hand down again, he winced in response and pressed his eyes shut momentarily. Danica instantly glanced down at his left forearm where she'd touched, realizing he had a large bandage underneath his shirt. The vision of Carrick violently defending her against the mountain lion flashed to her mind. He could have been killed.

And now he's hurt.

"I can look at that for you," she offered, leaning in to look at the bandage.

"No," he scowled, pulling back.

Frustration built inside her, and she narrowed her eyes at him. She realized he wasn't the type of man to accept help, but he would probably always offer it.

Danica couldn't explain why, but in that instant, tears filled her eyes. Maybe she was just overwhelmed by what had happened between them. Maybe she'd just reached the end of her rope with him. It was hard to admit it, but the man had awakened something inside her. And now, here before her, he was focused on her, every inch of her, making her feel something she'd never felt before.

She took in a deep breath, trying to collect herself.

He risked his life for me.

"Why are you doing this?" she whispered, needing answers.

Carrick flashed her an expression that screamed he might be doubting her sanity. He tightened his grip on her, telling her things that he clearly couldn't say.

She knew that feeling.

Absently, she ran her hand up his biceps and shoulder toward his neck and the rough stubble on his cheek. A tattoo that clearly sprawled across his chest poked out of the V-neck of his long-sleeved shirt— some sort of dark writing, but she couldn't see more than a few edges. It was a tattoo that was as mysterious as he was. In that moment, gazing back up into his dark blue eyes, a strange feeling overtook her. She wanted him to kiss her more than anything. There was just something so raw between them in that moment. She needed to feel him *closer*. She needed something to believe in.

But he never would. He was too damn professional.

She bit her lip, pleading and begging him with her eyes. Surrounded by the bathroom fog, she angled her chin up toward him.

Please, Carrick.

He didn't miss her movements when she shifted in his arms, but he seemed to snap out of it. Blinking rapidly, as though he were trying to regain consciousness, Carrick reached to the towel bar, grabbed a towel and roughly shoved it at her.

"Checkout's in twenty," he growled, turning on his heels.

As he left her alone in the bathroom, tears welled in her eyes once more. His clear rejection drove hard pain up her chest, making it hard to breathe. Alarm bells rang through her mind and a realization washed over her. She knew nothing about the man. In that split second, Danica made a promise to herself. She would gain everything she could from him, but she would not, under any circumstances, let herself become vulnerable with him again.

It was too damn dangerous.

Chapter Eight

Danica

The passenger side of the red pickup truck wasn't uncomfortable, but Danica sure was. Right then, after what had happened in the bathroom, sitting beside Carrick was the last place she wanted to be. She crinkled her nose as the bright Northern Californian midday sun shone through the windshield and washed over her face. They'd been driving—in silence—for hours through the interior wine country.

"So, ready to talk now?" His casual tone nearly toppled her over. "I'm going to have to make a decision soon...and a plan."

Unfortunately for him, every limb in her body still screamed from what had happened in the bathroom—how he'd come so close then abruptly torn himself away. It was damn clear to her that it was a metaphor for whatever it was between them—that the piece of her that had even been thinking about opening up to him had just as abruptly slammed close.

So she clenched her teeth, looked out of the window and tried to figure out how to respond.

Carrick broke the brief silence. "Well, look at this. I almost forgot. Reach back and grab that small black bag behind my seat."

She turned, saw a black fabric handle and reached back to grab it. *What is he up to?* Bringing it forward, she ran her fingers over the zipper.

"Open it."

She flickered her gaze up, trying to read him. He never let on much. So, she opened the bag, curious as a kitten. She couldn't conceal a gasp when she realized what was inside.

Pulling out her white ice skates, she burst, "I thought I'd never see these again!"

A wide, self-satisfied smirk crossed his lips. "We couldn't allow that."

She ran her fingers along the metal blades, clearly realizing how much care he had taken. He'd cleaned her skates so they wouldn't get rusty.

"Thanks," she replied softly, putting the skates back in the bag and tucking them back beside her backpack. "My mom bought those for me."

She almost allowed herself to feel the kindness of the moment, until she realized it was just another ploy to butter her up. He needed something from her.

Carrick continued, seeming to know he had her just where he wanted her, "I can't figure out why all this bullshit just to get you down to LA. What's the big fucking deal about this wedding?"

Heat began to rise up Danica's neck, but she wanted to remain circumspect. However, something about

Carrick's demands made it hard. She always struggled to remain cool under intensity like that. She was just too sensitive.

"It's not about the wedding, Carrick," Danica retorted. "It's about the Russian community coming together, and *who* is going to be there—who he wants to see me. That's how these things work—and it's always been like this."

And that's why I can't escape.

"Who he wants to *see* you?" Carrick repeated, catching onto the right words.

Realizing how deep she'd just gotten herself, Danica let out a low, frustrated breath. There was no hope trying to quell his questions now.

"Petrov has essentially promised me to the CEO of his business," she squeaked finally through a pinched tone. "And this is his chance to...foist me into a marriage that he wants me to be in."

"And you don't want to marry the guy?" Carrick followed up quickly. "Obviously?"

Shaking her head, she seethed. "But that answer isn't good enough for Petrov. He thinks he owns me. He thinks he controls me. And this marriage would be very advantageous for both men."

Carrick let out a laugh, as if the whole situation were simple.

"This is a free country. You should tell him to fuck off, and file a police report," he stated while his hands ran up and down the wheel, gripping and tensing, like he was ready to fight. "Or better yet—I can help you send a clear message."

She looked over at him, her eyes wide and in shock that he would suggest that. Clearly, the man didn't understand how her family operated.

"That won't work." She exhaled slowly. "He reminded me yesterday that I'm part of his family, whether I like it or not, and the only way out is…*death*."

"Death?" Carrick's eyes shot to her, seemingly incredulous.

She nodded, raising her eyebrows, "After my parents died, he told me that the only way I'd survive was if I obeyed him."

Be obedient.

Be controlled.

The words of the threat flashed across her mind, sending searing pain through her gray matter.

"You have to do something. You can't just sit back and take this bullshit," Carrick growled low as he continued tensely gripping the wheel. "I can't believe this."

Carrick's body flexed as the conversation continued, as though he was ready to fight then and there. Maybe she should just let him fight for her? It was the best chance she had. Her attention was again drawn to the bulky bandage on his forearm, and she shook away her original thought. *I can't get him hurt again.*

"Forced marriage? That's fucked up," he continued. "You should be able to be with who you want."

"I've actually never been with anyone," she mumbled to herself, thinking the words were inaudible.

He whipped his head over to look at her again. His eyes were as big as saucers, in complete disbelief. *He heard.* Danica shrank in her seat, embarrassed as hell, and pulled her black denim mini skirt down a little. *Why did I said that?* The meaning was clear, and those same goosebumps ran up her spine again.

"You're a virgin?" he followed up, his tone low.

She nodded shyly and couldn't help but notice how he trained his eyes to her lips. Something in his gaze grew heavy. He was a man, just a man — and she couldn't forget that.

A dew formed between her breasts, which were covered by a thin white tank top that barely concealed anything. She didn't miss how much tighter he gripped the steering wheel, and how his foot had fallen harder on the gas. They were hurtling down the back roads of the arid, mountainous countryside, liable to fly off the side of a cliff at any time.

Yet, the only thing she was scared of in that moment was the way he was looking at her.

And the way she felt.

And what she wanted him to do about it all.

Embarrassed, feeling like a child in front of a big, bad man, she shook her head. She was doing a terrible job at keeping her cards close to her chest. She snapped her mouth closed. Now he knew too much about her.

Suddenly, Carrick slowed the pickup truck to a full stop on the side of the sandy road. There was finally a break in the mountainous range running through the interior of California, allowing passage to the next state. To the left, they could head toward Nevada — and wherever else she wanted to go.

But, to the right, a sign marked the winding way back down to LA.

"What's it going to be, Dani?" Carrick finally asked, turning to her. "I'll drive you to the next state over or I'll drive you back to LA. Are you going to make a stand, fight for yourself — or are you going to keep running?"

Danica raised her hand to point toward Nevada, of course, but caught his gaze in the process. His intense dark blue eyes drilled into her, and she felt winded.

"You can keep running, but he will always find you, and whoever he hires next might not be so nice," he explained slowly, watching her reactions.

The truth behind his message shot pain throughout her body, and she nearly started hyperventilating. She was not combative.

The word itself made her want to pass out.

"I'm not a fighter," she admitted.

Black spots were taking over her vision, so she opened the door to the pickup and swung her legs out, keeping her peripheral vision locked into where Carrick was. Naturally, he was coming around the side of the truck as well but keeping his distance from her physically. She wasn't surprised. But she needed some air.

Her white tennis shoes dug into the dusty, sun-bleached dirt on the roadside, and a little sagebrush lizard climbed onto her toe. She knelt down instinctively, picking the little guy up so he didn't cross the road. His little brownish body slipped through her fingers, dancing around the back of her hand. He was so free.

That's what I want to be.

She moved toward a prickly desert bush and allowed the lizard to jump onto it. A tree swayed behind the bush from the gentle wind blowing through it, catching her hair. It was hot under the midday sun, even in February, but she loved it—loved the feeling of the rays on her face and shoulders. She tilted her face up to the sky, her eyes closed, and drank in nature, drank in Mother Earth.

The crunching of feet made their way toward her, and through her thick lashes she could see Carrick's fitted black jeans and crossed arms in front of her.

"You have a real connection to nature, don't you?" he asked, observing her.

"I love all things in the natural world," she exhaled, feeling the sun against her skin. "That's why I chose nursing, I guess — to try to help people, to take care of them."

"Interesting."

She opened her eyes, looking up at him. "And I love being outdoors. It grounds me. It feels like home. Sometimes I hug trees and just *feel* them."

The last words rolled off her tongue without permission, and she nearly stumbled back in deep regret. What was with Carrick that made her want to confess everything? She waited for him to react. The only thing was…that he didn't. Cool and emotionless, the stoic man in front of her just stood — watchful, assessing.

"It's time to make a decision," he explained, checking the time on his bulky black watch. "What do you want to do?"

Danica took in all the air around her, finding her roots in the soil. It was much easier to make the right decision with fresh air.

As she ruminated, she instinctively moved into tree position — her favorite yoga form when she needed grounding, when she needed to connect with the wisdom of nature. She bent her right leg to press her foot into her left thigh, and she stood only on her left leg with her hands in prayer position at her chest. Closing her eyes and taking a long, slow breath, she drew the air into her nose and down into the bottom of her lungs.

Whispers in the wind danced around her ears and into her mind. The wind was wise and old — and told her to be cautious and *not* to make waves. And those were things the wind knew about, because it was the wind that made the waves. She nodded as if understanding the words spoken to her by Mother Nature and tilted her head up to Carrick.

Holding the pose, she exhaled. "You already agreed to this with Petrov. The wedding is in a matter of hours. If we back out now, it's going to put a red-hot target on *both* of our backs. I won't even have a chance to run."

Carrick laughed like none of that mattered to him. "I'll do what I want. Don't worry about me. This decision is about you and *your* future. Are you going to make a stand?"

With his question, she fell out of tree pose. Her right foot slammed on the packed dirt underneath her as she looked up to the man in front of her.

She shook her head, pleading, "You don't understand these people. They are ruthless."

He shot her a confused look, like she couldn't be sane. He just didn't understand what she did. He didn't understand what her uncle was capable of, what he had done and what he was willing to do to her.

Danica added, her voice shrinking, "I can't fight them, Carrick."

"I'll show you how." He stood stall and alert, like a soldier.

She paused, playing with her bottom lip, thinking about what he was saying. He seemed so fearless, so brave.

"Who are you, Carrick?" she cautiously asked, studying him. "Were you in the military?"

Carrick shot her a sly grin. "I was."

"You've been trained to fight for freedom."

Carrick smirked but continued his narrative, power and intensity swelling in his voice, "I'll be there with you—at the wedding. I've got your back. All you have to do is tell Petrov to fuck off and you'll call the cops if he bothers you again."

"Just that easy?"

"Just that easy."

Danica exhaled slowly, a deep understanding of their dynamic taking her over. He was an aggressive fighter, and she was a passive avoider. They were a yin and yang. Wind blew up into her face, sending dust from the arid landscape into her nose and eyes, challenging her—screaming at her. However uneasy she was about it, Carrick was right.

He was her best chance.

"Okay," she whispered, barely able to believe that the word itself escaped her mouth.

Carrick grinned like a wolf that had finally caught its sheep, and he crossed his arms like a hard, sculpted statue.

"Let's go get your life back," he said, something feverish flashing across his eyes.

He nodded back to her, obviously ready to go to war, and turned to head around to his side of the truck. She licked her lips, watching him march with purpose. Her acceptance had obviously proven to fire him up. She couldn't disappoint him now.

As a willing but reluctant Danica jumped back into the passenger seat, she hoped that having the tall, strong protective man by her side would give her *strength* to face what she'd never thought she could. She kept that to herself as she watched him make the turn toward LA.

Why is he helping me?

She had no idea, but she suspected he had a deep need to guard and protect — and fight injustice, so long as she played on his side and listened to him.

Now, her next problem was to figure out what the hell she was going to wear, because she had not packed anything suitable for one of LA's hottest, richest weddings.

Chapter Nine

Carrick

"I'm just by that clusterfuck of crap in front of UCLA," Carrick grunted into his cell as the pickup truck idled on the side of the road in Santa Monica. "You know, that thing they are calling *art*."

"Oh, fuck—you're at the ugly statue." Delta chuckled. "Be there in a second."

Carrick ended the call and looked out of the window, across the street to where Danica was. He couldn't make out her form anymore through the glass windows of the trendy indie boutique and guessed she'd gone into the changing room. She wouldn't let him go in, complaining that his looming presence would stress her out as she desperately searched for something to wear for the wedding. He had no idea what she was after, but he knew they had less than an hour to be at the ceremony, and LA traffic wasn't forgiving.

Finally, in his rear-view mirror, he saw a dark pickup pull up behind him. Delta always came through. Always. There was a reason why Carrick relied on him.

Delta came around the front of the truck with a long, zipped-up suit bag in hand. Carrick opened the door and greeted him, taking the bag.

"Thanks, buddy," Carrick said, unzipping it and seeing his most expensive navy-blue suit, a dress shirt, tie and his shoes inside — the only one that would even begin to pass as fitting in at the Bel Air wedding.

Remaining silent, Delta put his hands on his hips, his face serious and hard under the beating Southern California sun. He looked tired, worn down. Carrick realized something was wrong and turned to face his crewmate.

"I don't like this," Delta warned, reaching up to run his hands across his face and over the long scar that started at his cheekbone then went up to his eyebrow.

That scar was a constant memory of heroism, Carrick thought, remembering the day Delta had gotten it. The man had done things that Carrick had never seen a SEAL do.

"There's something wrong with this job."

"I know," Carrick replied, feeling the same concerns.

"I don't trust Petrov. Did you read his AARs?" Delta questioned, keeping his tone cool. "I flipped you the intel. It was fucking hard getting my hands on that, so you'd better read it."

"I haven't had time," Carrick exhaled, keeping his eye out for Danica in the shop. He still couldn't see her...and that was starting to make him nervous. Two more minutes and he was busting in there.

Delta followed his line of sight to the shop, and looked back, assessing.

"Been distracted?" Delta asked, keeping his tone light.

Carrick shot him a warning look.

Delta flexed his jaw and stared down his friend. "You really need to read the intel. Don't go to that wedding. Cut this job *now*."

"Why?"

Delta discreetly looked side to side, seeming to check their surroundings, and said, "Petrov crime family—heard of them? Your buddy Kosta runs the Russian mafia here in LA. You do not want to fuck with this guy."

Carrick's mouth opened as he processed, narrowing his gaze back on the shop then back to Delta. Now, it was all starting to make sense. He knew a thing or two about the mafia—and it wasn't pretty.

"What about her?" Carrick nodded to the shop.

Delta shrugged, a dark shadow crossing his face.

"I can't just throw her to the wolves," Carrick said, his back stiffening. "You know what those people will do to her?"

"It's not your job to save her. This is her family."

"Well, we can't exactly call the cops now, can we?" Carrick responded, realizing his advice to Danica needed to be tweaked. Her options for fighting back were diminishing by the minute.

I'm her only option left.

"There's one cop I know..." Delta started, his head cocking to the side. That was a road Carrick didn't want to go down.

"You've burned that bridge, haven't you? She hates your ass," Carrick pointed out. "Look... I've run ops solo in five different fucked-up countries. I've fought my way out of foreign prisons and backwater torture camps. I can handle the fucking mafia."

"You're too distracted." Delta stepped forward, fiercer. "And now you're not just putting her at risk here. You're putting yourself at risk, too. The mafia will ruin you."

Carrick stepped a half-foot back, looking down at his friend—a guy who was like a brother to him, a guy who'd been there.

"I'm not leaving her."

"Then *read* the intel," Delta finally snapped, never letting up the intensity. "And focus, for fuck's sake. I didn't save your ass from a body bag in Syria just to watch you die in LA."

"Fine," Carrick retorted. "I'll read it when I get back. For now, I need you handle the office. McDonough wants an update on her missing son in Peru, and I need you to explain to her it's looking like a kidnapping."

And just as the last words rolled off his tongue, he noticed movement across the street. Danica appeared, coming out of the shop door. And damn, Carrick's jaw nearly hit the floor. She was fully decked out, ready for the wedding.

Christ, she was looking *unbelievably* fucking hot.

He had to keep it together.

He had to help her.

And what he *wanted* to do to her? That sure as hell wasn't going to help her at all.

"Oh look, a fucking sniper is about to take you out," Delta muttered sarcastically as the lithe brunette crossed the street, absorbing every ounce of Carrick's attention.

Carrick heard Delta's words but nothing registered, not even the fact that Delta was dead right that Carrick was brutally distracted.

All he could see was Danica pulling down the edges of her short, tight black dress and nearly stumbling as her black stiletto leather heels clicked across the pavement on the street. The cute-shy thing was killing him, and his cock hardened and lengthened down his pant leg. The thing that was almost his undoing was when she shot a shy grin at him and Delta as she waltzed over, like she had no idea what an absolute rocket she was.

"This is all they had that fit." She shrugged, looking down at the pavement and fumbling with her small clutch bag. "So…"

"It's fine," Carrick choked out and turned back to the truck, a hot flush running up his neck.

Back to mission-focused, Carrick immediately got down to business, unzipping the suit bag and whipping off his gray long-sleeved T-shirt. He'd changed in the middle of war zones and war ships. He didn't need a private dressing room to get ready.

"You look nice." Delta smoothly complimented Danica behind him, shooting up his ire.

Delta was moving Danica around the back of his truck, creating space between them. Carrick didn't like that, so he hopped into the truck and finished whipping on the suit as quick as he could, smoothing back his hair in the rearview mirror as he kept his eye on them. What was Delta going to say to her?

Within a minute after tying up his oxblood leather modern-styled dress shoes, he jumped out of the truck to collect Danica. They had little time left if they were going to get to the wedding and fly under the radar with the rest of the guests. That was the plan, after all — a show of face and a quick, quiet exit, keeping up appearances that everything was fine before he helped Danica figure out her next steps.

She was onto something. They needed time to plan her escape.

Danica looked up at him, tucking a lock of shiny brown hair behind her ear as he approached. Her long hair was almost down to her waist and had developed a beautiful, natural soft wave to it as they'd gotten closer to the ocean air.

But that wasn't all he noticed. There was something different about the way she looked at him as he stomped toward them in his blue suit, smoothing back his hair until it obeyed.

"Take a picture," he grunted sarcastically, rolling his eyes. "This doesn't happen often."

"You need a shave." Delta leaned back, looking at his friend. "Maybe some sleep."

Carrick rubbed his five-o-clock shadow, which had turned more into a two-day shadow. His dark, overgrown stubble and quickly styled hair made him look exactly how he'd looked jumping off the plane after a deployment. All he needed was a flesh wound, but then again, he already had that on his forearm, compliments of the mountain lion.

"Ready to go?" Carrick looked at Danica as she stood before him in her slinky black dress. He bit his tongue, not wanting to let his friend in on how deep his attraction was to her. He preferred Delta not know that he was right.

She nodded quickly, darting her gaze to the passenger side of the truck.

"You kids have fun now." Delta offered a shallow grin then shot a pissed-off look at Carrick. "Don't do anything I wouldn't do."

"That isn't much," Carrick scoffed.

"Difference between me and you is that I can pull it off."

As Danica started walking around the pickup with raised eyebrows, Carrick leaned forward to share some parting words with Delta.

"Fuck off."

Delta shook his head, grabbed his keys out of his pocket and turned to head out.

Spinning back to the driver's side of the truck, Carrick yanked on the door handle after he straightened his white open-collar dress shirt under his navy-blue jacket in the exterior paint's reflection.

Even for a wedding, he wasn't going to put on the tie.

Fuck that.

As Carrick whipped open the truck door, an unfortunately timed memory flashed to the front of his mind. Two years ago, his beautiful fiancée had been grinning back over her shoulder at him, asking him if he was seriously going to refuse to wear a tie on their wedding day. Wouldn't he make an exception just once? He remembered that they'd been at their condo on Coronado Island, a stone's throw from the West coast SEAL base. And in the memory, Carrick was grumbling back to her while reading the morning news and drinking coffee. Since when had planning a wedding been so divisive? Wasn't it supposed to be *their* day? Her gentle laughter in response punctured the moment, and Carrick found himself leaning against the truck door, winded.

Sucking in Santa Monica's dry, coastal air, he heard Danica's distant voice inside the truck, asking if he was okay. Carrick shook his head, regaining himself. Christ, the day was cracking up to be worse than yesterday, and the real fun was yet to come. It wasn't just ties that he didn't do. He didn't do weddings either.

Not since Lauren had died.

Not since their wedding had never fucking happened.

Chapter Ten

Carrick

I shouldn't have driven a pickup truck here, Carrick chastised himself as he approached the Bel Air Bay Club just north of LA. Every other vehicle lined up for the wedding's valet parking was some luxury car that was worth more than a Navy SEAL's salary, war money and retention bonuses included. They were in 'fucking rich-boy country' now, alongside the Pacific Ocean, not far from Malibu or Beverly Hills.

"What are you doing?" Danica said quickly as he pulled out of the lineup and drove toward the staff parking lot. "I don't think you are allowed to do that."

Lush green gardens shielded them from further onlookers as they pulled around the corner of the massive white stucco and glass clubhouse.

"We have to keep a low profile, Dani," he explained, watching over his shoulder as some guy in a white uniform came running out to talk to them.

Carrick rolled down the window and smiled at the club's harried employee, casually slipping a one-hundred-dollar bill into the guy's hand.

"Can I park here?" he asked knowingly, seeing the employee nod quickly. "I'm not a valet kind of guy."

Carrick shot a smooth, appreciative smile back, slipped another one-hundred-dollar bill into the guy's hand and moved to park in the spot where the employee was motioning. As he put the truck in park, he turned to Danica.

"Just follow my lead," he said, turning off the engine, and looking over at her. "Here's the plan. Today you are going to set the tone. You are strong. You are no one's property. You are not to be fucked with. Tomorrow, we will figure out the next step."

He watched her lips tighten, nearly turning white underneath whatever lip gloss she had on. She was nervous...scared. Carrick leaned toward her, stretching his suited arm across her naked shoulders, feeling the softness of her skin under his calloused hands. Reaching up to her chin, he gently turned her head to him and stared intensely into her eyes.

"Listen to me, *trust* me and everything will be okay," he furthered the briefing. "Don't go anywhere I can't see you."

As soon as the words rolled off his tongue, she shrank into her seat like a wounded creature. *Trust.* There was something about that word that she hated. And damn, he knew she had good reason to have trust issues — especially with men.

What did this Petrov character do to her?

Carrick pulled back, slowly dragging his arm across her shoulder, watching her reaction as he did it. She wasn't repulsed by him at least. No, she seemed almost to lean into his arm, taking the assurance he was offering. He grinned, never breaking eye contact with her. Carrick had been trained in reading people, in psychology. And, also unfortunately for her, he was on a mission.

Whether she likes it or not.

"How did you stay hidden from him for so long?" Carrick probed further, then waiting patiently for her to reply.

She was either going to lie or placate him. That was the game they played.

"I just stayed off the gird. I had no life," she replied curtly, but less than convincingly. "Let's get this done so I can just move on."

Carrick grazed his teeth across his lip, looking out over the grass, nodding in understanding. It was time to get shit done.

Time to turn Dani's life around.

Within minutes, Carrick had escorted Danica around the corner of the clubhouse toward the back, where the ceremony was set to begin shortly. Wedding guests milled around several stand-up serving stations, enjoying the open bar on the stone patio in the sunshine. It was now late afternoon, nearly evening.

A waitress passed him a glass of white wine, and he took it politely, narrowing his eyes on Danica as she leaned over the cocktail table before them to read the vegan options on the dinner menu. He didn't miss how her hands trembled. Looking back over the crowd and scene, he observed a wide, groomed yard that had a decorative floral altar framing the beautiful stretch of beach behind it. Everything screamed money. *Big money.* And as the birds sang above the Pacific Ocean and the sun cast a simmering amber glow over the guests, Carrick only had one question.

What kind of world does she come from?

There were enough chairs for five hundred people, Carrick guessed, realizing just how huge the wedding was. Everyone was rich and fake and painted. He leaned back into the bar, keeping his distance from a scene that was completely not his. Enough wedding guests surrounded him that he felt nearly camouflaged. Looking up into the large glass windows of the clubhouse, he saw more lighting and floral arrangements on wedding tables. That was where the reception would be.

As he looked back at her, watching her long, black lashes flutter, it really hit him. Danica was the black sheep here. She didn't fit in. She was one of those free-spirit types, happy with nothing—as long as she had sunshine and nature. Carrick couldn't wipe the admiring smirk off his face, watching Danica shut the menu in a huff, mumbling something about a lack of awareness for alternative diets.

Carrick leaned in, his elbows on the high table as he kept his voice low enough so only she could hear. "What do I need to know?"

Danica glanced up to him and spoke in a near-whisper, "The bride, Varya, is my father's cousin's daughter. She's marrying a Russian man, bringing him over to the States—someone who does business with the family."

"An immigration scheme?" Carrick asked carefully, keeping his voice low.

"That's what's expected of the women in this family," Danica replied, her voice lower. "And that's why I ran..."

"The CEO of Petrov's business... He's Russian?" Carrick replied, the wheels turning fast in his head.

"Yes," Danica replied, her big amber eyes flitting up to him, full of fear. "That's why—"

But before she could finish her sentence, she just shook her head and stared back into Carrick's eyes. While the west coast sun was dipping lower in the sky, Carrick drank in his date's beautiful golden tan as her skin seemed to sparkle. *Damn, she is something to look at.*

In a small voice, she finally whispered, "I just want out of this family."

The way she pursed her lips and seemed to beg for help through her eyes alone stirred that thing within him he couldn't control. There was something about her that made him want to fight all the harder, something worth fighting for.

"Need a drink?" Carrick asked, eyeing the bar behind them.

As she shook her head, he left his undrunk glass of white wine and moved toward the pop-up bar. It wasn't far, but his decision was strategic. He had to create distance from her. She was the most distracting woman he'd ever met. *Is it her fault? Or mine?* Her clear desperation shot to his core. That same need to protect the vulnerable crashed to the front of his awareness.

Carrick tried to flush the vision of her pert cleavage popping up and out of that slinky dress as he looked around, trying to keep an eye out for Petrov. Shit, it wasn't easy to stay focused. Delta might have been right.

Leaning against the bar, he ordered a Jack and Coke, more to blend in than anything. He hadn't had a drink in over a year. He wasn't supposed to. As Carrick brought the chilled mixed drink to his lips, taking a heavier swig than he should have, a familiar elderly Slavic man with a balding head and a slow, pained gate waddled up to Danica.

Petrov — the man, the legend, Carrick thought, as he nearly crushed the drink in his hand. But he leaned back, intent on observing the interaction. What was interesting was that Petrov wasn't alone. He ushered forward a lean blond man with a cunning face, who was draped in a sharply cut eggplant-colored suit.

Carrick had one good guess who that was.

Validating the theory further, Danica's reaction to the two men approaching her was visceral. She jumped back from the tall cocktail table and accidentally slammed into a woman behind her. Thankfully no glasses were smashed, but Danica quickly searched around, finding his eyes to plead for help.

"Keep it cool, Dani," he muttered, though she definitely couldn't hear him over the noise of the crowd. "Let's not blow it before the wedding even starts."

Clearly realizing that he wasn't coming to her side, she shot him a look of death and sank back beneath the intensity of Petrov and the young man. Carrick stood back, watching the scene unfold and gaining valuable intelligence while keeping his eye on her. After years of reconnaissance and black ops, he knew how to remain unseen if he wanted to. He stood back in the shadows, calm and collected. Proving he'd gone rogue wouldn't help Danica — not one bit. That wasn't the right card to play…just yet. This was his chance to simply observe.

Their conversation didn't take long, but Carrick learned some interesting things through their body language. Petrov was cold, dismissive and pushy. He sneered at Danica, uninterested in hearing anything from her, which seemed only to drive her further into silence and servitude. The blond, cunning man was handsy with her, even as she was clearly trying to shrink away. The guy acted as if he owned her, like she was a toy for him to play with, as though he was entitled to her body. It took everything in Carrick's power not to jump in, but he knew he had to stay back and see what Danica would do.

He was quickly learning that she wasn't willing to do much.

Watching her cower was the most heartbreaking thing of all. She looked like prey desperate to run, desperate to be free. She didn't deserve that. No one did.

It was a bad scene—and Carrick found himself feeling pretty rough by the end of it. Whatever he had in mind for the interaction did not come to fruition. She didn't stand up. She didn't exhibit power. She looked like she was under a spell.

Even when Andriy—the man Dani had told him was Petrov's choice for her—leaned in, grabbing her waist and bringing her in to kiss her on the cheek, her body remained stiff yet compliant. She didn't even refuse—and watching him hold her was enough to set Carrick off. As the guy slowly released her from his grasp, he scanned up and down her body—checking her out so obviously that the jealous, protective, possessive side of Carrick roared inside him.

Maybe Danica hadn't really ignored his advice. Maybe she didn't really have it in her. One thing was clear. She'd proved that she wasn't ready to fight Petrov...or Andriy.

That changes everything.

Finally, Tweedledee and Tweedledum took off, heading toward the chairs for the ceremony. Danica gripped the edge of the cocktail table, clearly struggling just to breathe. Carrick moved back in. After seeing the pupils of Danica's eyes dilated and her mouth parched, he grasped a glass of whatever off the tray that was floating by. As he held it up to her lips, she took a sip, clearly shaken. Then, she slowly took the glass from his hand, her fingers just grazing his for an instant.

Danica snapped out of it, slammed the glass down and pushed back from the table — pushing back from him. Her eyes narrowed on Carrick, and he saw something stewing within her.

"Why did you stay at the bar?" she vented, fast and furious, her eyes welling. "You said you would face them with me, and you left me *alone*."

He cocked his head back, unable to conceal his own discontent. "Why did you let him touch you?"

Her mouth parted, obviously grasping for words as she searched his face. But then she clamped it shut and turned her face away from him. He could feel her agony.

"Look... You need to listen to me," he started, ready to reiterate the plan. "You have to set the marker down that you are not his. It's just that easy."

"It's *not* that easy!" She inched back. "You don't understand."

But Carrick immediately shot back, "Don't go anywhere I can't see you."

"*Stop*." Her body stiffened and she turned on her stilettos.

He reached out but didn't catch her in time. She marched away from where he stood toward the chairs lined up on the grass. As he watched her leave, he only had two thoughts — *never before has it been so fucking hard to protect someone,* and *damn, that fucking ass.*

If she would only just listen.

Hot on her heels, Carrick followed in her wake, not wanting Tweedledum to corner her alone. Plus, Carrick wanted to get a good seat with a view of these goddamn rich people shenanigans. The wedding was cracking up to be ridiculously lavish. Right behind Danica, following her glide forward, he found a solid two seats on the edge of the far-right side. He reached up to tug her back, touching her smooth golden shoulder, uttering quietly that they should sit.

Her reaction was unexpected.

She elbowed backward, stabbing him in the gut. And he wasn't even *flexing*.

"*Fuck*," he ground out, a little winded.

Along with some granny beside him, Danica whipped around and narrowed her eyes violently at him, sending him that same look of death. As he mouthed a bullshit apology to the granny, Danica pushed forward as if she didn't care, like she didn't even know him.

He did not appreciate that, not at all.

However angry he had been before, now he was *really* pissed.

After slamming down beside her on a pristinely covered white chair in a row of dozens of seats, he observed as the hundreds of wedding guests found their spots. A hush fell over the crowd as gentle wedding music began with elegant harps and violins. The salty ocean breeze and relaxing nature sounds permeated through the air, hitting him in the bones — in the wrong fucking way. Just beside him, someone was releasing doves into the air to the tune of the harp. Sure, it was all pretty fucking beautiful and shit.

He was going to puke.

He crossed his arms tightly, wishing he'd taken Delta's advice and brought a gun.

Beside him, Danica also crossed her arms and sank back into her chair. He could tell she was upset. And really, he didn't blame her much. Her people were clearly assholes, and they were up to something — something Carrick really didn't like.

Things weren't going well.

He looked over the crowd, trying to get eyes on Petrov and his sidekick. But his view got stalled out by the bridesmaids starting to waltz down the aisle to some typical wedding tune. Little girls were throwing pink flowers and petals into the air, whacking guests in the face. Some dude caught one in the eye and started sneezing uncontrollably.

As Carrick exhaled in pure irritation, he remembered every reason why he hated weddings. The arch alone brought back vicious memories. *Lauren wanted an arch like that*, he thought, observing the decorative flowered piece at the altar. He'd always been against such a fussy wedding, and they'd had many arguments over it.

It was all so fucking stupid.

Lauren had never understood how he viewed it.

A wicked feeling flashed up his esophagus, and he found himself coughing into his fist, trying to keep it super quiet — but Danica noticed. Her wild gaze flashed to him, probably trying to figure out what was going on. And that was something she would never know. Thankfully, the urge to cough went away, and Carrick was able to catch his breath.

He carefully closed the steel trap in his chest and shut out the truth. When Lauren had died, so had his heart. That part of him was gone forever.

And it's never coming back.

Chapter Eleven

Danica

As the ceremony ended, Danica stood then turned to look around at the crowd. She was feeling even more nervous. Carrick's presence wasn't as comforting as it had been before.

From her vantage point, she could see white-uniformed employees starting to usher guests to the bars on the patio, just outside the clubhouse. Cocktail hour was just starting. It was going to be the worst part.

"We done?" Carrick grunted down onto her.

She turned to him, looking up into his cold face. As she assessed, she felt a chill running up her arms — but didn't know if it was the evening ocean wind or his dead gaze.

He was so damn emotionless.

Just heartless.

Straightening her back, she replied curtly, "I imagine we are expected for dinner."

"I don't give a f—"

But Danica spun away from him before he could finish. As she marched, her stomach dropped, turning violently as she started putting one foot in front of the other. Carrick had been her only chance. And now, what was he? She felt so alone. She'd known it was a terrible idea to come to this wedding. What had she expected would happen?

She was never going to be able to stand up to Petrov. *Never.*

She shouldn't have let Carrick convince her otherwise.

Her shoulders slumping, she saw her cousin Varya, the bride, getting ready for photos in the green grass against the ocean backdrop. At the very least, she had to congratulate her. And seeming to have a sixth sense, her cousin looked up in the distance, seeing Danica and waving effusively. Varya's eyes flickered up to the reception hall, pointing and smiling. Danica smiled back, a bit forced. It was going to be a big dinner, a big party.

And that was everything she didn't want.

As her cousin became distracted again with the photographer and her now-husband, Danica took in a deep breath and turned to the reception hall. She was expected to be there. There was no turning back now.

The distance between Danica and Carrick stretched as she moved through the crowd. All she could hear was Russian being spoken, and her abilities in that language were rusty, to say the least. It only intensified her isolation. Briefly looking backward, she realized that Carrick was quietly watching her, allowing a greater expanse to develop between them than ever before. The elastic band between them was ready to snap.

She exhaled sharply, knowing it had never been real.

As Danica found her way into the reception hall, she took in the hundred or so white round wedding dinner tables but found it nearly impossible to get a good look at the crowd to see who was there. The centerpieces were tall, flush with vibrant florals and greens. And that wasn't even getting at the other glittery décor. The entire wedding was a giant glitter bomb.

As she leaned in to read the table map, she realized that the fonts were too small, and she reached for her clutch to get her glasses. A man in a suit who looked like he worked there turned to her and asked what her name was.

"Danica Petrova," she responded, squinting back at the table map.

"Ah, Miss Petrova. You'll be at table six." The man nodded, as if immediately recognizing her name, and motioned to the far side of the room by the windows. "Please, may I escort you?"

"No," Danica shook her head quickly, stepping away. She didn't want the princess entrance.

Discreetly finding her way around the outside of the hall, attempting to locate table six and trying not to draw attention to herself, a young man around her age, with mousy hair and a very-LA cream-colored suit, stepped in front of her and she nearly slammed into him.

"*Izvini,*" the young man apologized in Russian as he turned around and looked her up and down. "*Ty zdes' s nevestoy?*"

"Bride's side," Danica replied slowly in English. She fidgeted with her clutch.

She was close — so close.

"Alexei." The young man shot out his hand, changing to English.

Danica took it reluctantly, shaking it as she offered a polite smile back. "Dani."

He licked his bottom lip as he grinned. "Want to get a drink? You look thirsty." His accent was thick, almost as thick as his charm.

And before she could say anything, he was flagging down a waiter for two glasses of crisp white wine. The waiter handed both over as Alexei slipped him a large tip, slick and impressive. He clinked Danica's glass and leaned in to ask her more about herself, laying on the charisma. Her reluctance to answer only seemed to make him all-the-more interested in cracking her.

She was in the lion's den — and anyone could be an agent of Petrov's organization, checking on her, testing her. She had to get out and get far away as soon as possible — and as quickly as doing so wouldn't cause more problems.

As Alexei talked about his life in Santa Monica, Danica realized the reception hall had filled up and guests were starting to find their seats. Then she realized Carrick was standing with his back against the far wall. She didn't notice him at first, because the man was incredible at fitting in when he wanted to be unseen. But when she did catch his tall, dark, muscular form, she noticed he was looking at her with that same frown on his face — quiet and unimpressed.

One of the ushers approached her, speaking in heavily accented English, "Miss Petrova, can I help you find your seat?"

Alexei's face dropped, and he immediately stepped backward from her. A look of terror flashed across his face. The usher gave him a sharp scowl. It was immediately clear that the young man had had no idea as to the territory he had been stepping into.

And Danica was someone's territory.

Danica quickly shook her head, taking the opportunity to remove herself from Alexei and the usher. With her empty wine glass, she found herself before Carrick's intense gaze as he leaned against the wall in between the large windows overlooking the ocean.

"I didn't see you there," she whispered.

The cold chill from him had gone into overdrive — and she shivered just being beside him. Things had clearly grown very uncomfortable.

"Need help?" Carrick asked, watching her try to read the table numbers across the hall.

"No, thanks," she replied quietly, bending to get something out of her clutch.

She pulled out her dark-rimmed glasses and slipped them up her nose. Finally, she saw table six in the middle of the room. She slipped the glasses off, but as she did, Carrick grabbed her hand, stilling her movements as they locked eyes.

"You wear glasses?"

"Looks like it, doesn't it?" She raised her eyebrow at him.

His eyes narrowed on her. "Don't put them away."

"Why?" She leaned back.

"Now is the time to be able to see properly," Carrick warned. "*They* are up to something."

Relenting, she slipped her glasses back up her nose and found everything was much easier to see. Carrick nodded subtly in the direction of Andriy, who wasn't even halfway across the room, hovering over table six. Her lips parted as she looked back to Carrick.

But he'd already looked away.

A waiter walked by, handing her a fresh wine glass, and she took it gladly, needing way more wine than what she'd had. She gulped the chilled substance, feeling it go straight to her bones. Guests slowly found their way into the hall, milling around to chatter and drink, smelling the arrival of hot appetizers. That meant that the formal dinner wouldn't be far off.

As she stirred uncomfortably, Carrick leaned in farther, as if to whisper something into her ear. Her whole body stirred as he got closer. But then he stopped and leaned back in against the wall — not saying anything.

"What?" Danica pressed.

Carrick just shook his head. He averted his gaze and stopped talking to her altogether. A distance grew between them once again. Danica hated how onlookers wouldn't even know they had arrived together. Validating that thought, a beautiful mid-forties woman with long blonde hair found her way next to Carrick and immediately started chatting, asking Carrick about himself, which led Danica to overhear and learn more about the man in that short moment than she had in all the time she'd been with him.

"Yeah, I grew up in Long Beach, just up the bluffs," Carrick answered the woman politely. "Nice place. You?"

Excited and effusive, the woman kept chatting about So-Cal families and surfing. Carrick got into the conversation with her on surfing, seeming to be more and more interested in talking to her. As the woman laughed, it was clear that she was flirting with him. But

Danica couldn't really hear everything that they were talking about.

And Carrick wasn't inviting her to join.

Danica wished she could switch spots with the woman and be having that laughing, flirting, fun conversation with him. And it hurt even more that he seemed to have forgotten about the reason why he was there.

So she quietly stood back, hurting, seething — and drinking wine that went down like water, and she realized that Alexei had been right. She *was* thirsty. Unfortunately, the more wine she drank, the more alone she felt and the more distant she was from Carrick. That feeling only got worse as cocktail hour continued. Considering that the man was more or less beside her, she didn't even know him. It seemed like she wasn't even there with him.

Which, in truth, she wasn't.

Finally, as guests were called to sit and the beautiful woman beside Carrick started proclaiming her need to dance later on, Danica couldn't take it anymore — so she pushed back from the wall, ready to bolt. She didn't look at Carrick, didn't say a word.

But she didn't get far.

Andriy swooped in out of nowhere and took her elbow. Looking down on her, he shot a wide, self-satisfied smile.

"Shall we?" he asked, putting his hand on her lower back.

Danica's skin crawled as she realized what he meant. He was ushering them toward table six. They were to be seated together.

But what about Carrick?

Turning her head over her shoulder, she realized what was happening but had no idea where Carrick was moving to. The same usher in a dark suit who had helped her had found his way over to Carrick, and as they both walked away, it was clear that they were having a tense exchange—even more tense than her interaction with Alexei. That was the last time she saw Carrick, as Andriy turned her attention back to the table and the dinner that was being served.

Assessing the glasses he'd never seen her wear, Andriy leaned into her, whispering, "Let's take those off." He reached up, pulling the dark frames off her nose, and took her clutch to stuff them back in as they approached the table.

"My fiancée," Andriy introduced her to the other guests, pulling out her chair for her, "Miss Petrova."

As the other guests at their table stood, greeting her like a princess, Andriy handed her clutch off to a man in a suit behind them. Shocked but unable to refuse, Danica obediently took her seat and occupied the position of Andriy's future wife. As he spoke, it was made clear that everyone believed her to be Petrov's real daughter—because no one, in the past nine years, had ever spoken her father's name again since the accident and not since Petrov had banished Ivan's memory.

And now she was the lost princess of the Russian mob.

Looking around, affixing a pleasant smile to her mouth, she realized that she was at one of the tables of honor and surrounded by ultra-rich executives both within Petrov's organization and key partners. Now she realized the reason why Petrov had wanted her to be there.

Andriy slipped his hand down her thigh, squeezing her knee with assurance. Something began creeping up her throat, and she was going to cry. It had all been a mistake, and she never should have come.

Now, their engagement was announced.

Now, it was official.

She flitted her gaze around and realized she was well and truly alone. Carrick had left — and it looked like he wasn't coming back.

Chapter Twelve

Danica

After a painfully fake and stiff dinner, Danica waited until Andriy got up to relieve himself, and she politely excused herself from the rest of the guests to refresh herself. She'd endured enough of Andriy's hand caressing her shoulders and landing on her thighs. The man treated her like he owned her.

She made her way to the edge of the reception hall as fast as she could without causing a scene and without Petrov noticing, as he was off in the distance — likely making business deals.

The first thing on her mind was retrieving her clutch, which she saw was being held by one of the men in suits at the edge of the room. Her second thought was, *How the hell am I going to get out of here? Where am I going to go?* A rush of emotion overtook her, and she was on the verge of melting down. She didn't know what upset her more — the thought of being forced to go home with

Andriy or the thought of Carrick dancing alone on the patio with that blonde woman.

Trying to be discreet, Danica found her way to a large floral arrangement decorating the edges of the hall next to the man holding her clutch. She smiled, holding out her hand to ask for it back, trying to be natural. The man nodded, speaking to her in Russian, and handed it over. Letting out a breath of relief, Danica slipped away, moving a little farther down the wall — plotting her next move. Fumbling in her clutch, she noticed that the contents were all intact. Why had they taken it? Danica chewed her lip, her only guess being that Andriy was embarrassed his fiancée would carry such a cheap-looking thing and even more embarrassed that she had taken out her dark-framed glasses.

Shaking her head, she whipped out her cell and found her roommate Addie's name, writing her a text.

I need help. She added a terrified emoji with it. *You're not going to believe this.*

Immediately, Addie wrote back.

Girl, where are you? What's going on?

Like a true sister, her roommate would be there at the drop of a hat if she asked.

My uncle hired a bodyguard to find me and bring me to my cousin's wedding. And now I'm here.

Holy shit. We need to get you out of there.

I need you to get rid of some of my things. Burn them. I'm not coming home...ever.

Addie stopped writing, and Danica stared at her screen, waiting.

Within five seconds, her cell was vibrating. Addie was calling. Danica answered it quickly, leaning back against the wall and keeping her voice down, though it was noisy enough in the hall that she couldn't be heard.

"Dani, are you in danger?" Addie's concerned voice carried through the line, forceful and demanding.

Danica paused, thinking, and finally confirmed, "Yes."

"I'm coming down to get you," Addie said quickly, and started planning out loud how to evacuate Danica from LA.

"You can't, Addie," Danica pushed back. "I won't bring you into this."

Addie paused, and a confused humming noise hit the line.

Danica continued, realization flushing over her, "This is something I have to do alone."

"You want to keep running?" Addie gasped. "Do you really believe Kosta will let you go?"

Danica's face grew hot as she thought of her past. She still didn't know if her uncle knew what she'd done years ago. And that was the most dangerous thing of all.

She replied, her voice shaking, "I have to keep going. It's my only chance."

Addie's next question was worse. "Would this bodyguard help you? Can he be on your side?"

Danica let silence fill the line, the only sound being her breathing.

"Dani?" Addie pushed for a reply.

Shaking her head, Danica replied, "I don't know."

Shock flushed over her as she saw Carrick coming in from the patio, looking as calculating as ever. Danica quickly told Addie she had to go, but that she'd call her later. Addie made her promise to text within ten minutes. Her concern was undeniable.

For good reason.

Danica's heart beat out of her chest uncontrollably, watching Carrick in the distance.

He's still here.

He scanned the dinner tables, and Danica knew that he was looking for her. *Her.* But she didn't want to face him…or anyone. He wasn't going to like what she was planning next.

Shuffling down a hallway adjacent to the reception hall, she heard Andriy's voice around the corner and panicked. *Terrible timing.* She immediately opened a door beside her and ducked into a small, dark room. As she tried to breathe, to make sense of it all, tears sprang to her eyes.

I have to get out of here.

Clearly, Petrov had strategized this. She had been announced to the entire organization as Andriy's fiancée at the wedding. There was no backing out now, not without consequences.

Laying her palms against the cool dark wall for stability, she heard Andriy's voice getting closer and closer in the hall and fear crept up her throat. That same creeping feeling ran up and down her limbs, and she darted her gaze around for an exit. There was none. She held her breath, praying.

Oh my God.

As Andriy's voice began to get farther and farther away, she exhaled in relief. Now, she had to make a move...no looking back.

Before she could escape, however, the door cracked open and a tall figure marched into the space. Flinching backward, she heard his angered voice.

"I told you not to leave my sight," Carrick growled, stepping into the room, letting the door close behind him. "Why are you in here?"

He stationed his muscular frame in front of her, and, in the shadows, she could see the intensity of his eyes. He was ferociously angry.

"I thought you'd left," she let out. "Where did you go?"

"That doesn't answer my question."

"I-I just need air," she whispered, backing up against the wall and grasping at the drywall behind her. "I couldn't breathe in there."

Carrick landed a strong hand on the drywall beside her head, and he loomed over her, breathing down on her. He obviously didn't believe her.

"You are up to something, aren't you?"

"Does it matter?" she cried out.

"It matters to me."

"Why do you care?"

He grabbed her jaw, roughly raising her chin to him. He wanted her to look at him—look him right in the face. Scowling and with his gaze on fire, Carrick dropped his head the final inches between them and he found her lips.

He worked her lips open, quick and determined, and danced his tongue in to play with hers. He was sending a message as much as he was tasting her, feeling her for the first time, like she'd always been his.

Holding her slender frame in his thick arms, she let herself fall into him, letting herself once again believe that it was real.

There was a groan in his throat as she let him kiss her. The deeper his kiss, the more she realized how bad she wanted him to do *everything* to her. He brought her tighter against his hard chest. As he ran his hands farther down her back, the coarseness of his palms filled her with sensation.

Reveling in the best kiss of her life, she felt his fire, his passion. Moaning and taking his rough handling, Danica experienced deep arousal in her core and a wetness pooling at the entrance to her untouched pussy. He dropped his hand down her throat, holding it firmly like a threat. The way he kissed her was like a promise. He seemingly wasn't going to rest until he had her complete attention and surrender. He appeared obsessed with her, needed her. And she was surely going to be in a damn lot of trouble if she didn't start listening to him.

Maybe he is really someone I can trust? Maybe I should just tell him everything – all my dark secrets?

He teased a moan from her that seemed to only heighten his response, and he kissed her that much more intensely. Never before had she felt so turned on, so needy for him. He grabbed her waist, holding her tight, her breasts pressed against him as she panted from his kiss. He pulled back just enough to squeeze and tease each one, working his fingers underneath her bra until he felt her nipple.

His touch was wild and out of control—and she responded in the same way. The roughness of his hands juxtaposed with the softness of his lips made for a delicious mix. Just as he started grinding his body against hers, his arousal seeming to be out of control, she cried out his name.

Then, as if hearing his name awoke him, he changed. He pulled away fast, and focus came back into his eyes, as though he'd just realized what he had done.

"Shit."

He stepped back from her, releasing her. As she slid down the wall and fought to straighten her clothing, even in the shadows, she could see the regret flashing over his face.

"I'm sorry," he said, causing a deep slice of pain to crack through her chest.

Then it got worse.

The door opened — and they were no longer alone.

Chapter Thirteen

Carrick

"What the fuck is going on here?" Andriy's voice echoed through the small space as his gaze snapped back and forth between Carrick and Danica.

Carrick crossed his arms, leaning back, tall and strong, as Andriy became visible in the ambient light permeating from the hallway. Watching the lean Slavic man, Carrick kept his mouth shut, breathing fire as he watched Andriy step into the space.

"What did he do to you?" Andriy asked her.

"Nothing." She flinched, shifting away—and the man's face twisted in vengeance.

Andriy *knew* what had happened. Any man would have.

Carrick stepped forward, putting his hand out between them.

"Give her some space."

"We don't require your *services* anymore." Andriy scowled as he turned to Carrick, a threat in his voice.

"Oh, I think you still do."

"*Leave.*"

"Not a chance."

Andriy stepped closer to Danica, and Carrick searched her for a response. Her eyes were wide, and she was out of breath and swallowing anxiously. She was frozen—in the same way she had been at the cocktail table. Andriy reached out to pull her toward him.

"Get your hands off her," Carrick roared, landing a hand on the collar of Andriy's purple suit and pulling him back.

A deep, vicious growl rose in Carrick's throat. Every muscle in his body caught on fire, and it took everything in his being not to take the Russian's life. Andriy pushed back on Carrick, but only sent himself backward—because Carrick hadn't gotten the name Moose for no reason. He was as tall, strong and sturdy as one. No one pushed him over.

As Carrick reached out to grab Danica, swinging her around behind him, she protested and cried out for him to stop.

"*Carrick!*" Danica called out, pure fear in her voice.

But he couldn't.

He had to protect her from this fucking goon. There was some greater need driving hard inside Carrick, something even he could not deny. And now Carrick stood face to face with Andriy. Carrick widened his frame, protecting Danica, who was now securely behind him.

"You're a dead man," Andriy snarled, straightening his suit from where Carrick's hands had been.

"Stay the fuck away from her," Carrick let out in his darkest, most intimidating voice, "or there'll be hell to pay."

As the last words of his threat fell, Andriy lunged forward to take a swing at Carrick, who caught the punch in his bare hand and threw his own. The only difference was that Carrick's punch connected hard with rich-boy's face. Blood splattered from Andriy's nose against the wall behind him, and he cocked his head back with a vicious, murderous look.

"Do you have any idea who you are fucking with?" Andriy spat out blood, reaching into his jacket. "She's *mine*."

Carrick knew exactly what Andriy was reaching for and he rushed him, taking control of the situation. He quickly whipped the man around, disarming him as the pistol from his jacket crashed to the floor. After a brief altercation, Carrick managed to get Andriy on the ground, and, boy, he was surely hurting.

That was when Carrick knew there was no turning back. He'd made an enemy out of the Russian mafia. In their eyes, he was a dead man walking. And if he didn't get Danica out of there, someone was going to find them—and he didn't want to see the extent of the mafia's firepower or the extent of Andriy's connections.

Andriy clearly was rich, powerful and had many friends...very powerful friends. Carrick was just a former Navy SEAL with too much to fight for.

Carrick grabbed Danica's hand and rushed her out of the room, pulling her down a deserted hallway, targeting the employee parking lot where they'd stashed the pickup. He had a GPS built into his head and could navigate even the most complicated mazes.

"What did you do?" Danica cried out behind him, pulling back as he dragged her forward. "Carrick, you have *no* idea what you've done!"

Making their way out of the building and to the truck, his heart was racing. Dani was breathing heavily, her eyes wide...furious. But he was too.

In the darkness of the employee parking lot, he pushed her up against the side of the truck, dropping his arms on either side of her to lock her in place. Feeling blood pumping through his veins, he looked down at her alarmed, heated expression.

"That guy is a fucking asshole." He growled low, dipping his head to get a good look into her eyes. "He deserved it."

"Carrick, I've never seen anyone take on Andriy and live," she cried out desperately. "Never. He's going to kill you."

She held his gaze, and he could see her look of pure fear across her face.

"I'm not scared of him."

"Did Petrov see what happened? He must know. I can't let this get any worse. I've got to do something." Danica's lips quivered as she shot a look back toward the clubhouse.

"You are going to do something," he snapped.

"What—?" she exhaled, searching his face.

"Look... I stood back. I watched." Carrick leaned in, tightening his hold on her. "I didn't like what I saw."

"What the hell are you suggesting?"

"You have to fight them. It's the only way." Carrick pushed off the truck, bringing her with him.

"Just...go." She waved her hand dismissing him, like she expected him to be done.

"You're coming with me. I've got a lot to teach you."

She shook her head in disbelief, and Carrick could taste the anxiety dripping off her.

"Why are you still here?" she cried. He didn't miss the hurt in her eyes.

The questioned lingered between them, and Carrick knew what was behind it. He'd kissed her, then he'd pulled away. He'd taken and injured her. And now, there was no point in being anything but honest with her.

"I'm still here because I *need* to be," he admitted, his head dropping a little lower. "There's a freight train coming toward you, Dani—and I can't sit back and watch it hit."

I can't sit back and watch you die.

An unspoken fear lingered in his mind as she lifted her chin to his. Carrick wasn't more than a few inches from her, but he couldn't—and he shouldn't. The first time had been a mistake. He wasn't going to make it again.

With a deep growl, he reached behind her, opened the passenger door and popped her into her seat. After slamming her door to make sure she was safely inside, he took action. He had to get them off the grid as fast as possible to regroup.

Jumping into his seat, he started the engine and pulled the truck out of the parking lot. Spinning onto the Pacific Coast Highway headed toward LA, he worked on the plan in his mind. Within minutes, Petrov was going to know what'd happened, if he didn't already—and he'd know Carrick had gone rogue. He'd just made himself an enemy.

As he ruminated, he caught Danica pulling out her phone, checking her messages.

"Now is not the time," Carrick ordered her, twisting in his seat to get a view.

She flickered her gaze to him. "Controlling much?"

"Who the hell are you talking to?" he demanded.

"That's your business, my lord?"

"You want to find yourself another ride?" he snarled, against his better judgment. But, before he could say anything else, she exhaled.

"My roommate is asking if I am alive," she confessed. "If I'm going to be okay."

"And are you?"

Danica shut off her phone, tucking it back into her tiny purse. "That remains to be seen."

The words fell like a ton of bricks on the conversation, and something about hearing her call him 'my lord' caused his cock to lengthen and throb. He knew that it was only going to get harder to stay away from her now that he'd had a taste.

He clenched his jaw, knowing that he wanted to take *full* control. He wanted her to give in to him, to let him lead. That was what he was good at. But there was a clear mistrust festering between them. It was going to be harder and harder to convince her to see his point of view.

Carrick narrowed his focus onto the coastal highway before him, assessing his plan. Well, everything had fucking gone to shit. Now, he had no choice but to take her someplace no one could find her, a location that was secure and untraceable — where he had immediate access and no one would ever know.

There was only one option.

And she isn't going to like it.

Chapter Fourteen

Danica

The small, private oceanside community of Sunset Beach came into view as Danica's new captor pulled the pickup off the Pacific Coast Highway. Carrick had driven fast as hell from Bel Air through LA, down to the south side of the coast. Sunset Beach was a surfing town where life moved a little slower.

Danica had been down this way before, in a camper van with nothing but close friends, a bikini and a surfboard. Still, she'd never caught a glimpse inside the gated, secure community that they were approaching. The community covered most of the beachfront property, where celebrities and athletes were rumored to live.

Leaning out of the truck window, Carrick swiped an access card at the gate.

"Where are we going?" she questioned, needing to understand the plan.

"Somewhere safe."

Carrick drove through the gates and up to a three-story home. It was tall and thin, sandwiched between a long row of expensive-looking beachside houses. Danica looked around nervously but couldn't get much of a read on what it looked like in the dark, especially since they drove right into a large garage that was big enough for two vehicles.

As Carrick turned off the truck engine, with the heavy reinforced garage door closing securely behind them, Danica saw that there was another pickup truck parked in the garage — black, with a surfboard sticking out of the back.

"Where are we?" she asked, her eyes wide as she shifted uncomfortably in the passenger seat.

"My place."

"And you surf?"

He shot her a look of disbelief across the truck's bench. "I live on Sunset Beach. I grew up in Southern California. I was stationed on Coronado island. Of course I surf."

She widened her eyes even farther as she started looking around. What else was she going to learn about her mysterious captor? As she put her hand on the door of the truck, starting to get out, she looked over at him. He'd flipped his cell out of his pocket and was quickly and furiously moving through his notifications. She couldn't tell for sure, but it looked like he had a ton of missed calls and voicemails.

He's in trouble.

Danica bit her lip, watching Carrick with a keen eye. How much time did they have before Petrov came knocking? Or Andriy? Then things would really get ugly.

Moving out of the truck, her limbs uneasy and shaky, Dani followed him up to the garage door, where he entered a password on a keypad and also unlocked a deadbolt with a key. It was clear that the place was tightly secured.

"Oh," she said as she stepped into the house, seeing how well appointed it was. "Nice pad." *God, it's expensive-looking.*

He grunted in response, throwing his keys onto a console and seemingly reviewing security footage.

Danica cautiously stepped onto the light hardwood floors, which looked as though he'd cut the birch trees himself. The entry level connected with a staircase leading up to the second level, which was modern and open concept. Carrick grabbed her hand, showing her up, and she realized the entry level was for the garage, mud room and what looked like an office in the back.

As they crested the second floor, she saw the living quarters — a gray-and-white kitchen with glittering quartz countertops and shiny silver handles bolted onto white cupboards. He flicked on the lights, illuminating a great room connected to a balcony. She couldn't see much farther through the dark sliding doors but guessed that his balcony overlooked a wide stretch of sandy white beach.

This place must cost millions.

As Carrick moved into the kitchen behind her, she glanced around the living room, at first in awe. But then something quickly struck her. It looked like a model home, like no one lived there. There were no family photos, nothing personal looking. Her stomach flipped with more questions of confidence. *How can an ex-military guy afford a place like this?* Once again, she was reminded of how much she was putting herself out on a limb with him, and how little he'd actually told her of himself.

She had no idea who he was...or what he did.

Turning, she casually prodded, "You own this place?"

He looked up from the sink after pouring two glasses of water, narrowing his eyes as he saw directly through her words.

"I bought it about a year or so ago," he stated very matter-of-factly — but cut it off there.

His tone bothered Danica, as she clamped her mouth shut. Clearly he was not taking any questions and there wasn't much she could do about it.

Obviously determined and on a mission, he grabbed her hand once again and showed her upstairs to the third floor. He took her into a bedroom that was long and narrow, with light-gray painted walls and dark-gray stained wooden furniture. Opening up through a patio door, there was another private balcony overlooking the ocean. The room felt cozy and warm, if not a little barren. There were hardly three pieces of furniture in the room, matching the tone of the rest of the house — like no one lived there.

At least there was a beautiful little happy green plant on the bedside table, which Danica silently mouthed a greeting to as she approached.

All living things are important.

Carrick sat her down with a glass of water, ordering her to drink and asking her if she needed anything. He laid out a T-shirt on the bed — one of his, clearly — that was a white V-neck. Then he left her alone — leaving the room and heading back downstairs, muttering something about grabbing her black backpack from the pickup for her.

She knew that wasn't all he was doing, though, because he was soon talking on the phone one level down, keeping his voice low, likely so that she wouldn't be able to hear what was going on. She could only imagine what was happening at that point, but was there really much point in asking Carrick any questions?

He's in damage-control mode.

Frustrated and alone, Danica picked up his shirt and suddenly, as if something cracked in her façade, tears started to stream down her face. Finally, she didn't need to be a big, tough girl. She could be vulnerable. She could be her soft, sensitive and emotional self. She didn't have to pretend to be something she wasn't.

Things had gone very wrong that night, and now she and Carrick were hot targets. The latter occupied her mind most of all, which was a truth she was almost unwilling to acknowledge. Andriy would spare her if she married him—but he would kill Carrick. And he wasn't going to rest until he did. Danica knew how her family did business.

They had too many friends.

They were too powerful.

It was almost impossible to escape them.

Almost.

She looked closer at the little plant on the side table and reached over to toy with a tag that was sticking out of the side of it. She pulled it a little closer to read what the tag said and realized it was a hand-written inscription. It looked like a gift card.

"*Carrick, for your new home,*" the tag read. "*A new beginning. Let the past be the past.*"

She dropped the tag, pushing back the plant, feeling like she'd stumbled across something deeply personal.

She looked back over her shoulder, wondering what his deep secrets were.

"Let the past be the past."

What *was* his past?

A question she was sure he would never answer — not for her.

Shedding her slinky black dress, she threw on his shirt and perched on the edge of the bed, sitting silently to hear the ocean. Her mind was spiraling. She closed her eyes, trying to breathe in the power of the water and its security and safety.

"Tell me what I'm supposed to do," she cried through whispers, pleading with the greater power of the universe that she deeply believed in. "Can I trust him? Please, guide me."

But, after a few minutes, she stopped praying. Even she realized how shaken she was — how high the cortisol was in her body. She couldn't think, let alone meditate, and it was clear that she needed to sleep. She just didn't want to, she realized, as she touched the soft pillow on the bed.

Behind her, she heard the bedroom door opening, and Carrick stepped toward the bed. His presence in front of her once again caused her senses to awaken, like she'd just been splashed in the face with cold water. There was just something about him when he was near. She felt an energy that she'd never felt before.

Carrick sat down on the bed beside her, but she didn't look at him, remaining curled up. She couldn't feel that level of intensity right then. She kept her tearful eyes on the ocean, unwilling to share with him what she was going through.

"It's been a lot, but you have to recover," he instructed her, all hardness and determination. "This fight is just beginning."

"I'm trying," she whispered as she looked up at him, her lip trembling. His untiring gaze locked on hers, and she quietly admitted, "I'm so scared."

She flickered her gaze up and down, noticing he'd changed into army green fitted sweatpants and a black T-shirt. She bit her lip, hating how her body responded to him so quickly.

And that kiss earlier? It had killed her, simply killed her — and she wanted more.

But he pulled away.

Danica pressed her eyes shut, feeling so alone, wishing he would leave. She tugged the blanket toward her.

Unexpectedly, she felt, his warm, wide hands run up her back. She inhaled into his touch, so vulnerable underneath him. He gently started massaging her back, then her shoulders.

As confident as he was serious, he said, "I'll figure this out."

"You don't know that," she replied.

He pulled at her shaking body and turned her onto her back. His gaze bored into her as he ran his hands down her body, tossing away the blanket. She kept her legs tightly clamped together as he found her ankles, massaging upward to her shins. As he hit her knees, goosebumps flashing across her thighs and arousal pooled at the entrance to her untouched pussy.

She shot her eyes open and saw that Carrick's gaze was locked on her legs as he ran his hands up and down the length of her. She'd never allowed herself to get this close to a man before. There was something about him that drove her instantly wild, giving her feelings she'd never before experienced. She wasn't used to being touched—and she sure as hell had never been touched like that.

His touch grew so gentle and caring—and it felt so real. And maybe that was what she needed to believe.

"Why did you pull away?" she finally whispered to him as he ran his hands up her thighs.

He frowned, considering her question—then finally he responded.

"I shouldn't have kissed you."

"Why not?" she asked carefully.

"Because this"—he motioned between him and her, sending a clear message—"isn't like that."

He doesn't want it to be like that.

"What if I want it to be?" she replied in nothing more than a heated breath.

He opened his mouth then closed it, training his gaze up her body. Being under his scrutiny alone was enough to take her breath away, and she shakily sucked in air.

"Just relax," he ground out, clearly holding himself back.

She watched his face grow intensely focused on her thighs and what he could see between them. She parted her knees slowly, and the shirt that she'd borrowed from him fell back slightly from her hips, revealing more of her lower body. She opened her legs a little wider until she revealed that she wasn't wearing panties anymore—not after she'd changed.

Carrick stopped his hand dead on her thigh as he stared at her wet pussy, and a groan rose in his unshaven throat.

"I need you to relax," he said again, but in a markedly different tone.

"I don't know how," she replied softly.

He leaned in, working his hands up her thighs higher and higher until he hit the base of her hips. He was so close to grazing her pussy, but she knew he wouldn't.

Will he?

"You have *never* been touched before?" he asked, his tone expressing a demand to know the truth.

She shook her head slowly, watching his hunger grow uncontrollable.

"You're fucking killing me," he growled, low and angry.

Like a werewolf changing under the moon, that familiar howl of need and desire grew louder in his throat as he looked back down at her aching wet center. It was damn clear that he had a fire lit inside him, and he likely wouldn't be able to resist.

Which was good—because she didn't want him to.

Running his hand toward her wet opening, she opened her legs even farther, inviting him, and, finally, he *touched* her. He drew a long line from her clit to her ass, seemingly reveling in her.

"Fuck, you are so wet," he let out, keeping his fingers pressing into her heat, "and hot."

Sensation filled her body from his touch, starting from her pussy but shooting all the way up her spine toward her mind. It felt incredible, and her own arousal beat harder. Then he drew a line back up to the front and found her clit, drawing gentle circles around it. His gaze became simply alive as she arched upward, responding to his touch, and his breath grew heavy. While he was circling her clit more and more, juice started flowing out of her, and she let out a deep, earthy moan. Visibly concentrating, he dropped his fingers toward her core and pushed one gently into her canal.

"Damn, so tight." He shook his head in clear disbelief as her pussy tightened around his single finger. "Unbelievable."

He found her hand and brought her fingers to her clit — showing her what to do. She complied, following his motion as he encouraged her self-discovery.

"Have you ever given yourself an orgasm?" he asked, dark and low, watching her work herself.

She shook her head as she circled her clit. "I can't seem to make it work."

He flashed his eyes, and she saw that animalistic need pouring out of him and consuming her. He obviously wanted to take her for his own, to show her things — to be her first.

"Like I said, I have a lot to teach you." He once again controlled her hand with his, showing her the motion he used, and she could practically feel the electricity between his body and hers. Sensations and feelings she'd never had shot up as he urged her to play with herself, finding what felt good.

She moaned, driving her head backward into the pillow.

"Do you like that?" he asked, his eyes growing hazy.

Biting her lip, she nodded and grasped his hand, pushing it toward her dripping opening. Desperate for his touch, she pleaded, "I need more."

He grinned and obliged, pushing a finger all the way up inside her again. As she gasped, tilting her head back, she kept working her clit. He reacted by adding a second finger, driving her arousal through the roof. She found herself wondering if that was what his hard manhood would feel like.

Once he worked her core enough to make space, he tried a third finger. Of course, his fingers were thick — and two barely fit into her virgin pussy. The third caused her to flinch in pain. Realizing that two was enough, he twirled them inside her, finding the spots there that made her want to scream out his name.

"Carrick," she moaned, rolling her head from side to side as he increased the intensity. She continued to work her clit, and the sensation was mounting to something she couldn't describe. It'd never worked before, but with him being there...

"Goddamn," he admired her as he moved his fingers in and out of her pussy.

As she lay underneath him, enjoying everything he was doing to her, he dropped his head toward hers. She moved her hand up to his thick, corded arm — muscular and strong. He replaced her hand with his on her clit, circling it rhythmically. Grinning, he took her mouth.

His kiss was ravenous and obsessive. It was hungrier and harder than he'd kissed her before, as though he was now allowing himself to do what he wanted. She opened right up for him, taking both his tongue into her mouth and his fingers into her pussy — and he brought her closer to where she imagined the edge was. A pressure was growing inside her, one that needed release.

Could it happen that fast? Was he already making her orgasm?

"I want to come," she groaned, bucking her hips under his hand.

"Then you will," he growled, working her even more intensely. "I promise."

As she was panting, losing her breath, he took his mouth away. She tried to follow him, sitting up, not wanting the kiss to end, but he gently pushed her back on the bed. She landed hard on the pillow, watching the confidence and determination in his face. Her orgasm had become his mission.

"Relax," he ordered with a tone of finality, and he moved his head down her body. Her knees shook as she realized what he was doing.

Kneeling on the floor, he shot his fingers in and out of her again, creating a puddle of her juices on the bedsheet beneath her ass. There was absolutely going to be a giant wet spot under her when he was done. Then she felt his hot breath on her clit and him dropping his tongue against it to draw slow, similar circles. She jolted as he took her clit and mound in his mouth, skillfully playing with her, using his tongue.

"Carrick!" she squealed, reaching down to weave her fingers through his thick, dark hair.

The sensations were too much already, and she couldn't handle them. He laughed and just kissed and played harder, bringing her closer and closer to *something*, as his two fingers pushed all the way up inside her, swirling and driving her insane.

"You said you wanted to come," he growled, reminding her of her choice.

"Oh, fuck," she moaned, trying not to shake any harder.

His mouth felt amazing.

It felt incredible.

She was losing her mind.

"You like that?" he chuckled between licking her. "Damn, you have the sweetest pussy. I could do this all day."

She tried to respond, but every time she opened her mouth, he fucked her harder and harder with his fingers, making her cry out his name again and again.

"Carrick, please," she pleaded, not even knowing why. She just needed to get there — wherever that was.

"I like hearing my name on your lips," he grinned as he slowed down the speed.

She was panting and hot, popping up onto her elbows to look down at him.

"Did I come?" she asked.

Then he laughed, blowing a line of air on her pussy. "Not yet. You'll know."

With that, he attacked her harder, faster — more intensely. He twirled and danced his fingers inside her, lapping up every drop that came out of her with his tongue and working her clit in the most exquisite way. Slowly, she felt something strange rising in her like a wave — like electricity or she had no idea what.

Then it started happening.

Her legs involuntarily started twitching and her back arched as something flowed through her veins, shooting massive amounts of pleasure from her head to her toes and back again. She couldn't explain it. It made no sense. It was like nothing she'd ever experienced before.

It was a slow burn and lasted too long for her to keep her sanity.

And he is making it happen.

As she came, sending rushes of sweet orgasmic juice out of her all over his hands and the sheets, he grinned at her and licked his fingers, groaning like he was eating some delicious gourmet dessert. She closed her eyes as he finished, kissing her gently on her mound and down her thighs, then back up to her taut abdomen.

"Time to sleep, Dani," he commanded, rising to stand, all business — like he was just going to leave her.

She shot out her hand and held on to his long, thick arm, gently urging him down onto the bed. He fell behind her and held her to his body, kissing her shoulders like a thousand promises.

Promises I want to believe.

Holding his arms against her chest, the last thing she was aware of feeling was the fresh bandage wrapped around his forearm from where the mountain lion had bitten him. The sacrifices he had made for her... The danger she'd put him in...

And she fell asleep with him to the distant sound of the ocean soothing her troubled mind.

Chapter Fifteen

Danica
Five years before

"Miss Petrova." An older nurse in blue scrubs spoke to her.

Danica jumped out of her chair in the waiting area of LA General Hospital's emergency room and stood face-to-face with the nurse, desperately trying to glean any information she could.

"Are Mama and Papa okay?" Danica asked quickly, stumbling over herself in the nurse's wake.

The nurse exhaled slowly and ignored her question, instead asking, "Do you want someone to wait with you?"

"I just want to see my mama and papa!" Danica shook her head and begged the nurse. "Please!"

"We need to let the doctors do their jobs, dear," the nurse replied calmly, obviously trying to assure her.

"You need to stay here and wait. I'll find someone to come sit with you."

"Are they going to be okay?" Danica sobbed, falling back into the uncomfortable chair in the waiting room.

Why isn't anyone telling me anything? Why are they leaving me in the dark?

The gray-haired nurse looked at her with sympathy in her eyes, but left without saying anything more, obviously unwilling to make false promises.

Danica vibrated in the chair where she sat, whipping out her crappy hand-me-down phone. *No cell service.* Hospitals were like bomb shelters.

Tears were falling from her face onto the floor when she heard the footsteps of a man walking toward her. Gazing upward, she rose before her uncle.

"Danica," Petrov stood, snarling down at her, "they are dead. Now, come with me."

Dead.

She sank back. "*No.*"

"Did you just say 'no'?" His voice grew livid, his eyes wide and crazed. "You will do as I say. I am your father now."

Danica shook her head again and again, feeling the burn of hot tears down her cheeks. She found the edge of the chair hitting the back of her legs, and she wished she could turn and run — to be anywhere but there.

"You will *listen*," he spat, switching between English and Russian, "you insolent brat. *Ne oslushaysya menya.*"

Before anything could leave her lips, her uncle had raised his hand high in the air, ready to crash down on her, but then he backed down — as if realizing they were in a public space. In that moment, Danica could see the pain in his eyes. The loss. The hurt.

He wanted to hurt someone. He wanted someone to feel his pain.

It was something she understood.

Because she felt it, too.

Mertvykh.

Petrov stepped to the side and motioned fiercely for her to follow him.

"They are dead, but you are not. You will learn one thing very quickly. There are rules in this family," he said, straightening himself. "If you want to survive, you will obey my rules."

"No—I want nothing to do with you or your *business*," Danica cried out. "That is how Papa died."

Petrov shot her a threatening look. "You have no choice. You were born into this family. The only way out is…death."

Danica's vision went black, and she cupped her face in her hands as she sobbed. The last thing she heard was her uncle's final threat.

Ne slushaysya menya, ty umresh odin.

Chapter Sixteen

Carrick
Present day

Carrick woke up too early. It was still dark out. Half of him wondered if he was in the bowels of a naval warship. He opened his burning eyes. They were dry and he was too tired to be awake. It was damn relieving to feel Danica's soft, warm body beside him, breathing rhythmically. At least she was okay.

He fumbled for his phone on the side table, realizing it was barely five in the morning. Still, he damn well knew he wouldn't be falling back to sleep. There was too much on his mind.

So, he moved off the bed—careful and calculated. The notifications blowing up his phone warned that he had far too much shit to do to lounge around crying over lost sleep. He made his way in silence down to the main floor to refresh himself, then into the office to start up his laptop. If the messages Delta had been sending him overnight said anything, it was that Carrick needed to read something as soon as fucking possible.

Carrick sank into his leather office chair, turning on the desk light. As he let his laptop boot up, he read the last message Delta had sent him just thirty minutes before. *What the fuck is that guy always doing up all night? Something is going on with him.*

Left something for you on your desk.

Carrick looked down at the folder in front of him, black and unmarked. It looked like something that had been smuggled. He curled his lips in distaste, wondering where the hell Delta was getting all the information from.

I have a strong guess.

He found the edges of the folder, opening it and revealing a printed-out report marked 'highly sensitive' from LAPD. Carrick nearly snapped the folder shut then and there, but he wouldn't stop reading once he'd started.

A confidential source has come forth with information pertaining to the death of Ivan Petrov, the intelligence report read.

Carrick's mouth dropped open as he read on, realizing that there was someone snitching from Petrov's organization…to the cops. And it wasn't a nice story.

Under the condition of anonymity, the source has disclosed that Kosta Petrov murdered his younger brother Ivan Petrov because Ivan disagreed on business matters with his older brother, threatening to leave the family business. No one can leave the family. The car accident was staged. Petrov has threatened family members with death if they disobey him. The report concluded, *This source has intimate knowledge of Petrov's organization but refuses to testify in open court due to fears of reprisal and his-her own personal safety.*

Carrick took the report in his hand, trying to understand it all. It was no surprise that Petrov was the real culprit behind the deaths of Danica's parents. The only question was, why was he trying to ruin Danica's life?

As he leaned back in his chair, studying the report, he realized that the question he really needed to answer was — should he tell Danica or not?

They were making progress, and she was learning to trust him. It had been a rocky start, but he felt like they were working toward a position where she might start listening to him. That alone was reason enough to tell her the truth. He needed her trust.

I need her to fight.

But then again, there was something at the back of Carrick's mind that gave him pause. What would this information do to her? Cause her more pain? Scare her into submission? And would these facts just send Danica down a spiral to rock bottom, knowing that her parents' killer had gotten off without punishment?

There was a reason why LAPD hadn't charged Petrov yet. Sure, there probably wasn't enough evidence, but Carrick suspected that there was a darker one.

Grabbing his cell, he shot a text to Delta.

Awake?

Within seconds, Delta was calling him.

"Do you ever fucking sleep?" Carrick grunted into the phone.

"I'm a monster," Delta replied, an amused tone in his tired voice. "You reading the report?"

"Yup. Got it right here."

"Look..." Delta began, his voice lowering. "There's a hit out on you and demands for anyone to bring her back to daddy. They've bought and paid for too many cops to count."

"Fuck," Carrick snapped, running his hand down the black folder with the intel report. "How much shit would we get into for having this information?"

Radio silence.

"Matteo," Carrick urged, using his friend's Christian name.

He heard a dog starting to bark in the background of the phone call.

"I've got to go," Delta said quickly. "Lie low. I'm going to keep digging. You need to figure out how the fuck you'll crawl out of this dumpster fire. Someone needs to deal with the girl."

"I'll deal with her."

"I'm sure you will," Delta replied a little too smartly before ending the call, driving Carrick's ire through the roof.

The phone call left him with more questions than answers, but one thing was damn clear. This wasn't going to be easy. Now, he had some serious decisions to make. What to do with Danica?

Carrick knew one thing about himself. He was a fighter. He was aggressive, dominant and didn't take shit from anyone. And her? That wasn't her. She was the opposite — and he knew it in his core. She had to be the one to stand up to her uncle. It was the only way.

He glanced again at the report in front of him. Her uncle had killed her parents. How much did she need to know? He played through the conversation in his head — imagining himself telling her the bad news, imagining her breaking down and crying, reliving all the pain of losing someone she loved. Carrick knew how that felt. And he knew he couldn't do that to her, not when she was just starting to strengthen up. His job was to help her be strong — strong enough that she'd be able to fight for herself...

When I'm gone.

And that was why Carrick folded up the report, deciding to tuck it away somewhere secret, somewhere safe.

Chapter Seventeen

Danica

The early morning came, and beautiful sunshine washed across the sky. Danica opened her still-tired eyes enough for her to see tender waves on the deserted beach—quiet even for a Sunday morning.

But, behind her…cold sheets.

She was immediately awake. She'd survived the night, but she was alone.

Stretching under the bedclothes, she realized that her pussy still ached from what he'd done for her the night before, and her heart sang from how he'd cared for her, how he'd wanted to make her feel so damn good. More questions sprang to her mind. Would he regret it? Would things be different now?

She had no idea. All she knew was that the previous night had been something special altogether. Never before had she met a man like Carrick.

As Danica moved out of bed with renewed energy, she was curious as to where Carrick was. Timid and hesitant, she found herself, still in his white T-shirt, tiptoeing out of the third-floor bedroom and down the stairs onto the second floor. He wasn't there either. *Where is he?*

As she snuck quietly toward the staircase leading down to the entry level, she finally overheard Carrick's voice coming from the office. He was arguing with someone.

"I don't give a shit," Carrick growled, then there was a pause.

Danica could only assume he was on the phone, and she cranked her neck to hear better whatever was happening. Listening to his hoarse morning voice float up the stairs, she experienced chills running up her legs. He was just so damn sexy.

"I'm not afraid of him. He can threaten all he wants," Carrick continued in a heated tone.

Threats. He was receiving threats. Danica gripped the wall, knowing what was going to come next.

Then she heard Carrick grumbling, "Get it to the lawyers. See if we have a legal problem here."

There was a longer pause and Danica thought the phone call was finally over, until she heard Carrick say one last thing.

"Look… I'm just trying to help a runaway girl who can't help herself," Carrick explained. "This is charity, man."

And Danica's heart dropped.

That was charity?

That's what she was? A charity case?

Every negative emotion crashed down on her as she collapsed backward, finding the doorframe of the bathroom behind her. Hearing Carrick moving around downstairs, she grabbed her black backpack that had been lying close by, jumped into the bathroom and locked the door. Tears once again found their way to her eyes, and she bit her lip so hard that it bled.

Turning to the shower, she flipped on the hottest water, ripped off his shirt and stepped in. She couldn't afford to let him hear her sob. Her question had been answered. Things were certainly going to be very, very different from that point on, now that she knew the truth about why he was helping her.

But why did he kiss me? Why did he put me in his bed? It all seemed like a cruel joke.

After letting it all out, crying under the hot water, she pulled herself back together. After getting out of the shower and toweling off, she pulled on a yoga outfit from her backpack. She hadn't packed much when she'd run from her apartment, but then again, she didn't have much to begin with.

Ran from my apartment — Danica thought through the words again, hating how she was starting to feel about herself. *A runaway girl. Helpless.*

After brushing out her long, wet hair, she wiped a homemade aloe lotion on her face as a matter of habit. She stood back from the mirror and took one long look at herself. This whole misadventure was making her ask a lot of questions. Carrick was challenging everything she'd thought about herself.

Adjusting the tight purple athletic tank top, she exhaled. *What type of woman am I? Am I the type to run and cry or the type to shine in the face of adversity?* She didn't know who she was anymore. Turning to leave the bathroom, she peeked out of the door. He hadn't come upstairs yet.

Good. She didn't want to see him. His brutal words were still fresh.

Danica reached to pull her clutch, sketchbook and pencils out of her black pack, taking them along with her as she made her way into the living area. Trying to take a breath and pushing down the anxiety that kept rising higher and higher, she took in the stunning ocean view. Carrick's beachside home broke out onto the long, white sandy beach of Southern California. She still couldn't get over how much this place would cost as she tiptoed toward the sliding door in the living room.

Maybe he really doesn't own it? Maybe he doesn't even live here?

Danica looked around and again found it odd that he had no TV, no personal mementos and no photos anywhere. It was like he'd rented a fully furnished home. *Let the past be the past* — the words from the housewarming gift on his bedside table rang through her mind.

What's he hiding in his past?

Danica had no idea, but she knew she was going to have to face him soon enough, so she had to find her center again and stop feeling like a sobbing mess. She reached out and grabbed a pillow, placing it on the little white rug in front of the patio door. It was time to sit and breathe. Just before she did so, she cracked open the door, ending the deafening silence of the house. Seagulls singing and ocean waves crashing emanated through the space, resolving at least a few issues within her, as she could always count on nature to do for her.

She set her sketchbook in her lap and popped on her reading glasses. Looking out over the scenic view, she began sketching what she saw...what she felt. Even from a seated position, it was easy to observe the ocean because the balcony was framed in glass. She allowed her breath to find the deepest parts of her lungs and her soul as she sketched a bird dancing in and out of the ocean before her.

Cross-legged while holding the sketchbook, she inhaled deeply, mindful of how her breath came in through her nose and went all the way down into the back of her ribcage. Repeating this for a minute or two, she tried to clear her mind, focusing only on the bird. She let herself enjoy the ambient sounds outside. Her mind wrapped around the natural world before her, and she drank it all in.

Just how Carrick drank in every last drop of me last night.

She immediately flashed her eyes open, a hot flush rising from her neck and into her cheeks. A rush of excitement filled her pussy with the thought of his fingers entering her, driving her over the edge. Her instant arousal couldn't have come at a worse time. Masculine footsteps echoed through the home as his lordship came stomping up the staircase.

She clenched her teeth, hating just how she felt about him and hating even more that it wasn't mutual.

"Morning," he grunted as he marched to where she sat.

She turned her head, forcing a stiff smile before turning back to her work.

"Whatcha drawing?" he asked casually as he took a seat in the chair right beside where she sat on the floor.

"Nothing," she responded too fast and slammed the sketchbook shut.

Carrick, smirking, reached down and slowly opened it. As he looked down at what she'd drawn, all she could do was study his solid profile. His scent filled her nose — *pure virility*. His body was so close. She found herself leaning backward, guarding her heart. His gaze climbed up to hers and he grinned with that skillful mouth of his.

"That's incredible. God, you are talented."

Panicking, Danica whipped off her glasses and searched for a reply.

Carrick shot her a sly look and stood to walk into the kitchen. She turned her head, involuntarily following his movements as he put on the coffee. While watching him work, the reality of her feelings hit. She did not want to talk about last night or this morning. She wanted to pretend none of it had ever happened.

I just have to get through this on my own.

As the coffee percolated, Carrick put his hands on the island, looking over to where she sat. He was still wearing his black T-shirt and army-green sweats, his dark hair disheveled. Danica hated how he always seemed to take her breath away.

"How did you sleep?" he asked, studying her.

Again, she smiled politely and replied stiffly, "Fine. And you?"

She waited for what he would say — if he would tell her about his phone call and the threats. He rubbed the dark stubble on his chin as his terribly blue eyes assessed her.

"Look, Dani... I'm ready to make a plan," he explained, "with what I dreamed about last night. I'm damn well ready to do something."

She digested his words — "*dreamed about last night*" — and stirred in her spot. She'd had dreams, too, the previous night. Her only question was whether or not his had been as hot as hers...

"I'm having visions of ripping heads off," he clarified. "Ripping these assholes to shreds."

Her voice fell into a low, hurt tone. "I guess you can do that."

Charity case.

His earlier words had been burned into her soul. Carrick raised his dark eyebrow as he must have seen her frown then look away. He leaned forward on the island, his arms and shoulders flexing.

"Dani, do you want to learn how to fight? Protect yourself?"

"Yes," she confirmed, and watched him nod in understanding. "W-we are in trouble?"

"We are."

"And are we safe here?"

"For now."

Standing, she locked eyes with him and understood that there was a lot more to that story, but he just wasn't sharing. She'd come to expect that much from him. Selfishly, she circled back to the reason why she'd played along in the first place.

She had to keep pushing. Her life depended on it.

"Can you also teach me survival skills?" Her tone was dead serious.

"Let's just focus on how you can fight to defend yourself."

"I think survival skills would be more…useful," she said, trying to stay circumspect.

Danica placed her sketchbook on the coffee table and crossed her arms, trying to look strong, but the look on Carrick's face told her he wasn't buying it.

"Useful?" he repeated. "Now I know you've got something on your mind, and I want to know what."

The way he looked at her told her one thing. She had something that he wanted to know. Under the intensity of his gaze, something strange got into her. He didn't deserve to know all her secrets. He didn't deserve to get the best of her. He didn't deserve to know all her plans.

Just so he can look down on me?

So Danica shrugged and pushed out her hip with a lot of attitude, enjoying the face he made as he leaned back from the island, that same hunger in his eyes that she'd seen the previous night. Charity case or not, he felt something. And she had decided that *her* plan was in part to get the upper hand and prove she was stronger than he thought.

"What's your plan, Dani?"

"I'll tell you mine if you tell me yours," she smirked, going in for the kill.

As his mouth opened, a confused look crossing his face, she turned around, flipping her nearly dry long brown locks over her shoulder as she slipped toward the patio door, seeking to swiftly step out onto the balcony, hearing him groan as she moved. The one thing she knew about men was that they loved watching women in yoga pants walk away.

If it was torture, she was glad to torture him.

He deserves it.

One point for Danica. She grinned to herself.

And just as she'd hoped, his heavy footsteps were apparent behind her, following her quickly from the kitchen. She lunged forward and shot her hand out to open the patio door farther, but she couldn't get it fully open in time. And that was when her plan fell through. Carrick was just too fast. He came up behind her, flipped her around and pushed her squarely up against the sliding door glass. Dropping his hands on either side of her, he trapped her in front of him, pressing her hard against the glass with his body.

One point for Carrick.

"I don't like surprises," he growled low, a warning ringing through his voice.

As intimidated as she was, she realized how much he wanted to know more. She forced a sly grin across her mouth, and though the unease was there, so was the temptation of empowerment. That was when she decided she was never, ever going to give in to him. He would rue the day he'd called her a charity case.

Runaway girl.

Helpless.

He continued, locking eyes with her, "I'm ready for answers. I'm ready to hear this plan of yours."

"And I'm ready for some coffee." She licked her lips, batting her eyelashes innocently. "Why don't we start with that and see where it takes us?"

And with that, she deftly slid open the door behind her and ducked under his arm, escaping his trap. She found her way onto the beautiful open balcony overlooking Sunset Beach. He hadn't followed her out, though, but had disappeared back into the house. Danica released a hot, pressurized breath.

A grin crossed her lips and a wild feeling flushed through her mind. *Two points for Danica.* She grinned. And that was something to celebrate. It wasn't easy to win against Carrick.

Leaning over the balcony, she took in the scene. The long, wide beach was seeing more and more beachgoers arriving to spend the morning, as was probably usual for a weekend. Danica enjoyed how the salty breeze wafted to her senses, bringing her into a state of deep relaxation. Rays hit her skin from the potent sun above, leaving a lasting feeling of heat on her shoulders.

She was a strong believer that vitamin D did the body good.

And she was proud of how she was turning the day around. She was starting to take back control, regaining a feeling of self-respect.

But she should have known that Carrick never lost.

"We'll head out in thirty." He appeared behind her in the patio door, bringing her a steaming mug of hot coffee. "I've laid some breakfast out for you, and I just need some prep time. From this point on, you are my apprentice—and there *will* be a test at the end."

"Where are we going?" she probed, taking a sip of the coffee.

"You'll see," he shot back, a devilish dark smile casting across his lips.

As his eyes spoke of scheming, she got hit with a feeling of insecurity—because he knew exactly how to get his way. And the man was clearly getting giddy at the idea of putting her through his own version of boot camp.

Clearly on a mission, he turned to head back inside, and she found herself anxiously jumping forward.

"Carrick, the point isn't to train me as the next Navy SEAL!"

As it came off her lips, that was when the question hit Danica. *Is Carrick a SEAL?* And his reply corroborated exactly that.

"That's the only way I know," he called back, a smirk in his tone.

"Wait—" she started, but he was long gone.

She parted her lips as she looked back over the ocean in pure disbelief. A former Navy SEAL...was protecting *her*? No wonder the man feared nothing.

Two points for Carrick, she realized — and now they were tied.

Chapter Eighteen

Danica

It was turning out to be an absolutely gorgeous day. Danica beamed as she rode shotgun in Carrick's truck—not the rental, but his own big, black pickup. Inside, it was new and had all the trappings of a fun, fast ride. With the music up and windows down, wind whipped into the cab, sending her long hair into a wild mess.

She felt *free*.

It helped that she had made it her mission to push back on Carrick—and prove just how strong she was. She'd temporarily closed off the aching part of her, hurt from his words and actions. Now, she was determined to live in the moment and soak in as much as she could. She was going to have to pass boot camp, of course, if she was going to take the next step in her plan. A former Navy SEAL teaching her survival skills? She couldn't ask for better.

Cruising the Pacific Coast Highway that, as its name indicated, ran all the way down the coastline, they passed all the hot beaches of Southern California — Huntington Beach, Newport Beach, Laguna Beach and San Clemente. By that time of day, mid Sunday morning, beachgoers were out in droves, flocking toward the wide expanse of fine golden-white sand that framed the edges of the sparkling ocean. Finally, as they seemed to leave the unending city sprawl of LA behind them, she noticed that they had found wild country. On her right, of course, was the Pacific Ocean — blue and white, far and wide. On her left, up a steep cliff, tall, arid hills with a lot of packed dirt and desert flora rolled on and on for miles.

"What's over here?" She motioned to the fenced-off hills, nearly yelling over the wind and music.

Carrick leaned forward and twisted the dial down, turning to her while he gripped the wheel with one strong arm.

"This is Camp Pendleton — a Marine Corps base." He nodded up the hills. "It's massive. There's no space down here that's not carved out and owned by someone."

"Is that where you trained?" she asked, dying to learn more about his military service.

He laughed like she was breaking into a secret inside joke, grinning so wide that his eyes wrinkled deeply. "No, my dear — it is not."

Before she could ask more, he leaned forward and brought the music back to loud. He'd streamed a hot-house list that she had started falling in love with. It fit perfectly with her taste, and really made her feel something she hadn't experienced in a while.

Upbeat.

Soon, he pulled off the highway onto what appeared to be a quiet intersection heading toward another beach. The sign read *San Onofre*. Her eyes widened as she realized where they were — a mecca for surfers. Real surfers, not just the tourists up in Huntington. San Onofre was known for the hardcore, and there wasn't much around it in terms of amenities. Surrounded by military land, it was a lone beach, but it certainly stretched on like all the other colossal beaches they'd passed.

Carrick pulled into the state parking lot, which was oddly quiet considering it was a Sunday. As he parked the truck and went to jump out, Danica just sat in awe of where she was. If this is where he was planning on training her, she was all in.

They unloaded what he'd brought in the back of the truck and hauled their gear toward the deserted beach. Their kit included two surfboards and three duffel bags. She had no idea what was inside them but guessed that her life was about to get interesting.

At one point, Carrick stopped on the sand, throwing the gear down. Danica looked around and realized that he had taken them to a private enclave, built into the landscape off the edge of the main beach area. It was like a secret little nook with an incredible view.

Carrick was making camp, and Danica lunged forward to learn and help. She'd camped a thousand times with her vegan yogi friends, but this was going to be different. She just knew it.

"Where do we start?" she asked, looking at the two black bags.

Shooting her an amused look, he started issuing orders, telling her to grab things and hold them for him. First, they set up a very small tent that he swore could fit two people, tucking it far back to be out of sight. Secondly, they organized and stowed food supplies and kits. She noticed a bag of apples and wondered if that was all he thought she ate.

Once that was done, Danica took a minute to look around, finding herself growing more and more excited at the idea that she was going to be camping on the beach. Maybe boot camp wasn't going to be all that bad?

Eager, she climbed into the faded green tent to help him roll out the sleeping mats and found him turning around to offer her a navy-blue wetsuit.

"Thought we should start on the water. That's what I'm best at," he grinned, shooting her that same wild smile she'd gotten used to. "Here... This is my sister's. You are about the same size."

Danica took the wetsuit in her hands, running her fingers over the thick, expensive fabric. She'd never been able to afford one, and surfing in the cold ocean without that added protection hadn't been easy. With a wink, Carrick moved out of the tent, giving her space to change. She wiggled out of her black yoga pants, folding them along with her tank top neatly beside one of the mats, and started getting into the wet suit. She didn't have a swimsuit underneath, but it didn't matter. As she pulled it on, she found it fit well. It was a feminine version, and her arms and torso were covered all the way through to the crotch, but her legs were bare.

Outside the tent, she heard Carrick's cellphone ringing—and ringing, and ringing. He didn't answer it. What if it was Petrov? Or Andriy?

After flipping up her hair into a ponytail, she focused on the plan. She stepped out of the tent to find

Carrick already in his own wet suit. His was full-body, black and had blue Hawaiian designs on it. She sucked in her breath to play it cool because the man looked un-fucking-believably hot. That was the hardest part, always.

She bit her lip when he shot her a sly smile and handed her a surfboard that was the perfect length for her. It was white and yellow and had a soft tether.

"My sister lives in Portland," he began explaining as they marched toward the water. "But she makes a point to come visit with her man, so I store her stuff at my place."

Was that the first time he'd offered up personal information without her prying it out of him? She didn't know but felt the winds had been changing since she'd pushed back on him at his place.

"Do you know how to surf?" he asked her.

"I'm a beginner," she admitted, feeling the sleek plastic of the board under her arm.

"I thought you grew up in So-Cal?"

"LA." She grinned. "Well, Bel Air. My parents thought ballet was better than surfing."

Carrick let out a chuckle, shaking his head, and they finally reached the edge of the water.

"All right, let's start easy. We'll paddle out and stay flat on our boards," he explained, pointing out over the water. "Don't pop up unless you feel it. Follow me."

And with that, he ushered her into the water. Once they were deep enough, they lay down on their boards and paddled out even farther. The hot sun roasted the back of her legs, but she loved it—every second of it. There was nothing better than being in the water, in the power of the world's largest ocean. She felt every living creature inside the ocean singing and the sunshine above encouraging her.

It feels right.

As she popped up onto her knees, paddling and catching the waves, she decided to try getting onto her feet—and she did, successfully. After riding out a smooth wave, she tumbled into the water near the shallower beach line, laughing hysterically. Catching her breath and the board, she looked around and saw him. He was laughing, too.

He called out, reassuring her, "You're doing great. Keep going!"

Warmth flooded her chest with his words, and she couldn't help but let it really sink in.

As the day drew on, Carrick taught her actual survival skills in the water—like how to handle dives and undertow and how to fish and hunt in the ocean. They moved onto the beach for a late lunch, and he showed her how to turn salt water into drinking water and cook a meal without fire. The outdoorsy lessons continued on and on—with everything from things she should do to things she shouldn't.

Finally, after changing in the tent into a spare set of dry clothes, she sat in the sand. It was early evening, and she was tired from the long day, so she leaned back on her elbows. Now in a fresh tank top and her black mini skirt, she soaked up the last rays of the day.

"Cheers," Carrick said, bringing out two aluminum cups full of some delicious sloshing liquid.

"What's this?" she asked, bringing it to her nose.

Whatever it was, it was hard liquor.

"Lesson number forty-five—always bring whiskey," he grinned, taking a sip, visibly enjoying it as she had every moment of the day with him.

Bringing the amber liquid into her mouth, she felt it burning like hell as it made its way down her throat, forcing her to cough.

"Take it slowly." Carrick grinned. "Taste it."

She nodded, taking another sip. As she drank, he walked her through it, teaching her how to savor. On the third or fourth attempt, she started to like it.

"I don't usually drink hard liquor," she admitted.

He raised his glass to her. "Yeah, well, I've been doing a lot of things I shouldn't do." And he took another swig of the booze, shaking his head.

She watched him, wondering who the man was behind the steel armor. She desperately wanted to know, and the whimsical part of her brain started filling in the blanks with wild stories.

Finally, Carrick cut into her thoughts. "Does Andriy even know you? The real you?"

She shook her head slowly. "No. Not at all"

"Did he threaten you...to stay untouched?" he followed up, anger in his voice.

"No, that's not why," she responded shyly, playing with the sand in front of her. Andriy had nothing to do with her virgin status.

"Then why?"

She shrugged, not sure how to answer. It was deeply personal.

"I think you know why," Carrick challenged, shooting her a knowing look. "I'm guessing that you don't trust anyone, let alone *men*. And that's why you've never given yourself to any man."

She looked up to him, her lips parting, realizing that he easily saw through her — and he was completely right.

"I wish I could read you like that." She sniffed, exasperated.

He leaned back, replying, "I'm a lot older than you. I've got more years under my belt, and I've seen a lot of things."

"How old are you?" she asked, curious as hell.

"Too old." He took his drink again. "Sometimes, Dani… Sometimes, I just feel like saying fuck *everything*. Sometimes I hate all the rules in life."

With those last words, he turned to her and licked his bottom lip as he looked her up and down. Butterflies fluttered uncontrollably in her stomach.

"But it's never that easy, is it?" he said, his face darkening.

"This doesn't need to get any messier," she found her defensive self blurting out, continuing to push back.

"I agree," he said, knocking his drink back and leaning forward so that his arms draped around his muscled legs. "Let's just do what we are *supposed* to do, all right?"

Deep disappointment ricocheted in her stomach. His eyes grew intense as he looked at her. The words hit her hard and the aluminum cup shook in her hands. She sipped on her drink, not knowing what else to do.

Then he stood and took a step. For some dumb reason, she stood as well. But the effect was poorly thought out. Turning around, he looked down on her where she stood. There was a lot of something in his eyes.

And Danica unfortunately was too taken by him to listen to the smart part of her brain screaming at her to stop.

"I think—" she said quickly, not even sure what to say next.

All she knew was that she desperately wanted him to kiss her.

But he wasn't going to.

Finally, in his detached and cold tone, he said, "It's time for the next phase of your training—learning how to fight. Show me your stance."

And with that, he pushed them right into a long session of fight training. She learned how to punch, kick and protect herself. He taught her self-defense moves and how to break free from holds. Danica kept her head down, obeying his every command and enjoying every time he touched her, reached his thick arms around her to hold her or held her hands up to show her how to throw a punch. He remained serious and focused, unbending.

Danica did everything she could to mimic the tone, though she had grown to feel very different about her time with him.

Hours later, Danica shivered as she sat near Carrick in the sand, watching the waves crash over each other underneath the night sky. The day had gone by too fast...way too fast. And now it was dark.

"Should we start a fire?" Danica prompted, rubbing her hands over her bare legs, which were even more golden from the day. "Surely that would be some sort of survival skill."

"No." Carrick shook his head, sitting strong and stoic in his place beside her. "We'd better not draw attention to ourselves."

Danica tilted her head, considering his words. The lingering threat couldn't be ignored. He was teaching her how to fight for a reason. She just hoped to God that she wouldn't have to use the moves anytime soon.

A silence fell between them, but he didn't say anything else. He just kept looking out over the water until, finally, she could remain quiet no longer and broke it.

"Tell me about you," she said.

"What's there to know?"

That same silence thickened between them, and more than ever she wondered what that cryptic message meant on his housewarming gift — *"let the past be the past"*. She'd grown desperate to know even the smallest morsel of information about him. Wouldn't he tell her?

"Have you ever been in love?" she asked.

"It doesn't matter. It's never going to happen again," he snapped with a tone of finality.

Her mouth dropped open. She was unwilling to believe it.

"Why not?" she pressed, chewing on his words.

"Because I'm never going through that shit again, so forget it." Carrick snarled with profound pain in his voice, pushing her away.

Before she could say anything, he got up and took three long steps toward the tent. The sand beneath her fingers seemed to shift and screech — screaming at her not to get up, not to follow him.

But she popped up out of her spot on the sand anyway.

"Wait, Carrick," she breathed, all the hurt from the morning rushing back.

He paused, half-turned around and gazed over at her — guarded as hell. There was maybe ten feet between them, but it felt like an ocean.

She quickly explained, "I don't understand why you won't just talk to me about yourself. You are less trusting than I am."

"This isn't about trust, Dani." His eyes flashed with fury and she knew the conflict between them had officially exploded.

"Then what?" The desperation in her caused her to grow irate. "Why can't you just fucking tell me a goddamn thing about you? Don't I deserve to know?"

He stood there, silent, watching her, as she laid it all on the line. Finally, he opened his mouth, and Danica found herself falling into his words.

"I'm an old vet, Dani. A washed up, broken sniper." Carrick spoke in a low, warning tone tinged with anger and pain. "I've been to war and lived some fucked-up shit. I have no business putting that on you. You have your whole life ahead of you—*without* me. Stop asking."

Then he turned around, moving back toward the tent.

"Without *you*?" Danica felt breathless, searching.

He shrugged her off, ignoring her.

She fell forward, stumbling closer to him, unable to let it go. "What do you mean—*"without you"*?"

He said nothing, as if she didn't exist. It drove her insane, and words she didn't want to say broke out of her mouth.

"I heard what you said! You think I'm a charity case!" she cried out behind him.

He stopped, turned and crossed his arms. A furious look expanded over his face as he looked down on her.

"Enough with the bullshit," he growled. "It's time for you to listen and learn how to defend yourself, because you and I both know that one day I'll be gone."

The reality of him eventually leaving just broke her.

"Then why did you do that to me last night? Why did you touch me?" She waved her hands frantically, tears falling down her cheeks. "Was it because I'm a charity case?"

Carrick launched forward, taking three big steps to close the distance between them. He wrapped one solid arm of muscle around her and yanked her close to him. After he'd hardening his grip and lifted her up and into him, she tilted her face up to his mouth—fearful but *willing*. His breath was a mix of whiskey and mint as it wafted down to her.

"Are you testing me?" he demanded. "Are you playing games here?"

"*No*," she cried breathlessly.

"This *isn't* charity."

He stared down into her with intense eyes, studying her. She could only guess that he was debating what he was going to do next. She squeaked as he tightened yet again around her ribcage, holding her harder and closer than she'd ever expected.

"Then what is it?" she whispered upward. "I don't understand why you are doing this."

He hoisted her slender frame up in his thick, strong arms so that her eyes were level with his and her tip toes were just grazing the ground.

"It doesn't matter."

He dropped her, her feet hitting the sand hard. With one last threatening look, he pulled away and moved down to the shoreline—leaving her absolutely breathless and alone.

Chapter Nineteen

Danica

Danica sat in the tent, trying to recover. In her mini skirt and tank top, she hugged her knees to her chest, and though she was getting cold, she couldn't feel it because she was sad, really hurt. He had hurt her, but she wanted him to come back to her all the same. Everything he'd made her feel that day and the one before came crashing to the front of her mind — like a teaser for something she'd never really get to have.

Finally, after too long, he stepped up to the tent, then he unzipped it and reached in. It looked like he was just grabbing a sweater, and she wondered if he was going to leave her to sleep alone.

"Carrick," she whispered, and he turned his head to her.

He shook it, clearly telling her to stop talking to him. She could feel the struggle within him because that same one was happening in her.

"I just…" she tried to say something, pure need coursing through her veins.

He paused, watching her.

But before she could find words to finish her sentence, she shivered, wrapping her arms tighter around her knees. His gaze trailed up her bare legs to her chest and her lips.

"Don't go," she pleaded, her voice barely audible.

He must have heard her because he lunged toward her, grabbing her and pulling her up and onto him as he fell back onto one of the sleeping mats.

"Don't you fucking think I want this?" he asked.

"I want this, too."

"Fuck," he growled and moved his hand up to the back of her head, bringing her face to his.

Then he took her mouth, kissing her like never before.

Lighting her on fire.

She straddled him and let him feel every inch of her. Acting hungry as hell, he inched her farther up his body, wrapping her even tighter against him and keeping his hand at the back of her head so she couldn't escape his deepening kiss. As he held her, she found his hand underneath her black mini skirt, which had hiked up as he'd pulled her onto him.

Never before had she let herself completely fall into a man.

"You have no idea what you do to me." He groaned low and hot as he slipped his finger underneath her panties, tracing the long, thin, wet line of her pussy's aching slit.

"Be my first," she begged with unchecked words from her heart, acknowledging for the first time what he meant to her.

"I shouldn't." Carrick worked his way down her jaw to her throat, running his teeth along her neck. "I really, really shouldn't."

"Do it anyway," she said, wanting to forget everything.

Wanting to change his mind.

Wanting to give herself to him completely.

"*Please*," she whispered as he pulled back to look into her eyes. "Just do this."

He held her shoulders, pausing as he studied her. Then he conceded, taking her mouth with his once again. With every lap of his tongue, more and more of her tension released. She tasted the sweet boozy flavor in his mouth, savoring it completely, like he'd taught her to appreciate whiskey.

With the sound of the waves in the background, he helped her slip off her mini skirt—leaving her with only a tank top and panties.

"You're perfect." He exhaled, running his hands up her soft shins. "Take everything off."

She nodded, starting to feel more nervous now that it had become a reality, and slipped off her tank top over her head, releasing her breasts. She didn't miss the sound deep in his chest as he watched her strip—or the hunger in his eyes as he stared at her gladly giving herself to him. She hooked her thumbs in her panties and slowly pulled them down, showing him what he'd already tasted before—her wet virgin pussy.

He helped her grab the panties when they were just at her shins, launching them into the corner of the tent, a sense of urgency in his movements. All the same, she could still tell he was holding back from what he really wanted to do—take her hard and fast. Looking down, she bit her lip as she saw how his board shorts had changed. Now, there was a long, stiff bulge that had made its own tent in his shorts — his rock-hard cock. He reached down to his manhood, probably adjusting it to a more comfortable angle, and he was running out of real estate down there. He was that big.

How's he going to fit in me?

After he whipped his hoodie off over his head, he revealed his bare chest and she sucked in an audible breath. She'd never seen him naked before. Sitting up closer to him, she reached out her fingers and ran them up a long tattoo on his torso. Like she'd suspected, he had some writing over the top of his chest, circling finally around his heart. She could only make out that there was a tattoo — not exactly what it said. She traced downward to his abdomen, which was ripped to all hell. *God, he's a statue of muscle*, she thought, salivating.

He grabbed her hand and pushed her back, taking her mouth with his in the process. Once again, he kissed her like he needed to taste every inch of her, like he cared. He laid her back down as he worked his way down her neck, running his teeth along her sensitive skin. She arched her back as he made his way to each breast, fondling, cupping and tasting as he groaned. He ran his other hand down her abdomen to her clit, using that same circular motion that had sent her over the edge the day before.

Soon, she was arching into him as he tasted and tweaked each nipple, all while pushing two fingers up her tight pussy to ready her for him. She already was about to orgasm under his skilled touch. The man knew exactly what he was doing, and he was doing it very, very well — or maybe he just excited her more than she ever thought possible.

He's the perfect guy to be my first.

"I can't wait." She exhaled, sensations pulsing up and down her limbs. "I need you now."

He laughed as he made his way back up to her mouth. "The wait is what makes it so hot. Lesson number sixty-six."

She shot her hands down, holding onto his thick wrists as he pumped his fingers up and into her.

"Carrick," she pleaded, "I need you *now*."

Again, he seemed calm and amused, circling faster over her clit and waiting for her to come. As she moaned, her pussy getting wetter and wetter, he pulled back a little, looking at her. The way he paused and watched her was unlike anything she'd seen before. He felt open for the first time...warm and raw.

I could get used to this.

"These past two days with you, Dani, have been the best days I've had in years," he confessed as he touched her, the scent of whiskey softly wafting down on her.

But before she could reply, he took her mouth again. Her chest filled with burning emotion, and she fought back tears of pure joy as they kissed. Quickly, she was pushing down his board shorts, releasing his long, throbbing cock before her eyes.

"Oh my God," she gasped, amazed by just how big he was.

When he kicked off his shorts and was naked, he laughed as he pumped his cock up and down, opening her legs with his other hand and moving between them. He hovered above her, one hand still working her clit, keeping her pussy warm and wet. She had no idea how he was going to fit inside her. He could barely fit two fingers.

"This might hurt at first," he warned, moving the twitching head of his hard cock toward her wet hole. "But it'll get better. I promise."

She raised her hips to meet him in desperation — needing to finally feel what it was like to have a man inside her. Aching and panting, she angled herself to make it easier for him, which he clearly understood. He held his cock at the base and slowly pushed the throbbing head into her while continuing to circle her clit. She cried out at first when he began, feeling her pussy immediately tighten around the intruder. But, slowly, she relaxed. Inch by inch, her dripping pussy allowed more and more of him in.

Then it felt like he'd reached a point where he couldn't go farther. She looked down and realized he was only halfway seated.

"This is the part where it's going to hurt the most." He drew down on her, and she heard it in his voice — the warning.

She bit her lip, nodding, but kept her hips up and ready to take him. He pushed in harder, quick and fast, probably to get it over with. She yelped, trying to catch her breath. The pinch was much worse than she'd thought it would be and hurt flushed up and down her body. But then it was done, and he'd slid his cock all the way into her. The pain slowly left her as he began pumping in and out. Whatever discomfort she'd experienced was replaced by pure pleasure — and a feeling that she could never have imagined.

No doubt seeing her pleasure reflected in her expression, he grinned and urged her to open her legs wider and wrap them around his waist. She complied, letting him have complete control. Once her legs were around him, he immediately started pumping into her again. As he plunged in deeper, his thick cock stretched all the way to the end of her canal, pulsing savagely. He was hard as granite and she was taking his entire length. The more he thrusted, the closer she came to orgasm, which she recognized now, thanks to him.

It didn't take long before she found those thrilling sensations running up and down her body, threatening what was about to happen. With his cock hitting the exact right spot, she came hard and fast, moaning his name in the process. Juice flowed out of her pussy as she throbbed and tightened around his cock. She arched once more, showcasing every inch of her body to him, which he met with a low growl and dropped to suck her nipples, one then the other.

As each pump of his cock blasted more and more sensation through her already-sensitive pussy, he found a harder and faster rhythm. Soon, his face grew serious and focused — and his breathing changed. His skin grew hotter, and his cock seemed on fire.

"Fuck, Dani," he groaned slowly, pulling out and releasing hot liquid all over her abdomen.

She just watched him refocus after the pleasure of his orgasm subsided. Keeping his warm, rough hand on her, he reached into the bag on the side of the tent to grab a towel and clean them up. Within moments, he'd collapsed beside her on the mat and zipped them both, naked, into the sleeping bag.

He pulled her close to him and kissed the tip of her nose before kissing her forehead and her hair. He reached up and affectionately caressed her face, closing his eyes with obvious exhaustion. In that moment, she allowed herself to just watch him fall asleep.

A spiteful little voice inside her tried to remind her that it was all temporary.

This isn't real.

She quashed any inner voices that she didn't want to hear and kissed Carrick's sleeping mouth before rolling over and falling into sleep, still held in his arms. The last thing she remembered before completely passing out was his sleepy lips grazing her shoulder and his thick arms tightening around her, bringing her into him as his little spoon, keeping her warm, keeping her safe.

Chapter Twenty

Carrick

On a bright Monday morning, Carrick sat on the golden white sand of San Onofre beach in Southern California.

He inhaled the breeze wafting off the waves before him and dug his heels into the grainy sand, which was hot on top and cool underneath. Already, the heat of the sun was mounting, and sweat slid his black sunglasses down the bridge of his nose.

There was something so peaceful about the beach in the morning, so soothing. The waves ebbed back and forth, a rhythm that was entrenched in his soul. He felt connected to the water in a way he couldn't explain.

It might have been the rising warmth or the sun beating on his back—but Carrick could swear that his core felt warmer than it had the days, weeks and months before. Who knew what it was, but it didn't seem to be all in his head. The feeling was palpable throughout his body.

For the first time in years, he felt *alive*.

He twisted in the sand, checking the tent up the beach where Danica was still sleeping. There was something about her that really pulled him in, made him want to break rules. He was doing things he shouldn't, but she made him feel something he hadn't in a long time. And the fact that she had given herself to him the previous night, begged him to be her first? Well, that had only made it all the better. He had no regrets. He certainly didn't feel bad about punching out the clown who was trying to force her into marriage. He'd do it again—harder—given half a chance.

He reached down beside him into the sand, running the warm, tiny grains through his fingers. Looking out over the horizon, hearing ocean birds singing, he was brought back to days aboard naval warships—his time of deployment, his old life. Maybe one day he could tell Danica about it all—when she could understand.

He'd seen more death than he could explain…for too long. And maybe his luck was changing. She embodied a vivacity that had been breathed into his existence.

Purity. Happiness.

Satisfaction.

And as he gripped another fistful of sand, feeling it against his calloused palms, his cellphone vibrated in his hoodie pocket. He fished for it, bringing it out, and saw that it was a text message from Delta.

Ignoring me?

Carrick opened the app and saw all the unanswered texts from his partner the day before. The reality of the dumpster fire he was in flashed to the front of his mind, drawing him away from the ocean's serenity.

I was busy. What's up?

The last time you ignored me, I found you hungover, broken and bloodied.

I'm fine.

God, I hope so. You'll be getting a call from her daddy shortly. Shit's getting real, man.

I'll handle it.

Will you? You're not yourself. Something's up.

Carrick read the words and exhaled sharply. His friend was damn right about that.

This can't go on. Are you going to deal with her or not?

Before Carrick could write back, a call started coming to his cellphone. Seeing that there was no caller ID, he knew exactly who it was. He sure as hell didn't want to talk to the fucker, but Carrick wasn't a coward.

And he wasn't about to let the asshole think he was faltering.

"Yup," he answered the call, pressing it hard against his ear so he wouldn't miss a word.

"You said you would call me," Petrov's unimpressed voice rang through the line. "It has been over twenty-four hours."

"Patience is a virtue" — Carrick kept his voice calm, not willing to show his cards — "especially on Monday mornings."

"I hope you have enjoyed your little *holiday*." Petrov wheezed into the phone, alerting Carrick. "Now, bring her to me."

"Not a chance," Carrick stated, his mind running with questions.

Little holiday? What the fuck does that mean? Does Petrov know we're at the beach? Carrick looked around, his mind working through any possible way Petrov could be tracking her, then decided the thug was just being a smart-ass.

Petrov let out a shallow cough then spoke in a low, deadly serious tone. "My jet is leaving for Moscow tomorrow, and I expect her to be on it."

"And what makes you think I give a shit?"

"*Poshel na khuy*," Petrov snapped, clearly growing irate. "Enough with the posturing. You've done everything I've asked so far, haven't you? You found her. You brought her to the wedding. I know you'll bring her to me once again — because, if you don't, you are intelligent enough to recognize what will happen to you *and* her."

A protective fury rose in Carrick as he slammed back against the threat. "Stop trying to control her. She's not going to marry Andriy."

"Won't she? She won't say no. You *know* she won't say no."

"I won't let her." The words slipped out of Carrick's mouth before he clenched down harder. "You don't deserve her — and neither does he."

Petrov laughed again. "And look at you — trying to control her life, telling her what to do. Remind me how you are so different from what you are criticizing?"

Carrick went silent, remembering how submissive Danica was, remembering that controlling her life was exactly *not* what she needed.

She needs to stand up to Petrov by herself.

Petrov added, with a tone of finality, "Andriy is a good man and will make a good husband for her. We take care of our own. Unfortunately, he is already displeased that he will have this black eye for their wedding reception this weekend. If I were you, I wouldn't give him any more reasons to be unhappy… It could *kill* your business."

Carrick flexed his jaw, removing the phone from his ear to hang up. Staring at it, he debated throwing the thing in the ocean. Something about that call left him feeling in way, way less control than he had yesterday…when he'd last spoken to the guy.

What the fuck am I going to do now?

Letting all the frustration inside him out in one long exhale, Carrick narrowed his vision on the crashing waves before him. He needed the cold water to wake him up. He popped up and zipped his phone back into his hoodie pocket. Whipping it off, leaving him in nothing but his board shorts, Carrick turned toward the tent to throw the hoodie up the beach.

But then he realized he wasn't alone anymore. A grin washed across his face as he watched Danica walking down the sand toward him, flipping back her long hair. She was so damn stunning.

"Morning," he called to her.

"Good morning," Danica replied, focused on him.

She stopped a few feet away from him, her expression apprehensive, awkwardly holding her arms across the chest of her pink hoodie.

Carrick immediately closed the gap and leaned in to give her a kiss, but she pulled back. He returned her intense gaze. There was no chance in hell she'd overheard anything. The crashing waves and strong breeze were enough ambient noise to drown out the conversation he'd just had with Petrov.

"Who were you talking to?" she asked, the words pouring out.

"It was a business call. How did you sleep?" he replied, keeping his cards close to his chest.

A frown shot across her face and she looked away. He knew for sure she didn't believe him and didn't trust his words. He bit his lip, regretting his response. In the blink of an eye, everything they'd shared the night before had disappeared—and they were right back at square one.

"So, what's the plan now?" Danica turned back to him, her voice stone cold.

"Well, what's *your* plan?" Carrick asked, pushing the conversation to where it needed to go. "What were you planning on doing with these survival skills?"

Her lips parted and he saw that she wanted to lie. He'd interviewed enough sources throughout the world, collecting intel, to know when someone didn't want to answer a question. And just like that, she seemed nervous and searching.

And that was when he decided he absolutely had to know.

"I think we are past the smokescreen, Dani." He laid it all out. "I need to know what you are planning. I need to know how to help you."

She flitted her amber gaze up to him, obviously relenting. "You're going to think it's stupid."

"So what. Tell me anyway."

She shifted in the sand, barefoot, and started fiddling with the bottom edge of her pink hoodie.

She breathed out, speaking quickly, "Look… I tried to face Petrov at the wedding. I tried to talk to Andriy and tell them to leave me alone, but it didn't work. You saw it. And now all I've really done is open the door even farther. They know I'll fold like a cheap tent."

"So?"

She pressed her eyes together as she finally said, "So, let's be real here. I only really have one option."

"Which is?" he asked through a clenched jaw. He knew what she was going to say and he already hated it. "What is your only option?"

"To run," she finally admitted, opening her gentle eyes to him once again. "Get off the grid. Hide somewhere they can't find me."

He exhaled as he let the truth sink in. She didn't want to fight back. She didn't want to make a stand. She didn't believe in herself. She was a flight risk more than anything, even at the cost of her own wellbeing.

I should have known.

"What does 'off the grid' mean?" he probed, trying to keep it cool.

"I've had friends who have lived an alternative lifestyle, and you know what? All it does is bring a person closer to nature and art." She was obviously trying hard to convince him. *And maybe herself?* "I can get up to the mountains and camp, either alone or with others."

"Living off the land? Living in a tent in the forest?" he shot back. "Is that part of your vegan crap?"

"Something like that," she whispered. "People do it."

Assessing her, he felt her deep anxiety. Unfortunately, he wasn't in a place for pussyfooting.

"That plan is dumb as fuck. Are you high?"

"What?" she gasped. "Listen… I recognize it's not a great first choice, but I'm looking at Plan B here. I'm trying to find a way to just be free."

"I'm not going to let you do something as dumb as that. You should have a real life." He waved his hand, holding his ground. "I'll help you."

But then *she* pushed back.

"It's not up to you," she snapped, crossing her arms tighter across her chest. "You can't run my life." Her gaze was fierce, strong.

Carrick leaned back, looking down at her in amazement. Why the fuck couldn't she stand up to Petrov like that? Didn't she see what she was already capable of?

"This is a free country, Dani. You don't have to run from anyone," he implored. "We can have them charged. We can fight back against them. There are grown-up ways to deal with this."

She stepped back, blinking out a few big tears. "I am not a Navy SEAL, Carrick. I can't do what you do."

"Yes, you can," he urged.

But she took another step back, accidentally stumbling and falling down into the hot sand. *Shit*, Carrick thought as he watched an expression flash across her face. He'd recognize it any day.

She feels helpless.

Unable to watch her break, he nodded sharply to the tent. "Go pack up your things. We leave in ten."

Her expression grew pained. She had no other words. And that was when it really hit Carrick. He saw something too familiar—a young woman who deserved everything in life but had been unfairly handed brutal hardship. As she scrambled off the sand and spun to march back to the tent, he found himself blinking rapidly, trying to get a grip on the present and forget his past.

I can't save her.

Finding himself alone again on the beach, Carrick realized how different he felt from when he'd woken up. He hated every problem weighing on him, every memory his mind threatened to flash before him. And with all that hatred, he walked toward the water, unable to be any closer to Danica, to think about her, to feel.

I can't watch her suffer.

As his feet hit the cold water of the ocean and it crashed against his shins, a chill shot through his body. But he wasn't cold. On SEAL Team Seven, he'd been on many, many dives in water that was frigid. He was used to cold water. The chill shooting up his body was because of what had just happened and the old agony that wouldn't go away.

Now waist-deep in the waves, Carrick dove in headfirst, finding his way underneath the water. The power and force of the ocean overtook him, holding him and pushing him forward. The undertow was incredibly strong, and he knew inexperienced swimmers could get caught up in a bad way. It was a good thing that he was very, very capable. As he swam back and forth, never too far from shore, keeping his eye on Danica packing up, he had to come to terms with what was happening inside him.

This was all too familiar. He'd been there before, been down this road. An unwelcome memory flashed to the front of his mind. As Carrick swam, he allowed the flashback to take over in full, knowing he just had to relive it...at least this once.

It was a little less than two years before, and he was standing over Lauren's intensive-care hospital bed, watching her stats on the monitors. She wasn't doing well. She'd had a stroke.

"Why didn't you take the meds?" he roared out of pure frustration, knowing his fiancée couldn't even hear him. "I told you this would fucking happen."

Her eyes remained shut. She was unconscious in her bed – vulnerable and weak. Her natural hair fanned out over the pillow, still messy and knotted, though Carrick had tried his best to brush it over the weeks she'd been there. Her dark lashes fanned out over her white cheeks, nearly lifeless. He desperately wished he could see those crystal blue eyes open to him once more.

"Lauren, I can't fight this for you. I can't climb into your body and beat the leukemia out." He broke. "You have to listen to me. You have to keep fighting."

Exasperated, he ran his hands over his unshaven face, feeling the pain of watching her get sicker and sicker before his eyes – the helplessness, the powerlessness, the exhaustion from living out of the hospital chair beside her bed. She wasn't supposed to get sick. She wasn't supposed to get worse. They'd just bought a house. They were supposed to get married. They had plans.

And they'd just painted the baby's room. They'd just started trying. Sure, the wedding wasn't until the summer, but they weren't too fussy about formalities. They'd been together a long time already. Lauren had just turned thirty, and she'd told Carrick she was ready to be a mom.

But then they'd found out she was sick. Really sick.

The lining of his throat started to stiffen as he looked down on the woman he loved, wishing she would just fucking wake up, that he could see any sign she would turn the corner and come out of it.

"Everything okay in here?" A nurse with pink scrubs and a reassuring, motherly feel walked in with a handheld scanning device. She walked up and started doing her checks on her unconscious patient.

"It's fine."

"It doesn't seem fine," the nurse replied, keeping a calm voice.

"She shouldn't have stopped taking the meds." He lashed out, his fist tightening on the IV pole. "I told her not to fucking stop taking them – and look what happened! How long is she going to be out for?"

The nurse reached over to the side table, grabbing a tissue from the box, walked around the bed to where Carrick stood, and handed it to him.

"What's this for?" he demanded.

"Your face."

Frowning, he reached up with his hand and realized his face was wet.

"Why the fuck is my face wet?" He pulled his hand back, feeling clear liquid on his fingers.

"You're crying."

Carrick gazed back at Lauren. She seemed so small. So white. So sick.

"When is she going to wake up?" he asked.

The nurse reached out and grabbed his arm, squeezing it in a caring way.

"I don't think she is," she said.

His eyes shifted to the nurse and his stomach convulsed. Lauren isn't going to wake up? What the hell? *His mind tried to process it, but he just couldn't.*

"She stopped chemo because she knew she was almost there," the nurse explained, holding on to his arm and looking up at him empathetically. "She just wanted her last days to be... well, without any drugs except those that keep her comfortable. Those were her wishes. We are still with her — right up to the end."

The end — *the words pierced Carrick's mind and he felt something snapping...something changing. He'd lost a lot of friends through the years in the war, but he'd never expected to lose his girl in a fight that he couldn't do anything about.*

I can't save her.

He refused to accept it.

"She should have taken the meds. She should still be awake," he panted, his voice distant and distraught. Finally, his voice cracked, "I need her to wake up."

She was still going to wake up. She had to.

He felt the nurse squeezing his arm tighter.

"She can't die. I never got to say..." Carrick choked then sealed his mouth. He couldn't fucking talk anymore.

His throat made a bizarre noise and the nurse immediately pulled in his stiff body for a bear hug. She must have been a foot shorter and a hundred pounds lighter, but the strength of her hug was undeniable. The strength of a nurse... He folded like a fallen soldier into her — dropping into something he hadn't felt for a while.

It wasn't fair.

It wasn't fucking fair.

Chapter Twenty-One

Carrick

Carrick heaved the last black duffel bag into the back of his pickup truck and stalked around to the driver's door. His movement was heavier and angrier than he wanted to show, but he couldn't keep it in any longer. The situation was all fucked up, and he was running out of the patience to deal with it.

A vibration came from his cell phone in his pocket, and he whipped it out. Delta was texting him again, and the message wasn't good — a shit storm had started that morning. Carrick gritted his teeth together as he read the words.

Lovely day today. Received several threatening calls from her daddy, and now I've got lawyers chasing you down for breach of contract. Hope you are having a great time at the beach.

Carrick ran his fingers over the cold glass of the phone, a knot twisting in his chest. He shouldn't have fucked off yesterday. He should have been there. He was asking too much of his friend.

Well, fuck. I'm on my way back. I'll deal with the critical issues. Do me a favor… Go home and get some rest. You've done enough for me.

Carrick jumped up into the driver's seat of the truck.

Slamming his foot on the pedal, he pulled out of the San Onofre State Beach parking lot, hearing Danica squeak beside him with the powerful movement of the truck. Everything was silent between them and had been so for an hour since they'd finished packing up camp on the beach. He reached over and flipped on the radio, finding some boring news station that wouldn't make him crazy.

But very clearly, he realized that was fucking unavoidable.

"Can you drop me off at the train station?" Danica asked, sending him over the goddamn edge.

He practically snapped the steering wheel in half from the pressure of his grip. Heat rising up his throat, he turned his head to snap at her.

"Where the hell are you thinking of going?" he grunted.

"I don't know yet," she slouched in her seat, avoiding his gaze.

"Jesus Christ."

Carrick clenched his jaw in disbelief as he found a way onto the highway. They were about an hour's drive from his place at Sunset Beach, but the train terminal was less than halfway there at one of the bigger beachside towns.

He could drop her off and be done with all the bullshit—let her deal with it in her own way, which was absolutely *not* going to work. He gripped the wheel harder, hating how deep he'd gotten, knowing that getting out now wasn't realistic for him—and there were many, many reasons why that was.

Chewing on every possible option before him, Carrick knew he needed to make a plan.

A better plan.

For that, he needed time to think.

"So, you get on a train—then what?" he challenged her, buying himself time.

She didn't reply and seemed to shrink even farther into her seat. The fury emanating off him had obviously hit her hard, and she fingered the door handle like she was ready to spring.

He continued, not waiting for her. "You know *Daddy* is just going to show up, yet again, harassing the shit out of you to do whatever he wants. Are you ready to finally tell him to fuck off? Finally going to tell him he's not welcome in your life?"

"He's not my daddy, Carrick, first of all."

"Might as well be, the way you're giving in to him." Carrick curled his lips in disgust, hating every moment of what was happening. "Letting him do whatever he wants."

She turned toward him, and though he wasn't looking at her, he could tell she was pissed. Indignant. Good—he wanted her to be pissed. He wanted to light a fire in her because that was exactly how he felt.

She needs to fight.

"I'm not giving in to him. I've never given in to him," she corrected him fiercely. "I ran as soon as I feasibly could and got myself into school to get a job.

That job, speaking of which, has probably already fired me for not showing up."

"You'd be fired anyway after you let Petrov fly you to Russia to be Andriy's little wife," he scoffed.

"Russia? What are you talking about?"

A silence filled the car briefly, and he knew he'd said too much.

She started again, realizing what was going on. "Have you been talking to him? Are you keeping things from me?"

Briefly, he flickered his gaze over to her. Wide-eyed, Dani slowly leaned against the door, clutching her seatbelt for dear life. He quickly whipped his gaze back to the road, too full of fury to keep his eyes on her.

Emotion rushed over him as he remembered her lips and how they tasted. From his peripheral view, he could see the softness of her thighs reflecting from the sunshine beaming into the truck. The memories of what they'd done the night before gutted him.

I took her virginity. What the fuck is wrong with me?

Angrily, he shrugged. "Well, there's no point in me telling you anything."

"And why is that?" her tone remained vexed.

"It's not like you'll do anything about it," he snapped back harshly. "Not like you are willing to stand up for yourself."

Realizing that he was too invested, he was plain furious. He couldn't sit back and watch her life crumble, see her make terrible decisions.

"Anyway, you are not getting on a random train," he commanded. "I will figure this out...alone."

She grasped the truck door handle and moved to take off her seatbelt. He knew she was bluffing, so he let her.

"Going to jump out on the side of the highway?" he asked in disbelief.

"It's better than being stuck with you in this fucking prison."

"Be my guest, then." He pulled off the highway onto a deserted offramp.

Slamming the truck into park, he turned to her, giving her a final salute. "Good luck, soldier."

She sat there, her mouth open, searching him.

"That's what I thought," he grumbled. But as he moved to put the truck back into drive, she opened the door and launched herself out into the sandy desert dirt on the side of the road.

"Jesus, fuck!" he yelled and jumped out fast behind her.

Running around the side of the truck, he realized she was bolting — on foot — up the arid hill. Her little hands were clawing at sandy dirt and desert rocks as she tried to scale the steep incline, trying desperately to get away from him.

"Leave me alone!" she cried back at him, slowly making her way.

He sprinted up the hill, looking up only to see a perfect view of her bare ass under the mini skirt, accented by light blue lacy panties. He groaned, feeling his cock harden.

"I'm going to teach you a fucking lesson," he roared.

His own violent desire was unstoppable, and he gnashed his teeth together as he reached up and grabbed her heel, pulling her back down the dirt hill toward him. In that moment, an animalistic instinct grew within him, overpowering his senses. God damn, he wanted to clamp her down on that dirt hill and fuck her — take her from behind, holding her down and biting her neck — showing her orgasm after orgasm.

"Fuck off!" she yelled, kicking at him as he slid her down the hill toward him, using one of the self-defense moves he'd shown her.

"No!" he yelled back, turning her onto her back and pounding her into the dirt underneath him. "You do *not* run from me. *Ever!*"

Tears were streaming down her angry red face as she whipped her body back and forth, trying to escape from under his hold—but it didn't matter. He'd pinned her down and was holding her wrists as he panted violent desires onto her. Her arms flexed, and her whole body tensed. All it would take would be for him to lean forward slightly and he could have her mouth under his.

"I didn't trade Petrov trying to control my life for *you* trying to control my life!" she screamed at him.

Her words hit him hard, but he chewed on it, letting the message bounce right off. He was lying to himself, of course—because her words were exactly what he feared.

He had become the bad guy.

He was a bully.

"You're coming home with me," he ordered, staring down into her face as she desperately tried to fight him. "And we are going to figure out what to do with you."

"What if I say no?" she challenged him, her eyes livid.

He felt his grin turning crazy wild. "Say no, then. Tell me *no*."

Her eyes widened as she apparently realized what door she'd opened. He tightened his grasp on her wrists and she winced, arching her back in that way he loved.

"I want to hear you say 'no'." He pressed his body into her, the hard ridge of his cock angry underneath his board shorts.

Realizing her fate, she relaxed her limbs, panting and locking eyes with him. Her anger was drinkable and so was her pussy. That same animalistic desire thudded hard in his cock as she gasped beneath his grip. All he wanted to do was slip his hand up her mini skirt and just feel how wet she was, rip her panties off — and fuck the shit out of her.

But no matter what the urge, he was never again going to give in.

He'd learned his lesson.

She tightened her lips together as she looked up at him, and he knew he had her in checkmate. She didn't really want to leave him, didn't really want to go anywhere.

She doesn't want to say no to me.

He eased his grip, freed her wrists and scooped up her body. Throwing her over his shoulder, he slid his hand across the back of her thigh to stabilize her as he clambered down the steep hill. She was relenting, though under protest. She didn't have much else to say.

Neither did he.

Both of them had pretty much said their piece.

And now it was *détente*.

He threw her into his pickup truck through the door she'd left open, not even caring how much dirt she brought in with her. Her pink hoodie was ruined up the front from where he'd grabbed her and pulled her down the hill. A snarl crossed his lips as he slammed her door shut and made his way back to his side. It was time to get on with shit, and he would tolerate no further shenanigans.

He was going to be her new *daddy* when they got back to his place, and she was going to quickly learn how strict he could be. It was for her own good anyway, wasn't it?

Chapter Twenty-Two

Danica

Danica breathed in deeply, looking out over the last remnants of the sunset as she pushed her dark-rimmed glasses up her nose. Her inhalation worked through to the bottom of her lungs as she held her yoga tree pose, trying to ground herself in Carrick's living room.

Why can't I fight back against Petrov? It was so much more complicated than Carrick realized.

As much as she tried to get Carrick's velvety voice out of her head, she just couldn't. All she could think about was the man who had made it his mission to change the course of her life. And it made it much harder to forget him, since she'd been hearing him all day long. His deep voice had been echoing through the house with every phone call he made.

They'd gotten back to his place at Sunset Beach in the late morning, and he'd dismissively dumped her upstairs to spend the rest of the day — alone. She hadn't seen him since. He'd made camp on the entry floor of the house, roaming between his office at the back and the garage at the front.

Well, she had sneaked a peek down — just once — and it hadn't gone well. A few hours before, her stomach gnawing, she'd tiptoed down to see him, desperate to talk. She hadn't known why. He was furious at her — and she at him. It had been icy between them since…she'd run.

When she'd snuck downstairs, he'd been on a call at the time, sitting comfortably and confidently in his leather chair at his long, wooden desk. Her nose filled with the scent of heady musk, rich cedar and leather when she'd stood at the entrance to his office. Before he'd noticed, she flitted her gaze around the room, observing a tattered American flag hung on the wall along with what appeared to be a series of plaques and trophies. She even saw some vintage guns and heavily used rope strewn up on the wall like decorations. It was only a few seconds before he'd turned around in his chair and seen her, jumping up immediately to push her out of his office and motion silently for her to go upstairs — never breaking from the call he was on.

That had been hours and hours ago.

Now, as she looked out over the Pacific Ocean at the purple sky that was quickly turning indigo, she tried to stay strong, to find her balance. Yoga and meditation always helped, but being stuck in a house alone with that man was dizzying.

I can't stay here.

The question she kept asking herself was, did she regret giving herself to him? He'd taken her virginity the previous night in the tent on the beach. He'd kissed her like she'd never been kissed before. He'd made her feel something brand new — like he cared, like he gave a shit. God, he made it feel so real. It had all been too good — until she'd climbed out of the tent that morning and realized where they stood. Nothing had changed. Well, everything had changed, but also nothing had. He was still keeping things from her. He was still pushing her to do what *he* thought she should do.

He was still laughing at her plans like she was a child, as though he was the only one who knew anything. He still expected her unquestioning obedience.

Danica dropped her foot from tree pose, and she wobbled to find balance, frustration and anger rising in her chest. It wasn't fair. She just had no idea what she was supposed to do — or what she could do.

Tugging up her yoga pants and readjusting her strappy purple tank top, she took her hair out of her ponytail, relieving some of the ache in her head. Her throat was tight and her face felt strained. No matter what she'd done, she'd felt two seconds from crying silently to herself all day, but she wasn't going to give Carrick the satisfaction of hearing that.

Suddenly, his office door slammed shut, and shortly after, his familiar heavy steps were climbing up the stairs. Immediately, panic rose in her and she looked around to…well, to appear normal.

She ran out of time.

Carrick, the monster himself, looking hotter than life in black jeans and a light gray T-shirt, crested the top step, pausing as he looked at her before moving into the kitchen.

"Did you eat?" he grunted at her, looking away just as fast.

She swallowed, knowing how rough things were between them. But she held her ground.

"I found some fruit in the fridge," she replied, not even sure if he'd care about her words.

"Fruit? That's not enough."

"Sometimes I follow a fruitarian diet when —" she started but stopped suddenly.

Just another stupid thing to say.

Carrick's eyes had grown big as he listened to her, clearly incredulous. But he said nothing and turned back to the fridge, opening and closing it without taking anything out. She watched him angle toward the corner upper cupboard, and he reached his defined arms to grab something. She narrowed her eyes as she realized what he was carrying.

Is he for real?

Marching over to her with a bottle and two shot glasses in his hand, he motioned for her to sit in the chair in the living room. He put the items down on the square coffee table, positioning himself on the couch. With the table between them, he reached out to organize the bottle and shot glasses in a neat row.

"I've done a lot of diving off the coast of Mexico," he started, his tone careful and guarded. "I brought this bottle of tequila back a handful of years ago."

He cracked the top, breaking the seal of the full bottle of liquor, and poured two full shot glasses. He pushed one toward her end of the table, watching her carefully.

"It's expensive. It's delicious." He rotated the bottle in his hands. "And I always found it was good for one thing."

"What?" she asked, her lips parting with her shallow breath.

"Getting the truth out of people." He looked back up at her, his violent blue eyes throwing her off her game, as they always did. He grinned, as if knowing his power over her, and continued his story. "Seeing people's true colors. And that's why we are going to play a little game here."

"A game?" She clamped her fingers tightly against her thighs, filled with pure nerves and anticipation.

"My house — my rules."

He pushed her shot glass over the table. With shaking hands, she reluctantly reached out and picked it up, trying not to let the golden liquid spill.

"I'm not much for shooters, Carrick." She looked up at him, nervously adjusting the glasses on the bridge of her nose.

That devilish grin crossed his lips.

"Even more incentive for you, then. We are going to play Truth or Dare. Play your cards right, and you can walk away from the game with only one ounce of this in you."

He picked up his own shot glass full of light-yellow liquid and brought it to his lips. "First, one just to get things started."

He nodded for her to follow suit and she did so as her brain tried to process what was happening — and how to get out of it. She absolutely did *not* want to play, but what was she supposed to do?

Carrick shot her a 'don't even try' look, threatening her to continue to cooperate, so she shook her head, accepting her fate. The last time she'd tried to run, it hadn't worked out. And maybe she could flip things around and get the truth out of him.

They both took their shots quickly. She winced as that familiar burn ran down her esophagus. Her stomach wanted to reject it and convulsed as she gagged, bringing her fingers to her lips to keep everything in.

"Don't tell me to savor it." She fluttered her watering eyes rapidly, feeling an instant rush.

Carrick let out an honest laugh, shaking his head.

"You want to go first?" He put down his glass and picked up the bottle, pouring two full shot glasses again.

"No." She snorted. "Definitely not."

"All right, truth or dare, Dani."

Her gaze darted back and forth as she debated it, and he shot her an impatient look.

"Dare."

"Take it all off," he growled, licking his lips as he looked her body up and down.

"No, wait — *truth*," she correctly herself.

"Why can't you just tell Petrov to fuck off?" he asked, throwing down the toughest question right out of the gate.

Fuck.

She sucked in air, realizing he wasn't messing around. This wasn't going to be a lighthearted game. This was business.

She opened her mouth to begin, but he leaned forward intimidatingly and said in his deepest, darkest tone, "There's a special punishment in this game for liars. You don't want to find out what it is."

Goosebumps ran up her thighs with a vengeance, and she tried to wrap her head around his question. *Why can't I just put Petrov in his place? Why?*

"I haven't spent a lot of time thinking about that," she began, connecting with his eyes as he listened, still as could be. "But I guess it comes down to the fact that he's my father's brother. My uncle. And I loved my dad more than anything."

"So, it's all some misplaced sense of blood loyalty?"

"It's just hard. I miss Mom and Dad. I want to honor my parents," she explained, and realized her throat was choking up. "Not to mention the fact that my uncle terrifies me. He's threatened to kill me before."

Blinking quickly, trying to get the tears away, she took a deep breath and kept her eyes on him. Was it the tequila? She wasn't sure. But suddenly, everything was coming to the top.

"I know this sounds so stupid."

"You know that what Petrov wants doesn't have anything to do with honoring your father?" Carrick demanded.

"Is that a question?" Danica caught on quickly and shot him a slick look. "I think it's your turn — truth or dare?"

"Dare."

He leaned back, his seated stance wide, and crossed his arms, gazing down his long nose at her. So she decided to make it harder for him.

"Off with your shirt." She licked her lips, knowing she was just being selfish and trying to make him feel equally uncomfortable.

His eyes hard on her, he tore off his T-shirt like he didn't give a fuck, exposing the long, curving tattoo across his chest. Now, in the light, she had a way better view of it than when she'd seen it in the tent. It was words and numbers — likely something meaningful to him. And now, she also had a way better view of his rippling, jacked body. Tan and defined, his chest flexed as he leaned forward.

"Not bad," she shrugged, shooting him a coy look.

Carrick shook his head with a grin then stared her down in all seriousness.

"My turn."

Shit, Danica thought, as she weighed her options. She didn't want any more questions. And she definitely did not want to drink any more of that engine grease.

"Fine. Dare."

"You know what I'm going to ask." He leaned back, his arm resting over the top of the couch. The view was delicious as his hard body shone under the soft amber light in the corner of the shadowy room.

"When exactly is this game over?" She caved back into the chair, eyes wide and shy as he watched her.

"When I'm done."

Danica grumbled as she reached forward and took the shot of tequila, sending the burning liquid down her throat. She was going to be drinking a bottle of tequila that night, apparently.

"Now, tell me, truth or dare?" she said, licking the last drop of tequila from her bottom lip.

"Truth." He shrugged like he didn't care, but she knew he did.

She'd guess he was just testing her to find out what her question was, so she might as well go for the jugular.

"What does your tattoo mean?" she asked, narrowing her eyes on the cursive writing across his chest. "Is that a date — from two years ago?"

Without hesitation, he reached forward, took the shot from his glass and poured them both new shots. He reached over and picked hers up, motioning for her to grab it.

"I forgot to tell you — any round where neither of us answer, we have to take another shot." He brought his to his lips. "And the punishment gets worse from there."

"Who invented this game? God, you are sadistic," she grumbled as she brought the second tequila shot to her mouth, slamming it back.

I can't take any more of this.

"You have no idea," he mumbled as he took his drink, winking at her.

A literal cold snap of electricity ran up her body and she parted her lips. That reaction only seemed to encourage him. *He likes being the bad guy,* she realized.

Now, three shots in, it was safe to say she was starting to feel it—and that all the things she really wanted were starting to bubble to the surface. Maybe she really needed to say some stuff. It didn't help that she wasn't far away from him, and she'd spent the entire day oscillating between hating and needing him. Her own resolve to have the upper hand was wearing thinner and thinner, and he was starting to look better and better by the second.

That was, until it was his turn again and he demanded she take off her clothes for the third time. She realized it was something he really, really wanted. He wanted to see her naked again. He wanted more.

Danica felt a rush up her chest as she considered her power over him. The man was undeniably horny and just as undeniably doing everything he could to control himself.

She wondered if she could make him suffer a little.

She decided having the upper hand was something that was really important to her—with him, anyway.

Danica stood up out of the chair, turned around and slowly peeled off her yoga top, revealing a light blue lacy bra underneath. Still with her back to him, she bent over the chair slightly, arching like a cat and smiling when he groaned behind her. He wasn't the only one who knew how to play games.

Feeling the rush of the tequila coursing through her veins, she realized fruit for dinner wasn't enough to keep her from getting absolutely wasted.

And maybe she was going to do something she was going to regret, but at that precise moment, she didn't really care.

Hooking her thumbs in the soft waist of the yoga pants, she slowly started rolling them down over her skin, revealing to him her lower back then her tailbone. Very slowly she popped them down over her naked ass, which she had covered only by the smallest patch of lacy blue panties. As she folded over completely, reaching down to her ankles to very slowly pull off her pants, she gave him a full bent-over view of her body. She'd expected his reaction and it was unmistakable.

He groaned savagely in the background, and she rose then reached behind her ass, innocently tugging at her panties to readjust them, showing a half inch of her raw, wet pussy. Just for fun, she slipped a finger underneath the fabric and pretended to play with her own wetness.

She knew how to compete in a game, all right. She was going in for the kill.

Turning back around, she sat down in the chair and brought that same finger to her mouth, taking it in like she was sucking on sugary icing.

"The fruitarian diet has its benefits." She grinned absently, as though she didn't have a care in the world.

The entire moment became absolutely worth it when he shifted in his seat to adjust the hardness in his crotch, his incredible erection. That part of his pants was tighter and more pronounced than it had been minutes ago. And she remembered how his cock had felt going in and out of her.

One point for me.

He looked her up and down, licking his lower lip, but kept on with the conversation as if nothing had happened. The man had fucking skills.

"So, you've got some misplaced sense of blood loyalty to Petrov, and he terrifies you," Carrick reiterated, machinations obviously working through his mind as he watched her. "Got it."

Under his heated gaze, she stirred in her seat, her arousal kicking in, but she couldn't be the one to relent. She had to be stronger than he was.

There was a silent game going on—one where the points really did matter.

"I think you are starting to understand me." Danica shrugged and leaned forward to push her empty shot glass back toward him, squeezing her breasts together to tempt him. "And maybe you are starting to understand why I can't just do what *you* want me to do."

"Then we will have to find another way." His voice grew dark, and she realized he was planning something.

Without her input, of course.

She clenched her jaw as she narrowed her eyes on him. "My turn." She took in a deep breath and stiffened. "You told me last night that you will never love again. What makes you think you can control that?"

He just sat, staring at her—silent as a grave. His lips and jaw tightened, and she recognized a familiar pain in his eyes. She knew the pain of loss anywhere—because she'd experienced it once, too.

Breathing out low, she whispered, "What happened to you, Carrick?"

Carrick pre-emptively reached out, poured himself an overflowing shot and sucked it back, shrugging like he didn't give a fuck.

"That's not fair," she gasped.

"Why not?"

"You can't just deny all my questions. You can handle more booze than me, so I'm at an unfair disadvantage," she cried out at the mounting injustice. "Don't be a cheater."

"I'm not a fucking cheater." His voice was hoarse, and his eyes were growing livid as he bounded forward, intimidating as hell.

But she wouldn't be frightened by him. She needed to keep her upper hand. She jumped up from the chair, staring him down.

"If you aren't going to play fair, then I'm not playing."

She moved to march away, but he lunged up from the couch, grabbing her.

"I'm a lot of things, but I'm not a cheater," he countered, the strong scent of tequila on his breath. "I've never cheated."

She blinked up at him, partially confused — and she realized that he wasn't talking about the game anymore.

And neither was she.

"Then what *are* you?" She pushed back. "What are you to *me*?"

He searched her, drinking in her meaning. The game had taken a sharp turn and things had gotten raw. *Real raw*.

She didn't expect he was going to answer.

Until he *did*.

Eyes locked on her, his face tense and serious, he growled, "I'm not the hero you want, but I'm the monster you need."

"What does that mean?"

"I'm going to marry you tomorrow morning. You'll never worry about Petrov again."

And that was when Danica realized that Carrick had just put her in checkmate, threatening to win their whole goddamn game.

Chapter Twenty-Three

Danica

"Carrick." She blinked up at him, in disbelief. *Marry him?* She was at a loss for words.

He remained stoic, steely.

"I thought..." she began, breathless. "I didn't think..."

Before she could finish her sentence, he reached down and grabbed her jaw, tilting her chin up to him.

"You in those fucking librarian glasses," he growled savagely, arousal deep in his throat.

And he kissed her.

She opened wider and wider as she received his kiss, which was hungrier than she'd remembered. It only matched her own desire and multiplied it. With enough tequila in him, his movements were less restricted, less controlled — more passionate.

God, she wanted him. Any woman would want him. There was no doubt. He was an absolute prize of a man — striking in every way. Determined, powerful and dominating... Her mouth watered thinking of what his rough, greedy hands had done to her the night before, and how he'd let his oversized cock fill her, taking her for the first time, forcing her to nearly burst at the seams.

But, sobering, she pulled back. While he held her shoulders as he looked down at her from his great height, she shifted under his gaze. He surveyed up and down her body, and the shade in his eyes shook her. She knew he was trying to figure out what the fuck her problem was.

Swallowing what felt like an acorn in her throat, she whispered something so quietly that she didn't think he could hear.

"I deserve love. I can't marry someone who is so vehemently opposed to the idea of love."

A laugh escaped his hardened mouth, like she didn't understand.

"You can—and you will," he commanded as he shifted her a few feet back to where the chair was. "This is the only way."

"Why?"

"Because it's the only way I can protect you."

His words crashed over her, and that same dark look took over his entire face. She knew then he was hungry...but not for food. He fell back into the chair behind him, holding her in front of him like a jewel to be admired—in nothing but her bra and underwear. He ran his hands up and down her body, as if studying what he was buying.

She realized then that it was her last chance. She had to do anything but give in, because the reality was that she couldn't marry him. She'd learned that the hard way. Being with a man who couldn't love, who refused to love? It was too dangerous.

Because I'm falling for him.

As her mind screamed at her to push back, to regain her upper hand, to run, Carrick cupped her ass down to where the wetness pooled in her panties, sending aching sensations up her spine. Unapologetic, he touched her as he pleased.

She breathed out, "I don't want a loveless marriage. I can't do that with you."

"I'll give you everything *else* you need." He unhooked her bra and threw it to the side, massaging each of her mounds and teasing each nipple with focus.

Then he pulled her down into his lap with ferocity, quickly grabbing her jaw. "And just so you know what you are getting into, I'll give you a taste of what marriage to me will be like."

His pupils were dilated with arousal, and he traced a line from her lips to her breasts. The same sound of hunger grew in his throat as he moved his hands to play with the edge of her lacy blue panties. He grazed his fingers over her crotch, down low, and she felt soreness in her pussy from the night before—from where he'd taken her virginity. Lifting her, he moved her to straddle him, her legs on either side of his.

"Fuck, Carrick." She arched backward in pleasure. "I can't do this."

"Then go." He released his grasp on her so she could get away.

But the painful truth was that Danica wanted nothing more than to feel his lips on hers again and to give herself to him completely. She nodded subserviently and fully immersed herself in the role he asked. He was the alpha in the room, demanding that she give in to his dominant play.

She moaned as he touched her. "I can't go."

"I'm going to start calling you Miss Paradox," he growled as he lowered his touch, caressing the skin on her abdomen in a circular motion, alternating between looking in her eyes and openly appreciating what was before him.

Adjusting his cock again in his pants, he said, "You need to decide—now. I can't handle you with those fucking glasses on."

She whimpered as he ran his finger over her panties, barely touching her throbbing clit. Goddamn, she needed what he was offering. It wasn't a fair choice.

And as he teased her once more, she breathed out, "Okay."

Carrick leaned back, a self-satisfied grin on his face, but then his expression changed and he laid out his conditions.

He grabbed her jaw again, staring her down. "This means you're mine now. Don't forget it."

The possessive words stirred a desire in her that she couldn't explain. She realized where his psyche had been all along. He'd always wanted her—all of her— for himself. And this was the only way he knew how.

As she relented, falling into his touch, he cupped her breasts and rolled his thumb over each hardened nipple. While he pinched and played, her hips jumped with sensation, a fire rising in her core. He was rougher, harder—and less forgiving. He drew her up to his face, biting each nipple, hurting and pleasing her all the same. 'Sadistic' was starting to sound less like a joke.

And with that promise, an aching grew inside her that she needed to be filled. Her pussy throbbed as she looked down at him, kissing and dragging his teeth across her flesh, and he seemed to know exactly what she wanted next without her saying anything.

He grasped her panties firmly. When his gaze caught hers again, she saw the determination, the power. He ripped them off, the lace easily tearing with his force. Then he tossed them aside, running his thick fingers farther down her body. He found the top of her pussy and moved his fingers toward her clit, roughly testing her wetness.

"My, my...aren't you wet?" he groaned, lust filling his eyes.

"Can you really do this without emotion?" she gasped as he drew his hand up and down her slit.

He licked his lips again. "I'll teach you how."

She refused to answer as he pushed his finger into her swollen pussy, which was still aching from being fucked so hard by him the night before. She arched as he did it, showcasing her breasts to him. That only seemed to please him more.

The same grin widened on his mouth. "I'm a fighter, Danica. I don't have emotions."

Danica moaned, tilting her head back. She didn't believe a single word he said, but it didn't matter what she believed. It only mattered what he did — and if he believed he couldn't feel, then he wouldn't.

And though the concern rattled through her mind, she was taken from the thought as he played with her clit so skillfully that it sent incredible shudders up her body. As she squirmed, feeling the pressure rising, he slipped his other hand behind her back to hold her steady — to keep her down.

She was that much closer to coming, since he'd teased it out of her the night prior. Everything felt so sensitive as he touched her.

"I *need* you," she breathed, the only words she could cough out as he fingered her harder and faster. "Just fuck me, Carrick. Let's get this over with."

He laughed, obviously enjoying how she begged and making her wait.

"Let's get this over with?" He laughed and scooped her naked body up in his arms as he stood up from the chair. "That's not what I want to hear."

He laid her in the middle of the couch and let his black jeans slide off, hitting the floor. With only his boxers on, his hardened cock was punching through. It was just too big to be held in.

He pushed her legs back and moved them apart, finding her throbbing pussy. Again, he pressed his fingers up her wet core and removed them to taste her. She squirmed with the tender soreness—but he handled her gently, with care, seeming to know exactly how she felt.

"Fucking delicious," he groaned as he licked her juice off the length of his finger. "Sweetest pussy I've ever had."

Before she could dream of asking how many that was, she rolled her head back in pleasure once again as he licked her all the way up to her clit. He rolled the sensitive nub with his tongue, lapping all the wetness that continued to pour out of her. *He's so damn good at that.*

There were reasons why he was so persuasive.

Danica's orgasm was mounting again as he licked until her legs shook and her hips threatened to leave the couch entirely. He held her hips down and laughed as she moaned, probably realizing how close she was.

"I could make you come all day long, and you think marrying me would be so bad?"

The agony of her swelling orgasm grew unmanageable.

"Carrick, please don't do this to me," Danica begged. "Just fuck me."

"I don't believe you really want my cock." He moved his head to roll her clit.

"I do," she moaned, digging her head into the couch as he rolled faster and faster on her clit, sending electric shocks throughout her body. "I really, really do."

Her pussy tightened and she screamed. She was so fucking close.

"I don't believe you," he teased.

She tried to protest, telling him to fuck off — but she couldn't.

As she screamed out his name, he grinned and continued eating her out. Finally, he ran his fingers up her pussy again, finding that certain spot that was her undoing. Her orgasm pounded to the surface and wetness poured out everywhere, dripping down her ass.

Letting his words sink in that he'd promised her a great life, she grew still for a moment then she flipped open her eyes, watching the gorgeous man at the foot of the couch stroking his long, rigid cock with his hand.

What's he going to do to me now?

"Close your eyes," he demanded, and she obeyed immediately, knowing what would happen if she didn't.

Within seconds, she felt something like a rope being tied around her wrists, and her body lifted. Her eyes opened and he noticed.

"I told you to keep them closed. What is it going to take for you to learn who is in charge?"

Turning her against the back of the couch in a kneeling position, he gently bent her over, pressing her head down to rest on the fabric. She grasped the back of the couch to steady herself as best she could with her bound hands. It was as though she was his prisoner. Then he brought her ass up to meet his cock, and she moaned with the realization that he was about to fuck her from behind.

"Could you do this without emotion?" He brushed his cockhead at the opening of her aching core.

I need him to fill me up.

"That wasn't an answer." He ran his cock up and down her wet slit, threatening to never thrust it inside her. It was blackmail, and she fucking knew it.

"I don't know," Danica cried, her legs trembling. She bit her lip, closed her eyes then became aware of his cock gently entering her pussy from behind.

"This is all I'll ever give you, Danica." His voice grew dark and serious. "Tell me this is enough for you."

She moaned a non-answer again, trying to push onto his cock. That only encouraged him as he reached forward to grip her mass of hair, drawing her head back. The way he touched her—dominant, controlling—was so fucking hot.

Because he knew she wanted it. He knew she wanted him to take care of her.

He knows how much I want him.

Pulling her long locks back, he leaned down to whisper in her ear as he pushed all the way up her wet pussy.

"Be good and I'll reward you."

He entered her as she gasped. It was a wicked feeling to be filled completely by a hot, hard cock, feeling every inch of her pussy's walls tightening around him.

He groaned in response but continued speaking, "You'll do what I want, when I want, and I'll take care of you, protect you. I'll save you." The last words seemed to escape his mouth with less force, revealing more than he'd likely intended.

"Oh my God! I'm so close, Carrick," she squealed.

A savage noise escaped his throat in response, and he quickened his pace. Moving in and out of her, he found a new rhythm that drew shocks from her — harder, faster, rougher. He wrapped his hand around her hair, like a handle, while he used his other hand to spank her ass. Just when she couldn't take it anymore, her orgasm finally burst down her legs, drowning his thick cock in her juices.

"Come inside me," she cried out through the lingering orgasmic feeling.

"Fuck, Dani." He tightened his grip on her, shooting pain up her side, and she expected that bruises would be forthcoming.

But I don't care.

All she cared about was how he was sliding up into her, pounding her, fucking her better than she'd ever hoped for. The carnal roars escaping his chest told her that he was going to come — and he was going to come hard.

"I think I'm falling for you," she suddenly confessed, drunk in the moment.

He gasped in response, and there was an explosion of his seed inside her. He panted, trying to catch his breath, as he stood over her, his grip on her hair growing more affectionate. He ran his rough hand down her long hair, down her back, cupping and caressing her ass with care.

I'm his now.

Finally, she looked over her shoulder at him. He locked eyes with her, and the room grew silent, except for his inhalation. Sobering once again, all Danica could think about was her passionate confession.

Did he hear it?

She hoped he hadn't.

Because it was true.

Chapter Twenty-Four

Danica

A deep heat crossed Danica's cheeks as she took in the meaning of her confession. She ripped her gaze away from him, mortified, yet still desperate to know if he had heard her.

If he heard me, I've played my final cards.

Carrick was already getting to work, untying her hands and turning her around to face him. Pulling her up into his arms, he planted one delicious kiss on her mouth. When he did, she tasted her own sex and cum, making her ache for him that much more. The way he kissed her felt different from before, but she couldn't figure out why.

He lowered his hand to her sopping wet opening and checked her. She winced as he did. Immediately, she sensed the change in him. It hurt, and he seemed to want to take care of her.

Carrick stepped back from the couch, holding her in his arms. Without hesitation, he took to the staircase, two steps at a time, and brought her to a large bathroom located on the third floor, at the front of the house. Exquisitely decorated like the rest of his home, the bathroom had the vibe of a nature spa. It was elegant, feminine — and the opposite of what she expected his style to be. It just seemed so unlike him. Expensive-looking flooring in a reclaimed wood style complemented a glittering granite countertop that was framed by 'his and hers' sinks. Of course, only his side of the sink was in obvious use.

Carrick carried her farther in and stopped at the big soaker tub that could easily fit two. He set her on the side of the tub and started drawing the water, hot and steamy. After pouring in Epsom salts and bubbles, he slid her glasses off, laying them on the counter. Then he placed her into the tub, leaving only the soft lights on above the sink as mood lighting. As she got comfortable in the soaker, she observed the artwork that hung on the walls — tropical, floral designs. That was when she knew... *There is no way Carrick selected those pieces.*

The former SEAL found his way into the tub behind her, holding her tight against his chest as he massaged her shoulders. His actions were caring and romantic...yet also very dangerous.

I need to stop this.

She should get out of the tub before she allowed herself to fall for him any further. But it was just too damn hard. Leaning back on his hard chest, she felt protected...safe. He was giving her everything to make her believe that this was real.

But he made it clear that it's not.

He massaged her slowly and she groaned with the pleasure of his grinding knuckles working out her muscle knots. Wrapped in his arms, his rough hands working up and down on her, she could almost slip into a coma. Never before had she experienced so much pleasure at one time. She just wished it could last longer than the few nights they had. She wasn't going to marry him. That was the most dangerous proposition of all. She needed more than just the physical side of him, but he'd made it perfectly clear that it was all she'd ever get from him.

"You're tense." He grumbled into her ear, driving those familiar shocks of arousal through her core. "Have I been too rough?"

He has no idea.

"Oh, that feels amazing. Thank you," she whispered back as he massaged her, moving his hands down her shoulders and over her chest.

"It's nothing."

She smirked. "You can never accept gratitude, can you?"

He kept working her, moving down over her breasts. "I don't like how it feels."

She turned slightly, looking up at his handsome face. "To be thanked?"

He shrugged, and though he'd refused to respond, she wondered why Carrick hated being admired or focused on.

At some point, Danica realized that she was starting to nod off in the tub.

In a haze, she went to get up, and he pulled her back down to him. "Going somewhere?"

She grinned in delight. "What time is it?"

"Bedtime." He wrapped his arms around her, stood then carried her out of the tub. Afterward, he grabbed soft towels to dry her off. "I've got a lot on the docket tomorrow."

Taking her by the hand, he led her into his dark bedroom, the silence broken only by the ambient sounds of the ocean in the distance. She guessed it was really late. The entire day had slipped by in a haze of anxiety, punctuated by tremendous pleasure — the latter masking the former.

She collapsed on the bed, unbelievably drained. As she curled into the blanket, he climbed in behind her, holding her to his chest as they lay together.

He tightened his arms, breathing down her neck. "What do you want in life, Dani? If you could have anything you wanted."

Her eyes shut, she confessed, "I've always dreamed of having my own tiny little art gallery, selling my work and supporting other local artists."

With that admission, she knew she was done for. He would never respect her. She was just a childish dreamer.

"That's different from nursing." He was slow to respond.

She bit her lip, knowing he'd see this as worse than being a vegan. Feeling defensive, she justified herself by saying, "Nursing was a smart choice — a way to get a paying job. And I like taking care of people. I don't have the money or the connections to open a gallery and sell art. It's just a silly dream."

But his response was surprising. "Interesting... I appreciate dreams. They gives you depth."

She was taken aback at the reception, the lack of criticism. "I thought you'd find my dreams juvenile."

"I've always been a dreamer."

"Really?"

"Once, I dreamed of getting into the SEALs," he explained. "Do you know how hard I had to work? All the way through the Navy — from scrubbing the bowels of a warship to finally getting a place in Special Forces, one of the most elite teams in the world. Damn, it was a fucking journey."

"Your dreams made sense, though. Mine are unattainable."

Carrick let out a low laugh. "Not at all. You are very talented. You *should* have a gallery and your art *should* be featured there. Maybe it will happen one day."

She almost gasped in disbelief. That was the most he'd ever said about himself, and it was the nicest thing he'd ever said to her. Coming from him, it meant the world.

Is this progress?

When he moved his hand down her body to find hers, wrapping his fingers around it, she had no choice but to let herself sink into him. He held her against him tightly, kissing her hair affectionately.

In a sleepy grumble, he finally said, "Never give up on your dreams, Dani."

Finding her eyes fluttering shut again, Danica let out, "I dream of real love, of the white picket fence, the kids — someone who loves me like I love them..." But her mumbling trailed off, her mind growing hazy. "Someone to share coffee with every morning, share life with..."

The last thing she remembered was him tightening his arms around her. He didn't say anything in response, but she was sure his heart was beating a little bit faster.

Chapter Twenty-Five

Danica

The muffled sounds of male voices woke Danica from a deep sleep. At one point, someone had drawn the curtains on the glass sliding door, leaving the bedroom a dark, warm cocoon. A little fuzzy, she blinked a few times, trying to focus and realizing that she had no idea where she was.

Until she knew *exactly* where she was.

Carrick wasn't alone in the living room, and immediately she was anxious as hell. She raised her hands to her naked chest and hugged the sheets tighter. Her swollen, sore pussy reminded her just how much trouble she'd gotten into the night before — and with whom...again.

Why do I keep giving myself to him?

Lobbing her feet off the bed, she tiptoed to the master bathroom. Memories from the night before began pouring into her hungover, aching head as she eyed the tub. That bath... It had been the most intimate moment she'd ever had with him — or anyone.

Picking up a toothbrush that had been set on the unoccupied side of the granite counter, she found everything she needed to clean herself. After drying her face with the softest white towel she'd ever used in her life, Danica threw on a plush robe that was obviously cut for a man. She tied the robe as she looked into the mirror, trying to figure out if she was presentable. Her hair was voluminous — if not complete sex hair. Her lips were plump from all the rough, passionate kissing.

That was when she decided she would be better off just staying in the bedroom, waiting it out. She had no idea who he was down there talking with, and though she was damn curious, she was also apprehensive. Carrick hadn't exactly been one to show his cards, and she had no idea what the man had up his sleeve.

She returned to the bedroom and found her cell phone on the top of his dresser. She had a missed text from Addie.

Wellness check — still alive?

I'm present.

She didn't want to be melodramatic, but her mind was racing with another sex hangover.

Addie immediately responded.

That doesn't sound good. Just come home. We can move somewhere else together.

Danica smiled, knowing their friendship bond was deeply powerful. But her smile slowly dissipated as she acknowledged what she'd been feeling for a while — that she was a burden on Addie's life. Eventually, Addie needed to move on from having a needy, runaway roommate. What would happen when Addie fell in love?

He asked me to marry him.

Oh my God, he's in love with you!

No, he's not. He wants a marriage of convenience…to protect me, to save me.

Well, that's fucking bullshit. Look… I'm starting my shift, but I can be late if you want to have a call.

No, I'm all right. I'm not dragging down your life anymore.

You aren't, but okay. Call me at lunch.

Danica edged her teeth along her lower lip, worrying about how she was impacting her friend. Putting her cell down, she heard the voices growing heated downstairs. Clutching the robe shut, she put her ear to the closed bedroom door, trying to gain clues.

Who's there?

Unfortunately, she hadn't quite learned her lesson yet. Carrick was a former Navy SEAL — as in, Black Ops, on top of his game.

And she was no match for him.

With her ear up to the door, she bounced back as it opened swiftly. Carrick shot his dark-blue gaze down on her as he loomed in the space.

"Hi," she whispered.

"Morning." He nodded, cool and collected, and motioned for her to join the living space. "Coffee?"

Danica swallowed a lump in her throat as she gazed up at him — his steely face, his kissable lips...yet his lack of emotion.

"Come on," he said, turning to leave.

Danica, like a little lamb, followed her wolf down the hardwood stairs, entering the great room. A man she recognized sat at the edge of the living room in the chair, his hands clasped together with a serious look on his face.

The driver.

"Danica," Carrick announced her as she moved into the space, and he ushered her to sit on the couch, adjacent to the driver.

Casually, Carrick picked up and threw a blanket over her lap to keep her warm — or to keep his friend's eyes off her bare legs. Meanwhile, the driver grinned like a coyote as he watched her — but not in a salacious way like Carrick looked at her.

"I'm Delta," the driver explained as Carrick moved to the kitchen. "We met before."

"Hi," she replied, as if it was the only word she knew that morning.

"You living here now?" Delta asked lightly, like he was making casual conversation.

She looked at him, trying to find the right words, and she observed the long scar that ran up the side of his cheekbone.

Delta, seeming not to notice, looked back and forth between her and Carrick. A little mortified, Danica clutched the robe tighter and slouched down in the sofa — wishing like hell she could just disappear. What was she doing there? She kept her eyes away from the spot where she'd left a big orgasmic stain from the night before.

Carrick then brought over a steaming coffee, handing it to Danica, and nodded to Delta. "When it's done, notify me. Don't answer any calls."

Any calls? Danica's mouth parted as she took the hot mug from Carrick. Her mind once again started piecing together all the evidence she had before her, pointing to the fact that they were in boiling water.

"Roger that, Moose," Delta acknowledged, standing up to adjust his belt and looking down on Danica.

Carrick turned on his heels and grabbed a sweater off the edge of the couch, throwing it over his black T-shirt and army green modern-cut cargo pants.

Moose? She found her lips forming the word, wondering if that was Carrick's nickname. There was so much she didn't know about him.

"It's a call sign," Delta explained it to her, recognizing her curiosity. "They stick with you, unfortunately. Just have to hope you don't end up with a shitty one."

Carrick turned around after throwing his wallet and phone into his hoodie pockets and nodded curtly to Danica with the appearance of goodbye, alarming her. She shifted forward in her seat, realizing he was getting ready to leave.

Where is he going?

Her lips parted as she held the mug, but something about the two men looming kept her quiet. She wasn't used to being with these kinds of men.

As Carrick started marching toward the stairs leading down to the main floor, Delta asked, "And what about her?"

Carrick didn't look back, but his voice carried as he moved down the stairs. "Keep her safe."

All Danica heard was *'keep her quiet'*.

After Carrick marched out through the garage door then turned on the loud engine of his truck and pulled away, Danica found herself alone with Delta.

"I cook, you clean?" He shot her a wild grin.

She shyly nodded, feeling more shaken than she wanted to admit. She flitted her gaze to the beach outside and had the sudden urge to run.

To follow Carrick.

Delta gave her a questioning look, as if he saw something curious in her. She realized then that she'd been so consumed by Carrick that she hadn't really paid attention to Delta. He was just as tall, but a little more charismatic—straight, slicked-back dark-blond hair and deep brown eyes. A little more playful. A startling white, straight smile. Likable. Relaxed. He held himself like a hero but had the gaze of someone who knew how to get into trouble, someone who didn't always play by the rules.

Danica found herself wondering if a tendency for rogue antics ran through the blood of special operators—or if it was just her luck.

"I'm not holding you prisoner, you know," Delta broke into her thoughts, searching her.

It was clear that the man wanted—or needed—to know exactly what she was thinking.

"So, I can go?" She stood up slowly, the blanket falling off her thighs.

Delta shrugged as if she played right into his trap. "Sure. Just give the boss a call before you head out."

She crossed her arms, processing. That wasn't what she'd expected, but the words were clear. Carrick didn't want her to do anything unless he knew about it and approved. *And yet I'm not a prisoner?*

Yawning and stretching, Delta moved toward the staircase heading down to the first floor.

"Wait," she said quickly, looking at the man she knew nothing about but wanting to know more about Carrick, who she barely knew.

Delta turned back, offering her a slight, expectant grin. As he looked at her, she drank him in. He had tattooed arms and that same rough-and-ready look that Carrick had.

"How do you know Carrick?" she asked, playing with the edge of the fabric of a sofa pillow.

Delta leaned against the wall, crossing his arms, killing her with the pause — and his dark gaze.

"We were in the same troop," he explained. "On the same team."

"In the SEALs?" Her lips parted, her tone innocent and searching.

Delta nodded, and there was a brief silence. There was something so different about him and Carrick, but something still the same. She got that same tortured feeling from both of them. Then he continued, reaching to his face to touch the scar that ran up his cheekbone.

He continued, "We've seen a lot together. Syria, Iraq, West Africa — you name it. We've both spent more time away than home…for a long time."

"Wow," Danica said. But learning something about Carrick's past only made her hungry for more.

But before she could ask any more questions, Delta turned to head down to the entry level.

"I'll be in the office if you need anything."

As he rocketed down the staircase, Danica found herself in silence. She had chills running up her spine.

It was incredible to hear that snippet of information, but where did that leave her? Carrick was still a steel vault. And she had no answers. No plan.

She suddenly felt very alone. She wondered if Carrick would be back any time soon. But why should he be? He had things to do. She was an afterthought. That was what marriage would be like with him. Transactional. Emotionless.

A frustrated sound escaped her lips, and Danica didn't know what the hell she was doing anymore. All she felt was hungry, tired and anxious. She felt like a toy in a greater game that she wasn't really a part of and didn't understand. Collapsing back against the couch, she wrapped herself in the blanket that Carrick had put on her legs.

And she sat.

And thought.

And sat.

And thought.

Until she couldn't be there anymore, and she got up — moving silent as a mouse upstairs to the bedroom where she found her laundered clothes folded neatly in a pile on a wooden dresser. *What time exactly does Carrick get up in the mornings?* He seemed to live a secret life before he even put the coffee on.

Clenching her teeth, she hauled on the freshly laundered set of panties and a bra, along with her black mini skirt and a loose-fitted knit sweater. She was getting out. No more. And Carrick?

I'm just an afterthought to him. This isn't love.

And as she stood in front of the dresser, pitching what little stuff she had into her black bag, she felt a pang of self-doubt — the most insidious of all the doubts.

What will happen if I leave?

She drifted her fingers down the dresser, tracing elegant metal knobs with embossed floral patterns. Again, there was no way he'd chosen that dresser. It was simply too feminine. She didn't know him well, but she was sure that he would never choose anything like that. Did he have an interior designer? Would he care enough to pay for that service? It didn't seem to fit his personality.

As she traced one of the dresser's knobs, she found herself questioning more and more. What were his secrets? What didn't he want to tell her? She tugged on the knob, opening the small top drawer, and inside she found a whole mess of things—belts, knives, empty and tattered leather wallets and what looked like Navy insignia. Now, that made sense. Couldn't be more Carrick even if it had growled at her.

She pushed the drawer shut and pulled open the one underneath. It was his socks and boxers drawer— neatly arranged and organized like any good SEAL would have it. She avoided the urge to rip out his boxers and smell them, so kept moving her way down, finding a shirt drawer and what looked like a drawer full of workout clothes. Of course, that checked out, too.

Huffing, Danica wondered what exactly she expected to find in a man's dresser. *Dildos and red panties?* That wouldn't even really alarm her as much as she would once have thought.

Then she realized she only had one drawer left to snoop in.

The bottom drawer.

She stood still, looking at it—debating if she should just stop. It wasn't right to pry. She shouldn't.

Right?

Immediately, she whipped open the bottom drawer, frantically searching for evidence. What type of evidence? The jury was still out on that. She just needed to find something—anything—that would tell her what she already knew. He had a dark past, and he was never going to tell her a fucking thing about it.

Rooting around, she found that the bottom drawer was stuffed with more clothes, but then she saw it. The edges of a small, torn cardboard box stuffed to the back of the drawer came into view, hidden underneath a shirt. It screamed 'secrets'. It screamed 'the past'.

Danica had to look inside.

I just have to.

Slowly pulling the box out of the drawer, she tried not to disturb the rest of the contents. She was going to need to put everything back to hide her crime. She ran her fingers over the dusty box and read his name written on it—block letters written in black marker on top of old, ripped packing tape. And sure enough, the box wasn't sealed anymore. It was simply folded up like it didn't matter.

And that was exactly how Danica knew that it mattered very much.

She carefully peeled back the flaps of the cardboard box and realized quickly that it was a box full of old cards. But then she realized that they were not just any type of cards. They were sympathy cards.

Someone important died.

She picked up a yellow and muted green card that had some sort of scripture on the front. She traced the gold embossed words with her finger and breathed in the truth. Once she opened that card, there was no turning back. She would know his secret. Know his pain. But also, she would know she betrayed his trust. She put down the card, looking at it. She shouldn't.

But I have to.

Snatching it up again, she opened the card. She read a message from someone named Aunt Kathy.

Carrick, I'm deeply sorry for your loss. Lauren was the bright star in all our lives, and this world is a lesser place without her. There are no words. An unimaginable tragedy. I'm always here for you, if you need me. In lieu of flowers, we have donated to the cancer foundation in her name.

Oh shit.

Cancer? Danica gasped. *God.*

She picked up a few more cards, reading similar sympathy messages, then dug through the box until she found a funeral service leaflet. It had a picture of a younger, happier-looking Carrick on the front — holding a beautiful brunette in his arms. The two were a gorgeous, healthy couple sitting on the beach somewhere. They looked so happy. Danica didn't miss the engagement ring on the woman's finger.

Tears welled into her eyes, and she felt moved beyond words. Immediately, she found herself crying for him and for her.

As she batted back tears, she read on, unable to stop herself. The leaflet described a young woman who'd suddenly become sick with leukemia and tragically died within weeks, leaving behind her fiancée. She had been loved by all and denied a life she deserved.

Died suddenly. Tragic loss.

Danica bit her lip, dripping a few tears onto the box. She cried for Lauren. She cried for a young woman who should have lived, should have gotten married, should have had children, been a mother.

It isn't fair.

Immediately, Danica wished she could trade places with her. It wasn't okay that she had died and Danica would live—taking her place with Lauren's man, a man who couldn't love her. It was so clear now why he was so sure that he'd never love again.

Danica knew then and there that her father would be ashamed of her if she let Carrick throw away his life for her—not to mention her own. *What an embarrassment.*

Crying harder, she felt the agony of her emotions. She was falling for him, but he didn't love her—and he wasn't going to. Once again, Danica looked down at Lauren's picture, and knew she had to do right by her memory, to do right by her parents and the people who loved them. And that was when Danica made up her mind.

Chapter Twenty-Six

Carrick

"How much is the property?" Carrick spoke into his truck's handsfree speaker, driving fast down the highway to make it home as soon as possible.

He'd already been a busy boy that morning and had more things to get done.

"It's listed at a million, and you'll share the building with a popular coffee roastery," Kathy, his aunt and real estate agent, explained into the phone. "This is a real hot buy—and a great investment. Want to put in an offer?"

"Damn, that's not cheap for such a small property. I knew commercial property down here was pricey, but come on," he scoffed, stopping at a red light on the Pacific Coast Highway, looking at his hands as he gripped the steering wheel.

A few of his knuckles were cut open. And unless he was planning on wearing gloves, Danica was going to have questions about what he'd gotten up to that morning — things he didn't want to tell her about.

Kathy continued musing on the call, "Well, you'd be able to buy it in cash if you sold — "

"Don't." Carrick cut his aunt off before she could continue.

"Carrick, listen… I was so happy to sell the house on Coronado island to you and Lauren, but I need to say something. Please just take this as coming from someone who loves you." Kathy pushed, telling him things he didn't want to hear. "The San Diego market is raging hot right now. I've never seen it this active down there. Your old home — and you are not even living there anymore — would sell *so* fast. I've been batting off unsolicited offers on it for a year. You are leaving big money on the table."

He exhaled, frustrated at how pushy his aunt could be. But she was right. She was a top-tier agent and knew her shit.

"Look," he grumbled, but pivoted. He was going to be married in a few hours and had a lot more to think about than himself. So, he just said, "I'll figure something out. I'll call you later."

As Carrick flicked off the call, leaving him in silence, he thought about what had been said — and what he should do. He hadn't stepped foot in his old place in nearly two years and was bleeding money every month to pay a property manager to deal with it. When Lauren had gotten sick, he'd lived at the hospital. When she'd died, he'd never gone back to the home they'd shared. The place had turned into a tomb — with all their stuff — all the stuff they'd bought together.

He knew he should just sell it and start fresh. It was just that in all those years, he hadn't been able to. He'd transitioned his life from San Diego to Sunset Beach, up the coast, and never looked back.

The traffic light turned green, and he hit the gas, his thoughts turning back to Danica — the woman he'd never expected to fall into his life. He started working on logistics — getting her to city hall and getting married. Carrick was nothing if not determined, and he'd made up his mind the previous night. He was going to do something that she couldn't do for herself. He was going to make Danica unavailable once and for all, something he'd promised Petrov and Andriy that they wouldn't like one little bit.

As Carrick pulled up to his place in Sunset Beach, he was ready to get shit done. Today, he was killing it, securing a lifetime of Danica — which promised to be amusing at the very least.

Jumping out of his black truck in the garage, he moved swiftly into the house. Purposeful. Driven. Inside, Carrick darted his gaze left to right, like it was a damn night raid. Where was she? The place was dead quiet except for Delta in the office on a call. Intent, Carrick moved on and took the stairs up. Dani wasn't in the living area.

What's she doing?

Carrick immediately hit the upper stairs, taking two at a time. The door to the bedroom was closed. In that instant — he couldn't explain why — his instincts lit on fire. He pushed open the door, revealing Danica standing by the bed. She jumped, just as surprised to see him as he was to see her. With her black backpack over her shoulder and white tennis shoes on, it was clear that she was getting ready to bolt.

"Going somewhere?" he pushed.

"Yes," she replied, her lip quivering as he stalked closer.

Unwilling to believe the words, Carrick marched right up to her, close enough to see the camouflage glint of her eyes, feeling that familiar rising hunger for her.

"Where?" he demanded.

"Anywhere not with you."

"How's that?" he rumbled, merely inches from her. "It's time for us to go get married."

Unable to control the growl rising in his chest, he drew out their marriage license from his pocket, as if to prove how serious he really was. He pushed it into her hand for her to review its legitimacy — and come to understand that this was happening.

Whether she likes it or not.

She gazed at the marriage license and back up at him, her eyes wide and her face immediately flushed with what looked like fear. "Why would you go do this? If Andriy finds out..."

"I've dealt with him," he confirmed and crossed his arms with a tone of finality.

"What?" she asked, arching her eyebrows as she watched him do so.

Reaching out, Danica grabbed his right hand, which was crossed underneath his left elbow. He realized what she had seen. Her face grew full of unease as she observed the blood on his hands for the first time. He clenched his fist, feeling how it ached. Even he was not immune to pain.

"You're hurt," she gasped, running her finger over the scabs on his knuckles. "Why are you hurt?"

"I had a conversation with Andriy," Carrick conceded, but remained circumspect. "You don't have to worry about him anymore."

"What does that mean?" she said breathlessly, fast and desperate. "What did you *do*?"

Carrick kept his face cold and serious. There were things he'd done that she didn't need to know, things he didn't want to tell her.

"All you need to know is that I dealt with it, and now we can get this done."

Danica dropped his hand and leaned back, though she was stuck by the bed and unable to retreat any farther. She was not happy.

"What do you think of me?" she gasped. "Don't you think you should have talked to me first? Don't you care about what I want?"

Then she started to cry.

Carrick watched as she reacted — knowing what he had done had been for the best. Sure, she was taking it harder than he'd expected, but what else did she want? This was his job. So he stood firm, his arms tightly crossed and his gaze narrowed on her. He wasn't wrong. She would learn, and she would come to understand.

And he watched…and waited.

And she ran her hands over her face, still crying.

The longer he stood, waiting for her to relent, the more he came to realize that there was something different in the air between them. He shifted in discomfort as he held his arms across his chest, watching her shake her head, clearly frustrated.

Not willing to wait longer, he pushed, "Like I said, I've got everything ready. Let's go get it done."

She finally stopped, wiping the tears from her face. He figured that she had come to understand his point of view. He reached to pull her into him. She immediately shook her head and backed away, turning so he couldn't take her mouth with his. That was when he knew. Something was very, very wrong. It was more than he thought. She didn't speak. She didn't say anything.

The intensity within him tripled, and he demanded, "Is there something you need to say?"

"I-I just... I can't afford to do this with you anymore because — "

"You can't afford to do anything else and I — " he cut her off, scanning her face.

"You can't love me."

He didn't reply, growing hard and angry, and just stood firmly planted. How the hell was he supposed to respond to that? Why the fuck would she say that?

She watched him, slowly shaking her head. "We deserve more than *this*. You are a closed-off, locked-down vault that I'll never get the code to."

He assessed her, his tone as emotionless as ever. "And what specifically do you feel you need to know?"

"About her." The words spilled out of her mouth as she turned, reached down and pulled back the crumpled mess of sheets on his bed, revealing sympathy cards and the cardboard box. "About what happened."

Holy fuck.

Fury filled him, as he was betrayed and broken by Danica. He gazed back and forth between his private past and the woman standing before him, unable to process what it all meant.

"What the actual fuck?" He clenched his jaw and was livid. "You don't need to know."

"I don't need to know about *you*? About your *past*?" She pushed herself away from him. "About why you need to keep emotion out of this? About why you want to marry me, but can't ever love me? I don't need to *know*? Then what *do* I need, Carrick?"

As he reached out to pull her against him once more, goosebumps rose on her arms and chest. Her reaction to him was equally visceral.

"You have no idea how you make me feel." She stiffened her spine, holding his gaze as raw emotion rose in her tense face. "I can't do this with you. I can't let you in anymore."

Carrick realized she'd made up her mind. She was leaving.

She was leaving *him*.

Her gaze falling from his, Danica pouted and showed a deep sadness he'd never seen before. She appeared defeated. She peeled herself from his hands then took a step to the side, moving toward the bedroom door.

"You can't leave," he choked out as she walked away, then sealed his mouth. He couldn't fucking talk anymore.

She snapped around, turning to look at him over her shoulder.

"I'm falling for you, Carrick — and I've realized that there's one person you can't protect me from," she said as big tears rolled down her cheeks, "and that's *you*."

Then she turned back to the door and walked out.

And he made a bizarre noise that he'd only heard himself make once before.

As he watched her disappear, he stopped feeling anything. He stopped hearing the ocean, the seagulls. He barely felt a drop fall onto his forearm as he looked down at his aching, bloody hands.

Reaching up to touch his face, he realized that his cheek was wet.

But it wasn't from blood.

Chapter Twenty-Seven

Carrick

Carrick stood in silence for minutes after she'd left — frozen in place.

A long-forgotten part of his mind was trapped, flipping back and forth between the cardboard box on the bed and Dani walking out of the door. Essential life support took over, turning up his survival instincts and turning off emotion. His body knew it had to survive because his mind…was just *breaking*.

He found himself moving down the stairs, numb, looking from side to side for any detail he needed. What had happened when he was gone? How had they gotten to where they were?

His gaze moved from the chair to the couch — where he'd had some of the hottest sex of his life — the way her body curved underneath his, the way she took every inch of his swollen manhood and made him feel…

Before the thought could finish, Carrick drifted to the tequila bottle that still sat in the middle of the coffee table from the previous night. He moved toward it, picking it up, rotating it in his hands. He wanted to break shit.

He wanted to thunder.

And that was exactly why he'd found himself at Petrov's office tower that morning in downtown LA, the place where Carrick had signed for the search and rescue job. Sure enough, Andriy — the CEO — had been there and Carrick had given him a piece of his mind. Carrick wasn't a 'sit back and take it' kind of guy. He was a 'determined, no bullshit' one — and Andriy had gotten to know exactly what that meant.

Tilting his head back, he raised the tequila bottle and took three big gulps. It burned on the way down and tasted amazing. It reminded him of taking her mouth, tinged with tequila, and wrapping his tongue around hers. He hated reliving the memory right now, under the new circumstances of her departure. He hated it so much.

He whipped the bottle against the wall, watching it shatter into glass shards, leaving a lasting scar.

Fuck it.

He looked around his place — his perfectly decorated place, thanks to Aunt Kathy. He'd told her he'd pay her anything to set the place up because he didn't want it to feel like his old house, his past…like Lauren.

He needed to forget.

Immediately, Delta was bolting upstairs, clearly having heard the shattering bottle. Carrick didn't give a shit. He couldn't give a shit about anything right then.

Not even his best friend.

"What the fuck happened?" Delta's voice echoed behind him.

Carrick shot a fierce glare over at the shoreline, ignoring the question and the ball of fire inside his chest.

Delta didn't relent as he approached. "What the fuck is going on with you? She stormed out?"

Carrick remained silent, as Delta's feet crunched the glass.

He stopped in his tracks.

"What the fuck is this?" Delta roared, and finally Carrick turned to him. Delta's gaze dropped to his bloody, scabbed knuckles. "You *didn't*. Tell me you fucking didn't."

Carrick stood firm, staring his friend down — daring him to say it.

"Yeah, I paid Andriy a goddamn visit," Carrick said, cold and hard. "Thanks for letting me know where he was."

Delta's expression grew incredulous. "I told you we would be putting lives in jeopardy if we acted on that intel. You told me it was to make sure your girl was safe. I *trusted* you."

"I didn't lie. You misunderstood," Carrick sneered at him. "And maybe it's time for you to cough up who the fuck is your intel source?"

It was the one question Carrick knew would have the effect he wanted. Delta backed off. Immediately, the man stepped away, crunching more on the broken glass. His face said it all.

"Doesn't matter." Delta exhaled, his eyes wild.

"You're not getting it from your cop girl, are you?" Carrick growled, stepping forward, determined.

"You're bad news for her. She's a good girl. Leave her alone."

Aggression felt fucking good.

Delta bellowed, "That's a little rich coming from you!"

Carrick cocked his head and threatened Delta to say more. He was just looking for a reason to fight.

Delta carried on, his voice breaking with anger as he stepped closer to his friend. "Are you fucking awake? Do you realize what you've done to your company?"

"I don't give a shit," Carrick countered, and he turned to glare out over the water again. "I did what I had to do."

"You don't give a shit?" Delta lashed out, now yelling. "Aside from the mob hits now on both of our heads, aside from the girl you've let run away, despite the threats she's facing, let me get this straight. You don't give a shit that we've got Petrov's lawyers threatening to sue the shit out of you for breach of contract? You don't give a shit that you're at risk of losing millions? I don't know if you remember, but the last time I saved your ass, I said it was going to be the last time."

Carrick whipped toward his friend and snarled, "I remember a lot, buddy—*too much*. I don't want to remember anymore."

Delta looked down, kicking at the broken glass. "Yeah, that's what you said when Lauren died—when you quit the SEALs and started drinking booze like water. And now, you're hitting the bottle again?"

"I retired. I didn't quit." Carrick jumped forward, ready to punch his friend. "And it's none of your damn business."

"You need to wake up, brother. Life is moving on without you." Delta lunged forward as well and pushed Carrick hard on the chest. But since they were both tall and strong, neither of them budged.

"You've been blind since the beginning," Delta challenged. "Petrov used you. He didn't want you to protect her. He wanted you to control her. And that's exactly what you've done, isn't it?"

Control her — the words hit the back of Carrick's mind as he flexed his neck and shoulders, still wanting to punch someone. It hit a little too close to home.

"I told you not to try to save this girl," Delta followed up, his fists up. "I told you this job was nothing but trouble. And here we are. You've fucked it up. You're collapsing. And where is she? Where the fuck *is* she, Carrick?"

Carrick heard the words, but he didn't feel them. He was numb. They stared each other down, frustration and old problems rising to the raw surface of their friendship.

"She left," Delta stated, leaving the words to linger in the stale air. "And so am I."

Hearing the words, Carrick felt nothing. Whatever man he had once been, he was no more.

Delta turned and headed back down the stairs, furious as all hell. Not only had Carrick lost his girl, but he'd also lost his best friend. And the constant vibrating of his cell in his pocket told him that his problems were just about to climax.

Chapter Twenty-Eight

Danica

"Just one ticket — Klamath Falls," Danica replied in a sullen tone to the attendant at the train station kiosk, handing over her credit card. She'd just transferred in downtown LA to the long-distance line.

"Oregon?" The attendant swiped the card then typing into her terminal. "With the wildfires, expect the trip to take longer than the usual one day, three hours."

"No problem," Danica mumbled, holding her clutch wallet tight against her chest. An entire day stuck on the train was the last thing she needed, but her options had run out.

The attendant stopped typing, leaning back from the terminal with a confused face as she gripped Danica's card. She looked back up at Danica, inquiring, "Do you have ID?"

"Not on me," Danica said slowly, confused. "Is there something wrong?"

"It's declined, Miss Jacobs." The attendant eyed the card suspiciously before looking up.

Danica found herself searching for words. Her fake names were starting to pile up, and so were the bridges she'd left burning in her wake. Slowly, she shuffled backward, explaining that she was going to come back with ID. As she walked quickly through the terminal, she checked her phone, seeing that her accounts had all been frozen.

What the hell is going on?

Zipping her clutch back up and stuffing it into her black backpack, she looked around at the bustling urban train depot. Quickly making her way outside the exquisitely designed art deco metal-and-stone front entrance of the downtown LA station, Danica ran across the concrete sidewalk in the city park garden. She frantically looked back and forth, wondering if it was Carrick. He was a SEAL. Wouldn't he have connections?

Her mind racing, she decided that she had to regroup, to think things through—make a new plan and act fast. Damn, she needed to take her mind off the burning hole she had in her heart. But, more than anything, she had to keep going.

I can't stop now.

Danica wasn't thinking about where she was going. She just ran—with her pink hoodie Carrick had washed but that still had a little dirt stain on it, her black mini skirt that he'd watched her slip off before he'd taken her for the first time and with her glasses sliding down her nose, the ones that Carrick said made her look like a sexy librarian.

People darted out of the way as she hurried through downtown, tears falling from her eyes. No one seemed all that surprised. Obviously, it wasn't the weirdest thing downtown LA would see that day. Finally, she hit a red light and had to stop to catch her breath. Something about few calories and little caffeine had debilitated her athletic prowess.

Panting on the street corner, feeling lonelier than ever, she knew there was something about being downtown that made it all worse. She needed nature. She needed something to guide her.

What am I doing?

She heard her cellphone's text sound and pulled it out of the pocket of her pink hoodie. It was her roommate, Addie.

What's going on with you and Rambo? I miss you. It sucks here without you.

Danica exhaled slowly, missing Addie as well but wishing the words had come from someone else, that someone else missed her. As throngs of pedestrians whipped around her, busily moving to wherever they needed to be, Danica leaned against a metal post off the curb. She inhaled, slowly reliving the whirlwind of the past few days. She found herself struggling to put together coherent thoughts, especially when her betraying mind let in visions of Carrick's delicious smile, twinkling eyes and wide, strong chest.

Danica let out an exasperated moan, closing her eyes as the world moved about around her. She pushed Carrick out of her thoughts — or tried to. She needed to stop remembering how he'd held her down and run his tongue along her body, what it felt like to fall asleep in his arms, in his bed — and how desperately she wanted him to love her, how she wanted to just marry him.

But I can't.

Because... Because I love him.

Pressing her cheek against the cool steel of the street pole, Danica felt like the lost child she once had been. She was a runaway girl all over again. A deep pain rose in her throat and she desperately wished her mom and dad would pull up on the side of the road and pick her up, like how they used to get her from school. They'd bring her snacks and hug her and kiss her cheeks until they were tender. An only child of immigrant parents, she'd never had anyone else. It had been just them.

Until they were gone.

Feeling a wet trickle down her cheek, Danica opened her eyes briefly — just as arms were reaching around her. Masculine arms grabbed her, throwing her into the back seat of a dark SUV. She screamed, but it didn't matter. The engine roared and they were already moving. She realized what had happened.

I've been kidnapped.

"Andriy!" she cried out, seeing the tall, blond man's face as he held her down. "What the hell are you doing?"

He had a black eye and cuts on his cheek — consistent with the injuries on Carrick's knuckles that she'd seen earlier.

"You're late," Andriy snarled at her, grazing his hand over his purple, swollen cheekbone.

"For what?"

"Our wedding."

Danica's eyes widened with horror as she realized that the worst had happened. She had been kidnapped by the two people on earth she wanted to see the least.

"You can't do this." She grabbed for the SUV's door handle. She'd jump out. It wouldn't be the first time. She could still run.

Andriy pulled out a pistol from his jacket.

"I hadn't wanted this to be at gunpoint, but your boyfriend's visit this morning changed my mood," he barked, narrowing his eyes on her with a viciousness that she couldn't describe. "Cooperate now and marriage won't be as bad as you think."

"Marriage is for people who love each other!" she cried, shrinking back from him as she adjusted the frames on her nose.

"Marriage is not about love," he snapped, his vicious gaze falling back on her. "Marriage is a legal contract — and we are going to have exactly that. And these will be the first to go," Andriy lunged forward and snatched her glasses off her face. He snarled as he looked at them in his hand just before crushing the frame and whipping them out of the window. A vain man, she knew he hated the way she looked in them.

As Danica heard the glasses Carrick loved smashing onto the pavement, the SUV turned into the parking structure of a downtown office building, not far from where they'd kidnapped her. Gutted, she shrank back, more helpless than ever.

Once the SUV found a parking spot, she knew her fate was sealed. There was no getting away now. His pistol still drawn, Andriy pushed her out into the concrete structure, moving her through the lot and into a dark elevator. The driver stayed behind in the SUV, probably waiting for his next orders.

Danica darted her gaze back and forth as she tried to imagine how to get away and save herself. There was no way Carrick would ever find her.

"Have you been following me?" She stumbled as Andriy pushed her out of the elevator when they hit the fourth floor.

"We didn't need to," Andriy snorted. "We just had some friends trace your credit card."

"How?" Danica asked, searching for ways they could have found out her false identity.

"Varya's wedding… I should have thanked you for letting us look through your clutch." Andriy snickered off her question as he ushered her to the modern building where he was the CEO. "I would have never guessed your fake name."

An incoherent cry left her lips as he pushed her on, still obeying his every demand. The more she walked along, the more she hated herself for it. He led her through the wide, vacant hallway toward a corner office where her uncle was probably waiting. Petrov shakily stood up from behind the desk, an oxygen tube under his nose, and grabbed his walking cane as he motioned for her to sit.

I need to run.

Danica unwillingly entered the room, pushed forward by Andriy, as she watched the sick old man who had once scared her more than anything.

"Are you ready?" He coughed then steadied himself.

"Yes." Andriy stepped forward, pushing her toward the desk. "Where do I sign?"

Andriy slammed her down in the chair before the desk then leaned forward to sign a marriage certificate. As the two men exchanged words in Russian, Danica's mind spiraled.

"You can't do this," she cried out again, tears streaming down her face. "You can't make me do this."

Andriy turned his face to her, looking her up and down slowly, a slippery, lecherous look crossing his mouth. "I am so looking forward to fucking you. Be nice, and maybe I will be."

Petrov waved his hand dismissively. "Get the paperwork done and you can do whatever you want with her. You'll own her then."

"The paperwork?" she pressed, lunging forward in her seat as she tried to look at what was on the desk.

"You don't think I'd marry you unless I had a good enough reason?" Andriy asked lazily, turning his nose up at her.

"You are my heir, Dansa," Petrov said, gripping his cane as he struggled to breathe. "I'm dying. I don't have much time left. My company and all my assets have to pass on to you, my only American blood relative."

Petrov bent over to sign a document, barely able to hold himself up.

"As Andriy's wife, you'll make him American. Then Andriy will arrange to have it all transferred to him. This is your duty to your family."

Danica's mind raced, a familiar stabbing pain of hurt in her chest. Petrov and Andriy leaned over the desk, flipping through the different pages where signatures were needed, mumbling in Russian to each other. Neither of them cared what Danica wanted, of course. She didn't matter to them. She never had.

I can't run anymore.

The tears on her flushed cheeks turned sticky, and anger rose in Danica's chest. It was that same anger she'd seen in Carrick. A hunger. A passion.

"My parents wouldn't let me throw my life away," Danica lashed out, leaning forward in the chair. "My parents wouldn't let me marry a man I didn't love in lieu of the man I am in love with."

Andriy and Petrov stopped, frozen, and turned to face her, realizing her admission. Danica felt her hatred. It was the angriest and fiercest she'd ever been, thinking about what Petrov had done to her parents and was now trying to do to her. Upon seeing her expression, the old man started coughing uncontrollably.

"You *will* sign this. This is the only way." Andriy seemed to realize that she was pushing back, that she wasn't going to obey him as easily as he'd once expected. He continued, pulling his pistol back out of his jacket. "Even if you need to be persuaded."

As he moved forward, pressing the cold steel of the pistol against her head, Danica twisted in revulsion. She was disgusted by what Petrov had done to the memory of her parents, by his abusive, controlling behavior and at herself for never fighting back. Violence flashed across her eyes as she came to a sudden realization.

Carrick was right. I should have done this a long time ago.

"Sign the fucking document." Andriy pushed the barrel of his gun harder against her temple.

"No." Danica straightened her back and she shot fire at him.

Petrov stood, hateful disbelief in his eyes. He uttered a familiar threat, one that used to terrify her. "*Ne slushaysya menya, ty umresh' odin.*"

Fear rushed over her body, leaving her feeling like a small, helpless child once more. *'Disobey me and you will die alone.'* Her gaze flitted over to Andriy's scowling face, then back to her uncle. She had never doubted that Petrov would actually kill her.

Yet, everything Carrick had ever said to her and every way he'd made her feel rushed across her mind. That was the moment Danica knew that she had to fight back, because if she didn't, she was already dead.

Petrov pushed the documents across the table at her and threw down a pen.

Through clenched teeth, she growled, "Go to hell."

Chapter Twenty-Nine

Carrick

"Fuck," Carrick growled as he marched through his kitchen, whipping open every cupboard.

Where is the fucking whiskey?

He couldn't remember.

He stopped remembering.

All he felt was pure anger, pain—until he opened one door so hard that a picture fell from the inside of it. It was a corner cupboard that he rarely went into—one that had all that extra shit in a kitchen that he rarely used. And what fell out was a picture his aunt had taped there after he'd paid her to decorate the place. He'd only seen it a couple of times—and not for a while.

It's me and Lauren.

Carrick reached out and grabbed it. He hadn't seen Lauren's face in a long, long time. There were no pictures of her around—and especially no pictures of them together. For too long, it had burned him deep inside to even think of her.

He turned to the view of the Pacific Ocean. It hadn't been long ago since he had been diving with the SEALs—a couple of years. He remembered the long training days, weeks, months—and the longer deployments. The difficulty and toughness of it. He was away a lot. He was never home—all because he wanted to do his part for his country. Did he regret it? Carrick let out a long breath, knowing that he only really regretted not being home enough and missing all those moments with Lauren. He'd never expected that they had an expiration date. He'd always thought there was another day to do all the same stuff—until, there wasn't, until he was alone, until Lauren was gone.

And here I am—alone again.

Dani's gone.

Flexed and hardened, he grabbed his phone out of his pocket and called Delta. It was time to focus. Work. The hardened operator inside him was happy to take back control, beating out every last ounce of weakness inside him.

"Matteo," Carrick said once Delta picked up.

"No one calls me that," Delta scowled back. "What do you want?"

"Let's finish this. You still in?"

Delta took a minute to reply, leaving Carrick hanging to wonder if his friend really was out—in a real, irreversible way.

But, finally, Delta said, "Yeah, fine."

"Good. Mount up," Carrick ordered into the phone, moving toward the closet near the bathroom where he kept his gun safe. "Where are you?"

"Around the corner. We going after her?" Delta responded, anger still high in his tone.

"We need to do something first."

"Not Andriy again—"

"No, buddy." Carrick cocked a pistol, stowing it in his black jeans before grabbing a hunting knife, zap straps and extra mags. *Just the essentials.*

"Where the fuck *are* we going, then?" Delta yelled as Carrick moved into the garage.

Running down the stairs, Carrick grabbed the keys to the red rented pickup truck, still in the garage. He hoped to hell that Delta had gotten insurance.

"It's time to have a conversation with Petrov and lay this fuck to rest," Carrick growled into the phone, his former SEAL intensity driving hard. "Let's go see if the old man is still at his office."

Delta scoffed, "That's all the way to downtown LA. Traffic is already stifling. What the fuck do you expect from me? Magic?"

"Buddy, just do what you did last time we were in Iraq." Carrick pulled out of the garage, the evening sun hitting him across the eyes.

"You want me to break the law?"

"That's never been a problem for you before."

Delta let out a low chuckle, hinting at that latent monster within—the side of Delta that few people had seen.

Out on Sunset Beach boulevard, Carrick hit the gas hard, moving onto the coastal highway. Delta soon pulled in front of Carrick, throwing a fake cherry on the top of his truck. He turned on the flashing red light, parting the sea of traffic like Moses, as if they were emergency vehicles.

Speeding furiously into the downtown core, they were able to make it in record time. Swift as a wild fox, Carrick parked his truck as close as he could to Petrov's office tower, taking a street spot that had freed up. He nodded over to Delta, who'd parked his own truck a few spaces down. It was game time.

Tucking his keys in the pocket of his jeans, Carrick felt the cold steel of the pistol against his tailbone in the back of his pants. The way he was feeling, Petrov better be fucking scared.

I'll do whatever it takes to get Dani back.

Carrick called back to Delta, "Hold the perimeter. I'm going to see Petrov alone."

"Going to be long?" Delta replied, crossing his arms.

"No," Carrick shook his head. "We've still got to find her."

Delta hung back, visibly digesting Carrick's command. After running his hands up the scar on his face, a blank look came over Delta's eyes. Carrick knew what he was reliving — the last time Delta had needed to save Carrick's life — two years before in the wild back country of Syria. Carrick shook his head, determined.

It won't be like that this time.

Carrick nodded at his best friend, silently reassuring him. Delta narrowed his eyes — and Carrick knew that some scars would never heal.

Focused aggression pumping through his veins, Carrick marched through the entrance of Petrov's office building, turning immediately toward the stairs. The security guard at the desk didn't seem to notice him. That was no surprise, given Carrick's ability to remain invisible. He was a master at it, and few questioned him when he wanted it to be that way. Taking two steps at a time, he kept alert for any sign of danger or threat.

He thought back to when he'd been climbing these exact stairs to sign a fresh contract. It had been a big one — a big opportunity for his private security company. Little had he known then...

Carrick had come to realize enough about Petrov and Andriy, and their time had run out. Someone was going to make the first move, and Carrick was strongest on the offensive.

Finally, he reached the fourth level and opened the hallway door into the office space, where he saw the embossed glass entrance for Petrov's company. Stalking down the hall, Carrick avoided detection. It seemed that all the employees had left for the day.

Carrick reached into the back of his jeans and removed his pistol, keeping it covered under his shirt. Around the corner, he saw it — the corner office, the place where Carrick had been a month before to sign the contract. Petrov's office. And it was occupied. As he stepped closer, he saw Petrov sitting on a chair beside the desk, gasping for breath. The man looked like he was on the verge of dying, breathing with the help of an oxygen tank.

Carrick stopped in his tracks, realizing the old man wasn't alone. Andriy was standing in front of the desk, a vicious snarl on his bruised and bloodied face. A sadistic grin. A pistol in his hand.

And the pistol was pointed at Dani.

Holy fuck.

Rage fired up every limb, and pure violence coursed through his veins.

Her head was down and her hair disheveled. She looked like she'd been tossed around. Immediately, a hellacious desire to kill rose in his chest. Without delay, he cocked his pistol, tracking his prey like a goddamn panther. With his heavy boot, he kicked the glass office door open, sending it crashing into the wall and just fucking shattering the glass.

"Gun down! Gun down!" Carrick howled, pointing his pistol directly at Andriy, aggressively rushing him.

"Fuck!" Andriy's eyes widened, a touch of fear visible.

"Stop him!" Petrov flew off the handle, jumping toward Andriy. "Shoot him!"

Carrick swiftly took control of the room, moving to protect Danica. When she whipped around to look up at him, blood was dripping down her swollen cheek. She looked as surprised to see him as he had been to see her.

"Carrick—" she said, her voice trembling.

Still with a shaking arm, Andriy looked like he was ready to shit himself, his hand absently touching the black eye Carrick had given him earlier. Gasping for breath, Petrov desperately snatched the pistol from Andriy, pointing it at Carrick.

"Drop it or you both die!"

"Fuck you!" Carrick roared back at the old man, rushing closer to Danica.

"Carrick!" Danica screamed, but Carrick pushed her back, covering her body with his.

Petrov wobbled as he held the pistol, unadulterated hatred in his aging eyes. Wheezing, the weakened old man pulled the trigger several times, toppling over with the force of the recoil.

Carrick shielded Danica in place. After four gunshots and two bodies had hit the floor, Carrick held the crying woman tighter in his arms.

I have to save you.

"Carrick!" she sobbed into his chest. "Carrick—no!"

All he felt was searing pain.

Like he was in slow motion, he peeled away from her, assessing the scene. Andriy was shrieking, crumpled over on the floor, holding a bleeding wound on his shoulder. Petrov was convulsing on the ground, his eyes rolled back.

Hearing distant screams, Carrick was on autopilot. He had to get her to safety. Heaving her into his arms, unwilling to feel the pain tearing through him, he ran down the hall, calculating their exit. He ran like the goddamn building was on fire — down the stairs and into the lobby. The rear of his mind registered that he'd been injured. The only thing that felt good was Danica buried in his chest, grasping at him, leaving hot trails from her touch on his skin.

"You're here," she wept. "You found me."

He just squeezed her tighter, feeling a lot of things he had no words for. Once outside the tower, Carrick crashed onto a sidewalk bench, placing her down beside him. The wetness down his back had gotten worse. He was bleeding.

"You've been shot," Danica gasped, jumping up to assess him. "There's blood everywhere. We need to get you to the hospital!"

Carrick was keeling over, dizzy and losing touch with reality. Danica was leaning over him, holding his head and with blood up her arms. Delta came running, clearly laser focused on him.

"Call an ambulance! And the police!" Danica cried out.

"Well, shit," Carrick slurred — everything was growing hazy.

I saved her.

Danica held him as she compressed his wound to quell the bleeding. A large, appreciative grin crossed his lips as he looked up into her amber eyes.

"You're here," he grumbled, trying to reach up to touch her face. He drifted his hand to where blood was trickling out of a fresh wound on her brow. They'd hit her. They'd hurt her. He twisted in agony, hating himself for taking so long to find her, and he let out a pained howl.

"Stay with me, Carrick. Help is on the way." The look in Danica's eyes was not encouraging. She would know exactly how bad it was, being a nurse.

"I'll kill them if they aren't already dead," he growled, his blurry vision unable to focus on her cut brow anymore.

She reached out, grabbed his hand and brought it down to her cheek. "It's just a scratch. Don't worry."

He coughed and closed his eyes to ground himself. Blackness threatened to overtake his vision, and he knew he was losing a lot of blood. Delta shouted in the background at someone—something about Syria. Danica was anxiously yelling back at him.

"This wasn't how this was supposed to go," Carrick rumbled, his mind drifting to the last tour he'd been on with Delta. That rough battle and Delta's unbelievably heroic actions had saved much more than Carrick's life.

"I had to save you—" Carrick coughed.

"Keep talking," she whispered, seemingly trying to keep him awake.

Danica ran a hand through his hair, bringing him back to the present. The evening sun of LA shone on them, warming his cold skin. He was losing consciousness and a lot of blood. The shrapnel inside him was hurtling to his core. Of all the battles he'd been in and the war he'd tasted, he hadn't expected that he would die on a bench in downtown LA.

"I have to tell you something." He reached up to touch her cheek with his shaking hand.

Biting her lip, she held his fingers, blinking out tears.

"Her name was Lauren." He coughed, feeling unmanageable pain. "She was the one. We were engaged…"

She remained stoic on the edge of her seat as she caressed his face.

"But, two years ago—Valentine's Day—she collapsed," Carrick continued through haggard breaths. "I took her to the hospital. She'd had a stroke. They told us she had leukemia. She died weeks later—" He panted, clenching his teeth.

"I'm so sorry." Danica wept, holding him closer to her, the sounds of emergency sirens approaching.

"I never talked about it," he said then exhaled, looking up at her through blurred vision, "because I couldn't."

"I understand."

"She was two months pregnant when she died and—" But then he winced harder, feeling a shooting pain up his spine that he'd never felt before. "I never got to tell her—" he slurred incoherently.

Danica never let him go, breathing down on him as she kissed his hair. Carrick felt himself losing consciousness, in that weird place where he was slipping in and out. All he could hear was Delta shouting and sirens pulling up on the street.

Only semi-lucid, Carrick persisted, "I saw a picture of her today for the first time in a long time. But I'm a different man now. I should have told you…" He fluttered his eyes shut, unable to keep them open.

As Danica whispered distant, reassuring words down to him, Carrick saw a light in his mind. A bright light. It was probably all the natural painkillers his body was releasing. He was bleeding out.

His mind went back to when he had stood in his kitchen earlier. He'd held the photo in his hands, the photo of him and Lauren. Running his finger over her face, he realized that something had finally changed.

"You would have liked Dani," he'd mumbled. *"I wish you could have met her."*

With hurried voices surrounding him, Carrick's mind wandered to a place of serenity. He was sitting alone on Sunset Beach, watching the waves. For the first time in a long time, he thought about Lauren. Surprising the hell out of him, a grin tugged at his lips, like he was saying hello to an old friend. He felt something lifting away. Lauren was leaving him.

Carrick only could feel Danica around him, holding his hand, pleading for him as his body was raised. *This is what it feels like to die.*

"I should have told you that I love you," Carrick mouthed, but he had no idea if any sound had come out.

Chapter Thirty

Danica

Danica ran behind the team of paramedics as they rushed Carrick down the emergency halls of the LA General Hospital on a stretcher. In shock, crying and running to keep up, she watched them move his unconscious and bloody body toward the surgical unit.

It was just like a painful memory playing on repeat in her head.

"We're losing him!" a paramedic yelled at the ER nurse, who was running toward them with an IV.

"Shit." The nurse's urgent voice carried through the hall as she took the stretcher behind closed doors.

Danica burst out into sobs as she tried to sprint toward him, wishing she could be there to help, that she could be his nurse.

But she was stopped in her tracks. A heavy hand fell on her shoulder, and she nearly jumped out of her skin. Whipping around and afraid for her life, she flashed back on memories of her childhood, memories of being thrown into a room to await news that the people she loved had died. Relieved, she realized it was only Delta holding her back, a deeply empathic look on his face.

"All we can do now is wait," he said calmly. "Let's get you a coffee."

Danica couldn't stop hyperventilating, her face a mess of heat and tears. Holding her shoulders, Carrick's best friend ushered her toward the quiet corner of the waiting room. She was trembling as he sat her down on a creaky chair. He moved over to the coffee dispenser, inserting a bill and pouring out two coffees.

"It's not going to be like Carrick's brew," Delta uttered as he handed the steaming cardboard cup to her. He sat down across from her, sipping on his own cup as he studied her.

Danica dropped her gaze to the steaming brown-black mess of liquid in the cup. Coffee grounds were visibly floating to the top. He hadn't bothered with sugar or cream, and she didn't care. It was something, and she damn well appreciated it — something to clutch onto, something to distract her. Sipping on the bitter brew, she felt an overwhelming need to weep.

"I can't lose him. It can't end like this."

"I know," Delta replied, his own voice cracking. "I know."

Danica looked up and saw the same distress in his eyes. He wasn't going to sugarcoat it for her, wouldn't pretend everything was going to be okay or lie to make her feel better.

He's worried as hell, too.

And that was when Danica's face twitched and scrunched up involuntarily — when she felt the need to throw up, when she lost control. She glanced down the hall, reliving the trauma of seeing Carrick's bloody body disappear into the hospital's emergency surgery unit. She'd seen her mom and dad disappear down that same hallway at the LA General—but they'd never come back.

Not alive.

"God," she choked, her coffee sloshing out of the cup.

Delta lunged forward, taking a knee in front of her, his face dead serious.

"Look at me," he said, tilting her wet face up to his soft brown eyes. "I don't know what's going to happen, but you aren't alone. I'm here."

"It's not good. His injuries were serious...very serious."

Delta ran his hand gently up her arm. He remained silent, watching her, holding her.

"My mom and dad died here," she sputtered through the tears. "Just like Carrick might. Everyone I love..."

She pressed her eyes shut, shaking her head, trying to toss the pain away. The last words that had come out of his mouth were as much a mystery as their entire relationship. And in that moment, she broke down to a point she realized she was never going to come back from. As she sobbed, struggling to breathe, Delta drew his arm across her, holding her back.

"Miss Petrova," a voice called out in the waiting room.

Danica raised her head slowly, her cheeks sticky from the tears. She saw a fit, blonde woman in a dark suit standing there, flashing an LAPD badge. Delta stood and immediately his demeanor changed. He flexed his shoulders, and he was tense.

"Danica," the woman tucked a stray lock of her silky bob behind her ear, introducing herself. "LAPD IDENT, Sergeant Kendra Larose. Call me Kendra."

"IDENT?" Danica asked, standing up beside Delta.

"Forensic Identification Services," Kendra explained, holding out a business card for Danica. "I know this is a difficult time, but I need to talk to you."

"Not now—" Delta started, putting his hand protectively in front of Danica.

"Step *back*," Kendra bit at him, resulting in a stare-down.

Danica ran her hand over the card, breathing deeply and remembering everything Carrick had told her. *Fight for yourself.*

"Okay," she replied, wiping the tears off her cheeks as she looked up at Kendra.

As Delta grumbled, stepping to the side, Kendra took out her notepad and prepared to take a statement.

"Danica, what happened?" Kendra began, scribbling quickly on the paper.

"Well…" Danica responded slowly, collecting her thoughts. What should she say? The vision of her uncle flashed across her eyes—everything he had done to her. Carrick's words came to her mind, along with the vision of him losing consciousness. He'd risked his life for her.

She knew what she had to do.

Danica began recounting it all from the beginning— who Petrov was to her, how he'd hired Carrick to track her down and how Petrov had been trying to force her into a marriage for the purpose of transferring his American assets to a Russian.

"But I said no," Danica concluded. "I said I wouldn't do it."

"You didn't sign the documents?" Kendra raised her eyebrow.

"No—they tried to make me." Danica reached up and touched the scabbing wound on her brow, remembering Carrick's hand on her cheek. "But I didn't."

"Petrov has been pronounced dead." Kendra appeared to search Danica's face for response, being as sensitive as possible. "I'm so sorry this happened to you," Kendra sympathized, reaching out to gently touch Danica's forearm.

Delta moved forward again, seemingly unwilling to let Kendra touch Danica. "Give her some space."

A tense silence grew between Kendra and Delta, then she turned her attention back to Danica.

"Andriy will live," Kendra explained, closing her notebook. "LAPD is charging him with forcible confinement, assault causing bodily harm and attempted extortion...among other things. I guess his company will need a new CEO—but then again, you'll be making that choice now since you will be the company's sole owner."

"Sole owner?" Danica exhaled.

"Your lawyer will work through the inheritance with you." Kendra offered Danica one last look of empathy and turned to leave. "Please let me know if you need anything."

Danica nodded quickly, offering a grateful smile. As Kendra gave her a knowing look, she tucked her notebook into her tote bag and slung it back onto her shoulder.

But before the sergeant could leave, Danica observed Delta squaring his chest to Kendra. The two stood a few feet apart, face to face. A tension thickened the air, and Danica instinctively stumbled back a few steps.

"It's been a while, Kendra," Delta moved in. "I—"

"Not long enough," Kendra snapped through a clenched jaw, a tousle of her bob falling over her cheek. "And I don't want to fucking hear it."

Delta betrayed no emotion, standing and staring at the lively blonde, who was spinning to leave. Kendra flashed her gaze away, and Danica didn't miss the hurt screwed on her face. As the sergeant marched out of sight, Danica stood back wondering what the hell that had all been about.

Delta looked over at her, his tone far more stressed. "I'll be back."

"Where are you going?"

"To check in with the nurse."

Danica lunged forward. "I'm coming with you."

But then a voice called across the waiting room. "For Carrick Byrne."

They both spun instantly, watching a surgeon step forward, a serious and grim look on her face.

"Can we talk?"

Chapter Thirty-One

Carrick

Carrick slowly opened his eyes to the sound of machines beeping in a shadowy hospital room. The distant patter of rain beat against the hospital window. He was alone, he realized, as he opened his bleary eyes wider, wondering what the hell was going on.

Wondering where she was.

He tried to turn his head to the window where daylight had been grayed to rainy dullness, but his neck screamed at him — stiff and sore. Instinctively, he reached up to touch his neck, sucking back air through pain, and monitors started beeping faster and more angrily.

"Shit," he groaned, realizing that his back and ribcage had lacerations and sutures.

A young red-headed nurse in purple scrubs came running in with a worried look on her face. She started pressing buttons and scanning his connections, then leaned over his bed.

"How are you doing, Carrick?" the nurse asked as she flashed a tiny light into each pupil.

"Fine. Got any water?"

The nurse gave him a cup and he sloshed the liquid around his mouth and drank it. She moved her flashlight down his body, peeling back his hospital gown to check his incisions.

"We've got a lot to catch up on," she said. "Let me know when you are feeling up for a chat."

"Yeah—I just need to piss," he said, feeling the immediate need to urinate.

The nurse laughed and took his arm, securing him as he sat up. He pushed himself up off the bed, holding on to the rail for stability.

"Holy fuck," he ground out, feeling pain up his back as he slowly moved toward the small washroom in the corner of his private accommodation.

"It's going to hurt. You've put your body through hell," the nurse called behind him. "But this is a good idea—to get up for a minute. You've been down for a while."

Carrick finished and stood in the doorway.

"How long have I been out?" he asked the nurse as she wrote on his chart.

"About fourteen hours," a familiar feminine voice answered from the entrance to his room. "But who's counting?"

Carrick had to grab on to the bathroom doorframe for stability. There stood Dani, her eyes wide and red, dark circles under her eyes. She was still wearing yesterday's clothes, with his blood on her pink hoodie, and he saw that black bruise over her eyebrow from where she'd been hit. Everything in his body screamed to lunge toward her, to pick her up in his arms and kiss her until neither of them could breathe, but then Delta burst into the room with Carrick's tiny Aunt Kathy behind him.

"Carrick!" Kathy bounced forward, wearing a pink blazer, her gray bob bouncing and with a bright smile on her face.

They both rushed into the room, but Danica held back, watching from the sidelines, her face hollow and haunted. She seemed empty and exhausted — completely burnt out. All he wanted to do was grab her and order her to take care of herself. But she was holding back from him, leaning against the far wall for support.

Delta helped Carrick back to his bedside, holding on to him as he sat. Kathy chattered about how his surgery had lasted forever and Danica had spent the night in the hospital waiting room, unwilling to leave.

"LAPD came for statements," Delta began, but the inflection in his tone tipped Carrick off. Something else had happened.

Carrick locked his gaze on Delta, raising his eyebrow.

"We'll talk about it later," Delta grumbled under his breath. "Yes, it was her."

Kathy pushed forward to his bedside, bringing his side table up and over the bed. She fumbled in her purse for paperwork.

"Carrick, you know I wouldn't do this unless it was absolutely urgent, but our twenty-four-hour-window is closing. If you want to sell and buy, you've got to sign these now." She slammed two separate contracts in front of him with a pen. "They're both solid offers."

Leaning back in his bed, he flipped through the documents in front of him—an offer from someone to buy his place on Coronado Island and an offer for him to buy a commercial property in Sunset Beach.

"You've got to make a decision on this," his aunt rattled off quickly. "Sign both now and I'll just have enough time to make the deadlines before they go on to the next buyer."

Carrick picked up his pen, quickly signing off on his offer for the commercial property. That one was a no-brainer. It would be the best investment he'd ever make. But his pen hovered over the offer to sell his old house, and he raised his eyebrow at his aunt. It was a great offer—a private offer.

He looked up and over at Danica as her hollow eyes followed him. There was a lot still unresolved between them, and he needed to talk to her pronto. He had a lot to say.

His pen hit the paper, and he signed his name to the second document. It was done. Now, all he had to do was convince Danica to marry him this time.

Kathy scooped up the papers, stuffing them in her bag and running out to go send them to the other agents to make them final.

"Ready to blow this popsicle stand?" Delta asked, eyeing the nurses.

Carrick coughed then asked, "How many bullets did they take out of me?"

He shrugged and replied, "Fewer than I had to pull out of you in Mosul. You've got this." Then, moving toward the exit, Delta nodded to the room. "Let's get you released."

Danica offered his buddy a forced smile as he walked out, but things were far from being right. As

Delta left her alone with Carrick, she let out a breath she'd apparently been holding.

"How are you?" Carrick probed, trying to get her to open up and come closer.

"Tired," she replied, and he saw the pain in her eyes. "What was that all about with your aunt?"

"Ah, don't worry about it," he began, but swallowed, realizing those were the words she hated — so he leveled with her. "Look... I'm selling my old place."

The meaning was clear — and Danica's eyes widened. Carrick appreciated how quickly she caught on, which was something he'd come to value a great deal.

"Are you buying something new?"

"I'm investing."

But being circumspect wasn't helpful because Danica looked crushed. Carrick swallowed harder, hating it. The only reason he wasn't telling her was that he didn't want to give up the one good surprise he had up his sleeve. He wanted to blurt out what he was investing in, but he didn't want to ruin it.

"Dani —" he started again, trying to find words for what he needed to say to her.

But in trying to talk, he found himself coughing.

Danica leaped forward to his bedside, looking at the beeping on the machine before realizing it was fine. As a nurse, she knew how to read those damn things.

"Are you going to be okay?" she whispered, her skin tone white, as she fingered the machine controlling the IV drip.

Carrick let a wide grin cross his lips. "That depends on if you're planning on marrying me or not."

Her whole body froze, and she looked back to him. It wasn't the reaction he was hoping for.

"You didn't forget, did you?" he pushed on, trying to keep his tone light, but unable to mask the determination in his voice.

She shook her head sharply. "No, I didn't forget. I thought you did."

He slid his hand up, reaching for hers that dangled at her side. As he wrapped it around hers, he found she was cold and stiff. *Maybe she needs the hospital bed more than I do,* he thought, as his mind turned to bringing her into the bed with him.

She squeezed back as she connected with him, and he tugged her over to him until she was as close as she could get without falling in altogether.

"Hey." He held her hand close to his chest, feeling her despondency.

Her pain.

"Are you okay?" he asked.

She nodded fast—too fast. And she scrunched her face with obvious pain and tears started welling at her eyes.

"Hey, it's okay," he tried to assure her.

"What if something happens to you?" she cried, a small, vulnerable voice shooting through. "What if you don't get better?" Her eyes grew big and concerned as her breathing became heavy.

"I will be fine. I'm tough," he assured her, knowing exactly why she was so upset. "You've been here before?"

She nodded, using one hand to wipe her tears and keeping the other hand with his.

"Carrick, I can't explain what it was like watching your bloody body rolled down the same hallway where I last saw my parents…"

But then her words stopped, and she closed her eyes. His own throat grew stiff as he watched her break down. It was fucking impossible to see. How could such an amazing young woman be forced to go through so much? His jaw tightened as he experienced every feeling he'd never wanted to have for years.

Finally, her inhalation grew stable, and the tears stopped. He could only guess she was trying to control her reaction and not to completely lose it. Only when she'd recovered did she open her eyes, tilting her head as she studied him.

"Are you crying?"

"No." Carrick blinked his eyes, realizing they were dewy. "It's the meds."

A wide grin spread across her perfect lips, her gorgeous smile uplifting him in a way he desperately needed. It was clear that there was something everlasting between them, and Carrick knew what he had to do.

"I'm sorry, Dani," he conceded. "I should have told you everything."

Danica nodded, understanding and forgiveness crossing her face. It was then that he knew that he still had her…very much so.

But he damn well didn't deserve her.

"There's something else I should have told you," he began, watching her carefully. "Delta gave me an intel report from LAPD. Someone snitched about what happened to your parents. Petrov killed them."

Her face grew white, and he could see the deep loss in her eyes.

He continued, "I'm sorry, Dani. I should have told you as soon as I read the report."

He could feel her backing away, shaking. Her hand slipped away from his, and he feared that he would never have her again.

"I didn't know...that you knew." She leaned back, her body trembling, and her eyes darted to the window. A tear rolled down her cheek.

He sat up in his bed and pain ricocheted through his back—but he didn't give a fuck. Reaching out to grab her once more, he held onto her waist, afraid she'd run.

"I won't keep things from you again," he let out in a hoarse voice.

She bit her lip, cold and detached.

"I'm—" he started, but her angered face turned to him, cutting him off.

"I *know* about the intelligence report. I *know* Petrov killed my parents." She snapped at him. "I know because *I* was the snitch."

"What?" Carrick looked shocked, trying to process what she'd said as he pulled her back to him by her hand. "What do you mean?"

Fire in her eyes, she ground out, "I was in the car when it happened. I survived."

On pure instinct alone, Carrick dragged Danica's body onto the bed. Without asking permission, he took her mouth with his, breathing a thousand apologies. How could he have been so stupid? She was stronger than anyone he'd ever met.

"Stay with me," he exhaled between kisses.

She let him continue kissing her, and finally, after a minute of being held, she reached up to his shoulder and caressed his skin. Her touch sent a fire across his chest—but it was a damn good heat. That warmth hit his bones and rushed back up to his eyes. When he looked down on the beautiful brunette in his arms, she shot him a little grin.

"No more secrets."

He nodded, conceding—willing to do anything to get her back. "Never."

He kissed her again, taking her tongue into his mouth like he was never again going to kiss anyone. Her taste was delicious and immediately forced his cock into an uncomfortably hard place—one where he just wanted to fuck the shit out of her in his hospital bed. But before he could act, Delta's echoing voice came closer to the door with what sounded like the doctor in tow.

"Come home with me." Carrick gripped her ass tightly while Danica squirmed. "I need a nurse."

A little something seemed to cross her lips, but she quickly corrected herself and furrowed her forehead.

"I'm not *that* type of nurse."

As Danica pushed off the bed, Carrick couldn't shake the fantasy of what he wanted to do to her when he healed.

Chapter Thirty-Two

Danica

Danica stood outside Carrick's Sunset Beach home on the back patio, waiting for him to come out. They'd been back from the hospital for a few days, but he'd spent most of the time sleeping it off — recovering from the bullets they'd taken out of him and ridding his system of the painkillers. If he'd wanted her to play nurse, she hadn't been able to do much except trying to spoon-feed him homemade vegan soup and smoothies, which he'd complained about.

Finally, today, he'd held her hand and asked her if she wanted to go out with him — like, out of the house. He had something he wanted to show her.

She stood outside his place, waiting, in dressy shorts with a tucked-in soft white blouse. She'd taken extra care in her outfit, using a few things Aunt Kathy had dropped off for her. Carrick's aunt had impeccable taste, which had started putting it all into perspective. She'd been behind all the décor. That was now obvious.

Combing her long brown hair through her fingers, Danica nervously adjusted her blouse. *Tucked in or left out?* She gazed at her reflection in the sliding doors, trying it as half tucked in. She didn't know why this particular outing felt so important, but it did.

The sliding door opened, and a slick, scheming smile affixed to a familiar handsome face appeared.

"Ready?" He licked his bottom lip as he looked her up and down.

The look that never failed to give her goosebumps… She blinked at him in the high afternoon sun, feeling hotter under his gaze.

Nodding, he instructed her to meet him around front — where he was going to pull out the truck. As she walked through the alley between houses, she let out a breath, relishing how much Carrick had chilled out since Petrov was dead and Andriy had been jailed. Danica's testimony against him had been the nail in the coffin that LAPD needed to finish off a long organized-crime investigation. Of course, Danica had instructed her lawyer to donate whatever inheritance she received to an organization supporting women fleeing violence. She wasn't going to take that tainted money.

Smiling and feeling a sense of peace for the first time since her childhood, Danica turned onto the street where Carrick's black pickup truck was pulling around. He stopped, letting her jump up in — and hit the gas with purpose. She clicked in her seatbelt, offering Carrick a shy smile as he peeled onto the highway. Whatever it was that he wanted to show her seemed important, because she could tell he was still in some pain.

He risked his life for me.

Something she would never, ever forget.

After a short drive into the main stretch of the small beachside community, Carrick pulled in behind a well-appointed brick building that had a frontage on the tourist shopping drag and backed onto the long public beach. It was a duplex, a commercial property, and appeared to have a coffee shop on one half with the other half currently vacant.

Jumping out of the truck, Carrick came around the side and opened her door, helping her out like the perfect gentleman, despite his injuries. Well, almost the perfect gentleman. He let his hand slip a little lower on her back and lifted her up by the ass into his body.

"Fuck." He coughed in pain, seeming to realize what a bad choice that had been, and immediately let her slip back to the ground.

"Can't change your spots," Danica grinned.

Wincing, Carrick grabbed the side of the truck for stability and closed his eyes. As he loomed over her, collecting himself, there was something so raw and vulnerable about him, just like how he'd been since the day he'd fallen head-first into her lap, blood flushing over his back. He'd been real.

Things *felt* real.

Danica couldn't help but stand on her tiptoes to plant a little kiss on his cheek before retracting shyly. It drew a wide grin across his mouth as he touched where she'd kissed him, and he shot her a promising look.

"Coffee first?" he prompted, nodding at the shop. "Or surprise?"

Danica laughed but confusion crossed her face as he pulled her toward the front doors of the duplex.

"What—? Is the empty side the surprise?" she asked, nodding toward the dark, empty side of the building.

He raised his eyebrow like he wasn't going to tell her anything and ushered her forward to the door of the vacant space. He whipped out a key and unlocked it, opening it for her to go in. She moved into the dusty interior. It was small and dark—and it smelled like an old printer.

Turning to him, she asked, "Let me guess. This is the new investment property you bought?"

"Yup." He grinned, tucking his hands in his pockets.

"Nice," she said. "Your desk will go over there, and Delta's over here."

He laughed like she'd said something outrageous.

"Unless you fired him?" She gasped. "Please tell me you didn't. He's so much nicer than you."

"Delta's still enlisted. He's deploying in a few days." Carrick shook his head. "Anyway, I don't think you want me sitting here all day."

"Why not?"

"Because it would be bad for business," he said, a knowing twinkle in his eyes. "How are you going to run an art gallery all day if I can't keep my hands off you?"

"An art gallery?" she asked...then her mouth dropped.

Carrick shrugged. "I'm investing in *you*."

Realizing what he'd done, Danica immediately felt tears of gratitude and joy welling inside her. He was never going to be the type to check with her first. That was his way. And maybe that wasn't always a bad thing—because he was incredibly thoughtful and giving, in a way she'd never known.

Before she could say anything or move anywhere, he pulled a little bright blue box out of his pocket and toyed with it in his fingers. And she froze—staring at him, and what he was doing.

"I did this all wrong before, Dani," he said slowly, holding the box up. "I should have told you that I love you. And you know what? If this isn't the best marriage proposal, then I don't know what is."

As he finished, a wild smile crossed his lips, like even he couldn't believe he'd said it all. And Danica burst out laughing.

"That's not a good sign," he grumbled.

"It is— It is!" She beamed, tears springing from her eyes. "It's just that only *you* could propose marriage in a way that is so nonchalant yet so touching at the same time."

She took a step forward, reaching up to his cheek as he stood still. He popped open the box, showing her what he'd chosen. It was a stunning, thin gold band, delicate and feminine, with a gorgeous green emerald on it.

"It's so beautiful." She breathed in sharply, gently touching the gemstone.

"I figured you want me to find something with ethical origins," he explained. "I hope it fits. Sometimes fingers can seem smaller when compared to the girth of my…"

"Carrick!" She pushed him gently before he could finish, cracking up as he teased her. "Please. I don't want to have to tell our children how you *sized* my ring."

"Our children?" he said, a little twinkle in his eye.

"Well, I want at least two...to go along with the white picket fence you are going to build for me." She stood up on her toes, planting a kiss on his lips.

"I'll have to get started on the fence tomorrow," he said as he slipped the ring onto her finger, taking her lips at the same time. "Today, we can start on the kids."

And as he kissed her slowly, tasting the tip of her tongue, she moaned then said, "I didn't say yes yet."

"I expect some return on my investment, you know."

Danica sighed, letting the tall, protective man deepen their kiss, enjoying her mouth more and more. As she kissed him back, she knew she'd found herself home — and home was with him. Pulling back just so her nose was touching his, she looked up at him with a sultry gaze, locking and connecting.

"I love you so much," she whispered. "And, yes, I would love to be your wife."

Chapter Thirty-Three

Danica

"You look stunning," Addie gasped as she helped Danica zip up the back of her mossy green cocktail dress.

Looking into the bathroom mirror, Danica beamed at her best friend, who was flipping her long blonde hair behind her back. Danica was overjoyed that her former roommate could be there on the day of her wedding.

Danica checked her watch, her eyes widening. "Wow, time has really flown by today."

Addie reached to the counter, picking up and sipping her mimosa. "Bubbly can do that to a girl. Let's head downstairs."

Taking Addie's hand, Danica led them down the beautiful wooden staircase of Carrick's Sunset Beach home, which now was her home as well. As they crested the second floor, she looked out of the patio door and saw Carrick off on the beach in the distance, preparing for the evening beach wedding they had planning. It was simple and small—with just a few friends.

"He didn't want to wait too long." Addie chuckled, finishing off her drink.

Danica shook her head, grinning. "He said he wanted to get started on kids right away, but I know the real reason he wanted this shotgun wedding. He didn't want to give me a chance to plan a massive, fussy event."

Her heart warmed with the thought, watching Carrick, in his well-fitted collared shirt and slacks, organize chairs on the lower patio with Delta. As Danica turned around to find her way downstairs, the doorbell rang. Addie followed her down, grabbing her camera along the way.

As Danica opened the door, she was surprised to see Kendra, the sergeant with LAPD who was assigned to her case.

"Oh, hi, Kendra." Danica smiled, opening the door a little farther. "How can I help you?"

"Good evening." The serious, athletic blonde stepped into the entryway, looking around suspiciously. "Is he here?"

"Who?"

As Kendra searched for words, Danica heard the patio door open in the back.

"Sergeant." Carrick's voice boomed from the hall as male footsteps echoed through the level.

Danica spun on her heels, watching Delta and Carrick enter the space. Kendra stiffened beside her as though her veins had flashed to ice.

"Kendra." Delta exhaled, as if he'd been gutted.

Danica and Carrick exchanged looks, a concerned expression crossing his face.

Kendra shot him a murderous glare. "We need to talk."

Delta's jaw flexed, and he shook his head. An icy pause followed, and Addie silently backed up the staircase.

Carrick squeezed Danica into his chest, and grumbled into her ear, "Come with me." He pulled her through the garage door, leaving Delta alone with Kendra.

"What's going on with those two?" Danica asked as Carrick pulled her into a shadowy part of his garage.

"He didn't call. Just stay out of it."

But before she could persuade him to dish out more, he leaned forward and kissed her, stealing every ounce of her attention, drawing her into him. He ran his hands up and down her back until he found her ass, squeezing and bringing her tighter against him.

Pulling back, he gave her one last kiss before reaching behind him to a black sheet that was draped over something. He tugged on it, revealing a brand-new surfboard and wetsuit hiding underneath — with price tags still on them.

"For the honeymoon."

Her mouth dropped open as she reached out to feel the smooth surface of the gorgeous new surfboard.

"God, Carrick — you spoil me," she gasped. "How am I ever going to repay you?"

He laughed, picking her back up in his arms. He'd healed a lot in the past few weeks, though he still winced in pain when he pushed himself too hard. She felt his throbbing erection lengthening in his slacks as he took her jaw and kissed her deeper and deeper.

"I'll show you." He bit her lip and hiked up her dress. "You didn't think my generosity came for free, did you?"

She tilted her head back as he ran his teeth down her throat, licking and tasting every inch of her neck and collarbone.

His dark drawl continued, "I was never a good guy, Dani. I'm greedy. I'm jealous. I'm possessive."

He ran his rough, calloused hands up her thighs, pushing aside her panties like they were a waste of space. He immediately found her wet, eager pussy and pressed into her opening with determination. She moaned as he rocked his hand back and forth, drawing out her wetness then pulling out his hard cock. With the reminder of what he'd done to her in the past, hot need filled her, like she couldn't wait for the wedding night. Because she knew exactly what she was in for.

As he shot his thick fingers into her pussy, massaging her aching walls, he groaned lower, darker.

"I'm controlling," he confessed, biting her ear, "and I'm always going to be that way. I always get what I want—but you know that."

Lifting her farther and pressing her back against the side of his truck, he brought the head of his massive erection to her slit and thrust up into her, bringing her full body down on his length. As he slid up into her with ease, she could hear shouting coming from the entry level of their house—and remembered that his best friend was just feet away.

Excited and nervous, she took every inch of Carrick's member, letting him pound her body up and down as he tasted her mouth. Drinking her in, he kissed her hard and fast—and fucked her harder. Her breathing grew as fast as her moaning, coming so damn close to climax. He always knew when she was close and brought his fingers to her clit to drive her over the edge.

"You're a difficult man," she moaned back, kissing him and biting his lip. "But you're an amazing one."

He smiled into their kiss, bringing her body up and down his cock—harder and harder until her head was ready to explode.

"No, I'm a lucky man."

"I love you beyond words," she cried out, holding onto his shoulders.

It wasn't long before he drew out her orgasm then he came—inside her. As his hot cum mixed with hers and dripped down her thighs, she giggled as their noses touched. His dark blue eyes blinked back at her, serious and assessing, before he broke into a wide, satisfied smile. He would always be that way.

And she would always love him for it.

"I hope you didn't make a mess on my wedding dress," she teased.

He smirked, letting out a chuckle as he kissed her once more—long and slow, promising and caring. He held onto her like he would never let her go.

She believed him.

Then the garage door whipped open, Addie's face appearing in the crack.

"Dani—um, I need backup," Addie spoke with a tone of urgency. "Some of your wedding guests are trying to kill each other."

Carrick looked back at Dani, holding in laughter, before he burst out, letting those wild laughter lines form at his eyes. He held her, his bride, close to his chest—close to his heart. And Danica knew that she was going to be his happily ever after, just as he was going to be hers.

Epilogue

Six months later

Danica popped her knees off the ground, moving into full downward dog, stretching every muscle that ached in her pregnant body. She breathed in deeply, trying to ignore Carrick's griping on the mat beside her.

"Bend deeper," she instructed him as she pushed into her palms.

Carrick chuckled low and dark in reply. "I'll fucking bend you deeper if you keep talking like that."

A little grin crossed her lips as she moved back into a sun salutation, watching Carrick struggling to keep up out of the corner of her eye. The man was athletic, strong — but not flexible.

"Yoga is good for you," she reminded him, despite his complaining.

"You know what else is good for you?" he asked, reaching his arms above his head to match her. "Steak. Want some?"

"Babe, we talked about this. 'Vegan' means no meat," she replied, folding into a forward bend.

"Not even mine?"

She let out an unwilling laugh as her fingers grazed the floor. He took a step back and behind her, and he grabbed her hips to pull into his groin. His *hardening* groin.

"I can't do this," he groaned, playing with the waist of her yoga pants as she remained bent over in front of him. "It's just as much torture as watching you do it."

She pressed her ass backward, feeling the hardness of his ridge nearly bursting through his gym shorts.

"You promised you'd help me stay fit through my pregnancy. That means we have four more months of this to go!" She giggled, rising to a standing position as he hugged her into him.

Slowly he started his lips making their way up her shoulder to her neck, tasting and teasing her in a lazy and loving way. He placed his hands on her pregnant belly, feeling the bump that had pushed out in the past couple of months. Their child was floating in there — growing and thriving.

"I can think of another way to help you stay fit," he said, dropping a heavy insinuation. "Take off these pants."

She laughed a hearty, deep laugh — one that only he could draw from her.

As he found his way up the side of her throat with his tongue, he kissed her ear and turned the side of her face to him. His appetite had only grown since they'd gotten married. He'd welcomed her into his home like she'd always belonged there, and even she had to admit that it very quickly felt like she'd never lived anywhere else.

As intransigent as Carrick could be, there was just something so devoted about him.

Danica turned slowly in his arms, looking up into his beautiful dark blue eyes. He grinned, a sly, evil grin that screamed that he was about to practice his marital rights.

And, as it turned out, marriage to Carrick wasn't so bad after all.

He leaned down to kiss her in the way he always did — hot, fierce, passionate.

She was the luckiest woman on Earth.

Want to see more from this author? Here's a taster for you to enjoy!

Unbreakable Heroes: Under Pressure
Zoe Normandie

Coming November 2021

Excerpt

Matteo 'Delta' Valente ran out of his Californian bungalow a little too damn early in the morning. Hell, he'd only been home for a few hours. After jamming his aching arm through his hunter green utility shirt, he buttoned it, trying to multi-task as he unlocked the dark truck which awaited him in his driveway. He was running behind — again.

For fuck's sake.

Damn, sleeping a couple of hours a night is bound to catch up with me sooner rather than later. He grumbled as he slipped on his dark sunglasses to protect his hurting eyes from the blistering sun. Even in January, the sun was still beating down on him stronger than a direct RPG blast. Or maybe it just seemed that way because he was so damn drained.

"Matteo!" An elderly lady's voice called out quietly from behind him, her Italian accent pouring through.

He whipped around, checking to make sure she was okay. The tiny old Italian lady stood at the edge of her bungalow's stoop, a worried look in her eye. Using his hand to flatten back his chaotic dark blond hair, he regrettably realized another thing. He was way past due for a shave.

"Mrs. Romano." Delta attempted a polite smile at his neighbor, hoping she wouldn't notice the gashes on his knuckles from the previous night.

Mrs. Romano fretted, wringing her yellow dotted handkerchief as she batted her eyelashes up at him. He gritted his teeth under her gaze, willfully rejecting any concern she had — or judgment.

"Lovely morning, Matteo." Her voice fluttered, darting her eyes down her empty driveway to the street.

Every other neighbor on the street had bins out. It was garbage day. Immediately, Delta realized that she needed help — but she didn't want to ask.

"Want me to take your bins to the street, Mrs. Romano?" He shot that same, self-assured smile, like he was the most relaxed man in the world. It was a mask he was used to wearing.

A wide, relieved smile crossed her lips. "Yes, son. Please."

Wasting no time, Delta moved around to the back of her home and shuffled out her garbage and recycling bins. It was the least he could do to try to keep up the ruse. He wasn't an idiot. People had been looking at him funny since he'd rotated back from Syria again, three weeks before. Maybe it was the bruises that didn't seem to heal or the fact that he always looked like he'd been ridden hard and put away wet the night before. Whatever it was, home had stopped feeling like home. He didn't belong there anymore.

As he finished, Mrs. Romano waited at the top of her bungalow stoop with a homemade pistachio biscotti for him. Her kind eyes and compassionate spirit reminded him of his late mother's—the last memories he had.

"Thanks," Delta grunted as he took the baked good from Mrs. Romano.

His stomach was rumbling from the lack of sustenance. He was used to pushing his body to extremes, neglecting his own needs for the sake of his platoon, but things were going too far now.

"You're a good man, Matteo…a very good man." Mrs. Romano's voice cut into his thoughts, a knowing twinkle in her eyes. "When are you going to find a Mrs. Valente?"

Delta let out a loud, sarcastic laugh, sloughing off the question. Shrugging, he coyly took a bite of the biscotti and moved toward his truck, waving goodbye. All she saw was his façade, like everyone else. *If she only knew.*

Mrs. Romano's gaze didn't relent as he leaped into the cab. He was in a rush—but it wasn't just because of where he had to be. It was because of what he needed to get away from. He was damn sure that Mrs. Romano wouldn't think so much of him if she knew what lingered underneath the surface.

I'm not a good guy. Not even close.

Slamming the gears of his truck into reverse, he pulled out of the driveway of his place, saluting Mrs. Romano on his way out. The fun and games were over. Now, he really had to focus. He was on a mission that morning—and things could get ugly.

Barreling down Oceanside Drive, Delta flipped on the radio—local LA news—and listened to the newscasters talking about a body discovered in South Central in one of the roughest blocks. It had been on the news all morning—tragedy porn for LA'ers. Delta listened for any pertinent intel as he set his GPS for the crime scene. He had questions that needed answers.

Gripping the steering wheel, Delta rolled his shirt sleeves up to let a little heat off, revealing his winding tattoos. It was far too hot for long sleeves, even by LA standards. They were in the middle of a bizarre mid-winter heat wave. But he didn't have a choice. He had to cover up. There were things he didn't want *anyone* to see—like the fresh laceration on his arm that was only going to add another scar.

As he stopped his truck at a red light, he pulled off his sunglasses and absently traced his fingers over the long scar that ran from his cheekbone up to his temple and eyebrow. A little less than two years old, it was a reminder that he should have died in the Syrian mountains. Hell, he should have died in a lot of operations, but *undeniably* that one.

Now, he was on borrowed time. He could feel it. He was never wrong about those things. He was playing with fire and some sort of fucked up luck that was about to run out.

The light turned green, and he hit the gas hard, not wanting to think about how he was spending that second chance at life. It sure as hell would make a priest cry. His mother had always said that he didn't need to be led into temptation because he already knew the way.

The drive from his bungalow up into South Central wasn't fast, but he drove aggressively. He knew how to scare the piss out of LA's richest, stalling out the fast lane in their luxury cars.

Revving his truck and nearly eating up some dinky coupe in front of him, he peeled off the highway. Rounding the streets in the impoverished neighborhood, he transitioned into a different type of vigilant and cautious. Those streets bled a type of desperation that he'd only seen in war.

Delta drove up to the vicinity of the taped-off scene and chose to park well off in the distance to keep a low profile. Before jumping out of his truck, he popped a black baseball hat on, pulling the brim down low for as much anonymity as possible. He adjusted his long sleeves across his muscled forearms so his unpolished appearance would help him not to stand out too much. He looked like any hungover blue-collar laborer who spent too much time at the gym. Then again, that pretty much described any SEAL.

He walked up to the periphery of a building that police were investigating—an abandoned commercial warehouse. Delta guessed that whoever owned the aging building had been hit hard in the economic crash, so they'd left it to rot. From the insecure doors and broken windows, he would bet that criminals and drifters had been trespassing for a long time.

Delta gripped the police tape surrounding the epicenter and glanced around to see if the cops off to the side had noticed him. They had their backs turned, just for a moment, so he took his chance. As he slipped past, he slunk around the building into the shadows, and he observed. He paused in an enclave, watching cops come and go from the building, listening to the broken conversations of the investigators.

In all his years in the special forces, he'd become skilled at going unseen when he needed to. He could be a goddamn ninja. A lot of it just had to do with confidence—and looking like he belonged. That had turned out to be damn useful the previous few weeks. He'd been on leave from work, but it hadn't been a fucking vacation. He'd been working on something else—something serious. And, in true Delta fashion, he'd been going it alone.

Crouching low and moving slow, Delta approached a broken window near the back of the building. He checked inside, seeing the room was empty. A ton of blood was splashed across the concrete floor, but there was no body in sight. *Fuck.* Had the cops already moved the corpse out? He reached into his pocket, readying his cell phone to snap pictures of anything that could aid him. Delta scanned the room for pertinent info. The graying building interior had the feel of an unrealized horror film, and a chill ran up his back as he wondered what the fuck had happened there.

Voices echoed from the front hall of the building, and Delta ducked down outside the window. He could hear the voice of someone entering the room, calling back details of the scene to the front of the building. His first instinct hadn't been wrong. The victim had been using. And, unfortunately, his second instinct had been right too. *She* was there.

His body stiffened and his skin prickled, awareness flushing over him. He'd never forget her voice, even though he hadn't heard it for a while. He'd bumped into her at Carrick's wedding, just weeks after they'd hooked up, but that hardly counted. Had it already been a year? Hearty, feminine, sincere—every word she said danced out of her mouth. As he tried to regain focus, he slowly looked up and into the open window, enough to fully take in her candid, clever words. Her voice alone ran a wave of sensation up his spine that surprised him, after all that time. But it was nothing in comparison to when he finally laid eyes on her.

Sergeant Kendra Larose's natural blonde hair bobbed into view. Delta adjusted his position, getting eyes on the interior of the crime scene and a better view of her — a woman he hadn't seen since he'd deployed, spending the year fighting enemies with half the resolve that she had. A woman who had grown to hate him — and rightfully so.

I can't let her see me.

After she tucked a stray lock behind her ear, Kendra was focused on the warehouse floor. Delta's cock twitched as he watched her shift on her feet, her hips swaying. Blood pumped through his shaft as he drank in her body — a form that drew him to arousal so quickly, without fail. Never had he met such a natural beauty as her. Some guys might find her ordinary or plain, but he found her simply intoxicating. There was always just something about her — something that really got to him.

Even at a distance, he admired the machinations of her clever mind. She was looking down at a cluster of blood where a body once had lain, her lips and nose twitching that certain way that showed when she was really deep in thought. She was on to something. How much did she already know? Delta tried to see what she was seeing. He flexed his jaw, wondering if maybe it wasn't fate that they'd met again. On his own, tracing the source of the drugs had proven to be an impossible task.

And just as a familiar man's voice echoed through the space, Delta realized he was biting the side of his cheek, breathing heavier than usual and gripping the edge of the window like he was going to snap.

"This city is falling to pieces." The man scoffed, coming into view.

Delta recognized him immediately as Staff Sergeant Hunter Greenwood. Delta had met the guy a year ago, around the same time that he had met Kendra. The

Navy had put on a one-week training course for partners in law enforcement, extending the invite to LAPD. At the time, Delta had shown Kendra the ropes—training her how to safely rappel, while realizing that he needed to train her on protecting herself from creeps. Something about the way that Hunter looked at Kendra…

"He's another military vet." Kendra shook her head and furiously scribbled in her notebook. "They've already identified him."

Prickles ran up the back of Delta's neck as he watched Hunter stalk Kendra in the middle of the crime scene. Everything in Delta's body screamed for violence as Hunter licked his bottom lip, carefully examining her. The scowl on his face deepened as she furthered her point.

"What do you bet his blood has traces of doxycycline?" Kendra turned to her boss.

"Come on." He shook his head dismissively, straightening his jacket. "It's a common antibiotic. Stop."

"This is real, Hunter. We've seen traces of it in the other two bodies." Kendra glared at her staff sergeant, standing her ground. "There's a pattern here. Are they being targeted?"

"For what purpose?" he asked, an underlying threat in his voice.

"I don't know yet."

Hunter stilled, clearly judging her. The man looked damn tired, like he hadn't slept for weeks.

"Let's not start jumping to conclusions," Hunter snapped back, his eye twitching. "Anything is possible, Kendra. Let's check with the gangs first."

"Hunter, please. The first two have been soldiers, not gangbangers," Kendra replied slowly, flipping through her notes. "But why? Who's after them —?"

A flash of rage visibly taking over, he cut her off. "We don't have any reason to believe there are links between cases. This is LA. Murders happen all the time."

"But there must be a connection." Kendra glanced between her notebook, the blood splatter and Hunter, apparently confused by his messaging. "It's this doxycycline. Isn't it known to be used by the military as an antimalaria drug?"

"You're asking the wrong questions." Hunter strode toward her, his face darkening.

"Yes, but doxycycline —"

"You don't get it."

"They were soldiers —" Kendra countered again but halted as Hunter's hand whipped up into the air, matched by a growl escaping his lips.

For a split second, Delta's protective instinct thrust him forward, ready to fuck the guy up. But Hunter had recovered, using his raised hand to smooth back his hair.

"Fuck," Hunter grumbled, shaking as he regained control.

Delta stiffened, his eyes wide open. *What the fuck is he going to do with that hand?* Kendra stumbled back in surprise, audibly sucking in breath. But before Delta could jump to her side, the enraged staff sergeant spun and marched toward the front of the building. Whatever he was up to, Delta saw a man who was losing control — a man who posed a threat. He was a ticking time-bomb. Didn't she realize it?

Stunned, Kendra stood there alone, tightly clutching her notebook. She bit her lip, trembling, as if trying to get back to work. Delta sat back, confused as fuck at what he'd just witnessed. Delta knew right then and there that he had little choice. Things had just gotten more complicated.

I have to protect her.

Pulling out black gloves from his pocket, he slipped them on, preparing to leave no trace of what he was about to do. The scene before him had validated everything he'd seen since he'd been back from deployment. The body count was climbing.

Moving around the building a little farther, he gained entry to the interior. As he stalked through the shadows, making note of everything he saw, he was careful not to disturb anything, not even caked-on grime from years of abandonment. In stealth-mode, he slid out of the hallway into the darkest corner of the large room, not too far from Kendra. For a split second, he found himself just staring at her, drinking her in — the way she poured over her notebook then sharply analyzed the room before her. He had no doubt that her cunning mind was finding every anomalous detail.

And, yet again, he was proven right.

"And why are *you* here?" Kendra's exasperated tone echoed over to where he stood, though she didn't flinch or glance up from scribbling in her notebook.

Delta sucked in his breath, wondering if she meant…

"Yes, *you*." She turned her chin slightly and shot a warning into the darkness, seeming to slice into his core. "Do you think I'm daft?"

Releasing the air in his lungs, he stepped forward — confident and relaxed, offering her a sly look as he crossed his arms. His charming ruse was too goddamn easy for him to make people see his way.

"Sergeant." Delta shrugged. He narrowed his focus on her, giving her that grin that women loved. "Here we are, crossing paths again."

"Crossing paths?" She balked.

"That's right." He kept his gaze intense, his body squared.

Turning away, she scoffed, "You're acting like we've stumbled across each other at the grocery store."

She shook her head in deep discontent, seemingly impervious to his charm. A chill ran up the back of his neck, her rejection biting. He hated it — but deserved it. Still, he stood there, watching.

"I'm too busy for *this* right now." She spun, crossing her arms tightly, as if shielding herself. Her body language screamed of a woman who would not be fooled again.

"Too busy for me?" Delta pushed.

"I'll go back to my original question." She raised her eyebrows accusingly. "Why are you here? This is a secure crime scene, so *you* don't belong here. I don't care what security clearances you *say* you have."

All the air got sucked out of the room, and he found himself momentarily searching for a response. Her bright, intelligent eyes left no stone unturned and demanded answers. She anxiously chewed her lip, giving him a rare glimpse of her girlish vulnerability — the type of vulnerability that made him voracious.

"We have a mutual purpose." Delta let his face become stone cold serious, imparting the intensity he felt.

"Which would be?" she asked.

"Keeping you safe."

Home of Erotic Romance

Sign up for our newsletter and find out about all our romance book releases, eBook sales and promotions, sneak peeks and FREE romance books!

About the Author

I'm a mom with three sweet young daughters. I have three jobs - mom, author, and analyst. Years ago, I grew up in a military family, went to a military university, worked alongside the military as an intel analyst, and my husband is (surprise!) a veteran. I've tried to write for anyone who wants to feel what it's like to be with someone from that world - with all the good and the bad.

My heroes are grounded in reality, and are inspired by guys I know in the special forces. Guys who've been in combat, tasted war, and fought for what they believed in. They are really heroes, but raw and rough and broken in their own ways.

My heroines similarly come from the best parts of the women I know, and the challenges we all face. The relationships that they fall into have familiar characteristics for many, myself included. These heroines represent all of us, with our good and our bad laid bare.

In my stories, I illustrate, romanticize, and celebrate the harsh realities of duty, service, and sacrifice.

Zoe loves to hear from readers. You can find her contact information, website details and author profile page at https://www.totallybound.com